TWISTED PLOTS

By Bonita Y. McCoy

Copyright 2019 by Bonita Y. McCoy
Published by Gordian Books, an imprint of Winged Publications

Editor: Cynthia Hickey
Book Design by Winged Publications

All rights reserved. No part of this publication may be reproduced, stored in a retrieval system, or transmitted in any form or by any means—electronic, mechanical, photocopying, recording, or otherwise—without the prior written permission of the publisher. The only exception is brief quotations in printed reviews. Piracy is illegal. Thank you for respecting the hard work of this author.

This book is a work of fiction. Names, characters, Places, incidents, and dialogues are either products of the author's imagination or used fictitiously. Any resemblance to actual persons, living or dead, or events is coincidental. Scripture quotations from The Authorized (King James) Version.

Fiction and Literature: Inspirational
Christian Cozy Mystery

ISBN: 978-1-947523-69-2

Dedicated to:
My husband

Who taught me the value of perseverance

*Let us not become weary in doing good,
for at the proper time we will reap a harvest
if we do not give up.* Galatians 6:9

and to:
My big brother and two sisters
who taught me about my family roots

*He is like a tree planted by the water, that sends out its roots by the stream,
and does not fear when heat comes, for its leaves remain green...* Jeremiah 17: 7-8

CHAPTER ONE

Fire! What was I going to do? My heart raced as I peeled out of the parking lot in my ancient blue van.

How was I going to make payroll, much less the bank note? I didn't have an endless stream of money. Tears of frustration threatened to flow. This couldn't be happening. Twisted Plots had only been open three months.

Well, Amy Kate Anderson, it looks like your trouble magnet is up and running. I pushed the gas pedal a little harder.

The image of waterlogged books floated across my mind's eye. Would my beautiful bookshop be in ashes? I turned the corner and parked as close to my shop as I could.

I slammed the car door and hustled across the street. My chest tightened and my breath came in small bursts. The anxiety of what I'd find pressed in on me.

The remodeling had taken several months, but the wait had been worth it. The shop windows needed to be replaced due to rotten wood, so I put in some full-length windows to let in additional light. With the new carpet and the soft leather club chairs sprinkled about, the bookshop possessed a warm, welcoming feel. Now it was all lost, and I couldn't afford to start over since I'd sunk every penny into Twisted Plots.

As I rounded the corner, I couldn't believe my eyes. The scene was a circus. Police cars, fire trucks, ambulances, and news media vans littered the street in front of the three storefronts which shared the west side of Pine Lake's town square. The three shops—the florist, Twisted Plots, and the one in between—Beans and Leaves, the coffee shop—didn't appear too damaged. Relief flooded over me, but I needed to see the inside to be sure. There had to be something more or everyone uniformed person wouldn't be here.

Cops and firemen hurried here and there, doing their jobs. Barricades blocked off portions of the parking spaces in front of the stores to keep out any unauthorized personnel. Several reporters spoke into microphones, interviewing anyone they could persuade to stand still for a moment, including Mrs. Culpepper, who walked her dog, Alvin, every morning at five. She was busy fluffing her hair when I passed her.

When I reached the barricade, I glanced across the town square to the east section of storefronts where Elizabeth, my older sister, had her law office. I didn't expect to see her car there this early, but out of habit, I looked. No surprise, she wasn't there.

A smoke-filled cloud hung over the corner of Hardin Street and Adams Avenue, causing my eyes to sting, and the unmistakable odor of burnt coffee lingered in the air. I rushed past the cameras and reporters in search of a uniformed police officer. It didn't take long before I crossed the barricade, and one planted himself in my path.

"Sorry, miss, no one is allowed past this point."

"I own the Twisted Plots." I stuck my chin out daring him. "I need to get through."

"Hold up, ma'am." The young officer raised his hand to keep me at bay. "I'll check with the lieutenant. Give me a minute." He jogged over to a rather handsome thirty-something man, whom I presumed to be the lieutenant in question, and they talked together for a moment.

The lieutenant peered at me, nodded to the officer, and moved in my direction. His stride exuded confidence. He appeared at ease in the middle of the disaster. As he drew closer, I noticed his dark curly hair was mussed as if he'd been roused from his bed. His face was long, and a five o'clock shadow outlined the angles of his chiseled jaw.

"Are you Amy Kate Anderson?" His husky voice sounded familiar.

"Yes, that's me."

"The fire department is still checking the building. They want to make sure it's safe before they let any of the owners in."

As I stood listening to the lieutenant's explanation, my vision streamed into a single tunnel. Everything became a bright, white blob.

"Umm," I said when he paused, my head feeling heavy. My stomach churned and I teetered. I slid my hand to my abdomen and inhaled the cold January air, trying to stop the wobbly feeling.

"We've also come across another hiccup. We believe the fire originated in the coffee house next to your shop. Do you know—"

The lieutenant's words jumbled in my head. My knees shook and turned to noodles and my mouth went dry. I grabbed the barricade to brace myself. Between the stench of the burned coffee, the stress from thoughts of my store in ashes, and the cologne of Lieutenant what's-his-name, my world faded into black.

When I opened my eyes, a man's face hovered over me. I tried to get up, but the motion caused my head to swim.

The EMT pushed my shoulders gently back toward the concrete. "Why don't you just lie still for a minute."

I decided to take his advice.

"Are you all right?" I turned my head to the right to find the lieutenant kneeling beside me, his face full of concern.

The movement made my stomach lurch. I laid my hand across my middle, praying it would stop before last night's snack made an appearance. It took a minute for it to settle. "Yes, I'll be fine. I don't know what happened. I guess the odors got to me. I have an acute sense of smell, but it's never caused me to faint before."

The EMT popped back into my field of vision. "You aren't pregnant, are you?"

"Oh, my goodness, no." I screeched, coming to life. "No, no, no. I'm not even married. Good grief." I rolled to my side and propped on my elbow.

The lieutenant clamped his lips shut, but his dimples appeared. I glanced from him to the EMT and pulled myself to a sitting position. They rose, amusement playing in the EMT's eyes as his face contorted trying not to smile.

The lieutenant offered me his hand. Still not sure of myself, I took it. He lifted me to my feet with ease and held my hand a little longer than necessary. Once I realized what was happening, I snatched my hand from his. I couldn't help noticing the warm tingling sensation that lingered even through my mitten.

"So glad to see you both find this funny." I brushed myself off, done with this nonsense. I needed to go see the damage to my store. I needed answers. This wasn't the time to swoon like some wilting Southern magnolia. Like Aunt Maude says, "we Anderson women are made from Southern iron."

It was Aunt Maude who had given each of us a little surprise of a trust fund on our twenty-second birthdays. Because of her gift, I was able to remodel the bookshop and give the bank a nice down payment. Though money's so tight that I have a roommate and can only afford to eat meat once a week, it's a small price to pay for the thrill of owning my own shop.

Fully recovered, I peered around the crowd spotting Matt and Lilly Murphy huddled together near the front of the Beans and Leaves coffee shop. Where was Bryant his partner? I didn't see him among the people standing around waiting. Maybe he was at one of the other coffee houses they owned throughout the state. Looking at Matt, you wouldn't guess the two had become a big deal.

I threaded my way to Matt and Lilly, leaving the lieutenant chatting with the EMT. Being five foot two and petite has its advantages, one of which is the ability to squeeze through crowds with ease.

"Matt, Lilly, are you guys okay? Do you know what happened?"

"I was on my way down when I got the call," Matt said. "I was supposed to meet Bryant here this morning so he could taste test some new flavors I've developed. We were also trying to work something out about that infernal contract. I'm sure you received an earful from Kirk yesterday about what happened."

"Yeah, he said you and Bryant had a heated argument about taste buds, whatever that means, and then it turned personal."

"I'm sure you've heard through the grapevine Bryant and I

are selling the Java Vein Coffee Houses to a national chain owned by the Benson Company. The problem is I don't want to sell this shop. I'm happy with my little slice of heaven. I don't care what Bryant does with the other stores, but this one I want to keep."

Matt was right. I had heard from my usual source, Flora, about the sale. Both men would be well-off if the deal went through according to her.

"From what Kirk said, you took a swing at Bryant," I asked.

Matt's lips pulled tight. "It's true. I shouldn't have, but I did." He shifted his weight from one foot to the other.

"You lost your temper pretty quick then, and you don't strike me as the short-tempered type."

Lilly jumped in front of him. "No, Matt's not the type to let others upset him, but Bryant knows exactly what to say. He's been so worked up over getting the contract signed he's been a pain in ... well, I hate to say it ... the rear."

"Yeah, he's been more of a pill than usual, and on top of that, he's not here. Bryant never showed. I've been trying to call him, but he's not answering."

Watching a group of fire fighters emerge from the building, Matt sighed. "I wish they'd let me in so I could see the extent of the damage. My grandmother's teapot was on a shelf in the back. I hope it didn't get broken in all the excitement." Concern crept across his face.

"Oh, not the one your great grandparents brought over from Ireland?"

"Yep, that one. I brought it to the shop to use in a display case a couple of weeks ago but never managed to put it out."

I agreed with Matt. I just wanted in my shop. The suspense of not knowing was killing me.

The crowd parted, and a uniformed police officer made his way toward us from the direction of the Beans and Leaves. Two EMTs pushing a gurney carrying a body bag, followed close behind him.

I caught my breath. The officer pressed the crowd back to clear a path between the gurney and the ambulance. The crowd inched me back.

I glanced over at Matt and Lilly. Their faces had drained of

all color.
"Did you say Bryant was supposed to meet you here?" I asked.

Matt nodded, his eyes on the medical attendants hoisting the gurney into the ambulance.

We all knew who lay in that body bag.

CHAPTER TWO

"Oh guys, I'm so sorry."
Lilly turned toward Matt's waiting arms.
"I can't believe it." His voice sounded so hollow.
Lilly's soft cries melted my heart. I rubbed her back trying to comfort her but felt so helpless.

The three of them had been friends for a long time since college, and I hated watching my friends' world fall apart and not doing anything about it.

The lieutenant was talking with an early morning walker near the edge of the crowd, so I decided to ask him again if we could enter our shops. No, *demand* he let us in. I pulled my coat tight around me, squared my shoulders and marched to where he stood interviewing Mrs. Culpepper.

He didn't acknowledge my existence. Alvin, Mrs. Culpepper's dog, sniffed my ankles.

The lieutenant's voice was even, and his hip leaned against one of the police cars. His focus was trained on Mrs. Culpepper, and he jotted down what she was saying. "So, you didn't hear anything. No one calling out for help or anything like that?"

Alvin pulled against his leash, causing his owner to jostle to the right. "No, when I passed by the first time, I could smell coffee, but I didn't think anything of it. I can always smell coffee. Then, when I passed by on the way home, everybody was here."

It irritated me how at ease he was—as if he were at an afternoon tea chatting with the other guests. Didn't he know what this meant? It would be weeks before things returned to normal, and normal had changed forever for Matt and Lilly.

"Thank you, Mrs. Culpepper. If you think of anything else, please give me a call." He straightened and closed his notebook, taking a few steps toward the building.

"Excuse me, Lieutenant—" It dawned on me I never caught his name. He turned, and a slight one-cornered smile greeted me.

"Yes, Miss Anderson, can I help you with something else?"

"Something else? Are you referring to my moment of lightheadedness?" I propped my mitten-clad hands on my hips, daring him to mess with me.

"No, but since you mentioned it, I did keep you from hitting the concrete. Goose-eggs aren't fun." He turned toward me, and his eyes held a smug amusement. "You might be a little nicer about it."

"Yes, well, thank you." I bit out, refusing to be intimidated or sidetracked. "I need to check out my shop. I'm anxious to assess the damage."

"No one gets in, Miss Anderson, standard procedures." He stood to his full height.

As I debated what to do, thinking all kinds of unique things about the lieutenant, another detective yelled from the front door of my shop. "Hey, Lieutenant Cooper, I got something you should see."

"Excuse me." The lieutenant started toward my bookshop.

I followed him. I wasn't finished with him yet, and he was crazy if he thought he could get rid of me that easy. Then I realized he was going where I wanted to go. What could be the harm in tagging along?

I trotted behind the lieutenant a little to the left of his peripheral vision as if I belonged. No one stopped me because they thought I was with him.

So, this was Lieutenant Cooper of the Pine Lake Police Department. I had heard all about him from his dad, my new employee, Carter Cooper. He had Carter's height and build, but it was his easy-going manner that was most like his father's. Can you inherit a mannerism?

I let the thought slip away as I stopped by the counter of my bookshop near the north wall which was shared with the coffee shop.

    Everything looked the same as it had yesterday. The leather club chairs were undisturbed, still arranged around a small coffee table. The rows of cherry bookshelves were standing in their upright position, and the blocks were still scattered over the floor in the kids' corner next to the counter. No books floated in puddles of water, and the carpet wasn't squishy. The sprinkler system hadn't been activated. Hurray.

    Wait a minute. What if that's the reason Bryant was in a body bag? Were the sprinklers faulty? Had he died from the smoke?

    Guilt overwhelmed me. A picture of Bryant lying on the floor gasping for air flashed into my mind. I needed to find out what had happened. I headed toward the workroom in the back where we stored our incoming shipments and logged everything into our data system.

    As I crossed the threshold, the smell of singed paper and fried electronics permeated every crook and cranny. I put the cuff of my sleeve over my mouth and nose. Damaged books, damaged equipment, damaged shop. My heart fell.

    The wall connected to the coffee house had taken the brunt of the destruction. The heat from the fire must've caused the paint to curl and blacken. The smoke was heaviest here. *This is going to need a little bit more than airing out.* I'd have to make it work. My entire trust from Aunt Maude was tied up in this shop. I couldn't let this fire be the end of it.

    As I surveyed the severity of the scene, I caught sight of the back door. It was in splinters, pieces lying here and there, the cold air gushing in through a gaping hole.

    There was no question the firemen had entered through the back of the building. From this, I assumed the fire had originated in the back of the coffee house, not the front.

    I pushed back the tears that wanted so badly to spring forth and hugged my middle. The sick feeling from earlier threatened to return. I couldn't let it. I had to find out what happened for my friend's sake.

    The coffee house.

    I needed to find a way to get over there. Poor Matt—he already had to deal with the death of a friend and a partner. Now, his beloved coffee shop was in shambles, and what about his grandmother's teapot? I couldn't do anything about the others, but I could check on the teapot.

I glanced around for Lieutenant Cooper. When I didn't find him, I grabbed a clipboard off my desk and blended into the stream of police personnel. I tucked my head and walked with purpose out my front door straight into the coffee shop.

I faltered at the door when the bell jangled my arrival, then took a step. The squishy carpet under my feet let me know the sprinkler system had done its job. Glancing at my clipboard every now and then to keep up the pretense, I took in the sight.

Water dripped from various parts of the shop, and foam cups floated in puddles. Again, the smell overwhelmed me, and I placed my cuff over my nose. I walked across the front area, dodging overturned tables, and made my way into the back half of the shop.

The investigators milled around, not bothered by the odor. They were all business. Some took photos of the fire damage. Some took photos of the outline of the body and the surrounding area. Others dusted for prints.

Eddie Thornton, the fire marshal and longtime friend of my dad, was checking the structural integrity of the building. Lieutenant Cooper was in the corner by Matt's desk digging through a file drawer. He held several papers in his gloved right hand while he talked with a larger, older guy who looked familiar. He glanced my way, but my presence didn't seem to register. It became apparent the Beans and Leaves would need professional help. Elbow grease wasn't going to work. I was sure Matt's and Bryant's insurance would cover the cost of the repairs and the replacement of the mounds of burnt coffee beans littering the floor.

It struck me the actual fire damage wasn't as severe as I had imagined. A half-melted coffeemaker that looked like an overheated snowman rested on a heap of what used to be bags of foam cups. The wall beside the heap of foam cups connecting their store to mine was charred and smoldering, but the damage didn't look bad enough to have trapped anyone inside.

From what I could tell, the fire had not blocked the back door, and I knew the front door was accessible because I had just come through it.

What had led to Bryant's death? I ran my mitten hand along my chin. The only thing I could figure was he'd passed out from smoke inhalation and choked to death. But even that seemed to be a stretch to me.

I walked over to the work area where the coffeemaker once sat and noticed the contents on the counter had been knocked over. Packets of sugar and stir sticks were scattered across the floor, looking like discarded peanut hulls at Logan's. Many of them fused together into a wet, black puddle. The way things were strewn it appeared as though there had been a struggle or maybe Bryant had fallen against the counter taking the contents with him to the floor, spilling and breaking things as he fell.

My thoughts jumped to the teapot.

I scanned the shelves near the back, but it wasn't there.

My eye caught sight of something white under the edge of the counter. Thinking it might be a piece of the broken teapot, I stuck my hand under, feeling for the object. When I pulled it out, I discovered a broken piece of white porcelain. I scanned the area for other pieces, but I didn't see any. The piece had grooves that formed a dainty pattern. It might have been a chunk from a broken coffee mug since Matt and Bryant used thick white ones, but the stacks that sat on the green trays ready for the morning rush seemed intact.

Although I couldn't remember if the teapot was white, I decided to keep searching in case the piece I had found was part of it. I checked the two rows of shelving where the supplies were stored. To my delight, I discovered a slim teapot near the back of one of the shelves behind some large boxes of creamer packets.

"Miss, you can't be in here." I jumped, and my heart nearly leaped out of my chest. So engrossed in what I was doing, I hadn't heard anyone approach.

I turned to find a uniformed police officer staring at me. Since my dad had been a detective on the force up until last year when he retired, I knew most of the cops in our town, but this guy was new.

The radio on his belt crackled to life, and he turned his back to me to answer the voice on the other end. While he wasn't looking, I tucked the small teapot inside my coat and cradled it to my side with my right arm, then slipped the broken piece of porcelain into my coat pocket.

When he turned back around, he asked, "how did you get in here?"

"Oh, I'm sorry," I apologized. I didn't want to say I didn't know because it would've been a lie. "I just wanted to see the damage since I own the shop next door."

At this point, the officer took charge of my left arm and guided me to the door. "That's no excuse for contaminating our crime scene. No one is allowed in until the all clear is given."

By this time, the officer had whisked me through the door and deposited me outside, closing the door firmly behind me.

I took the teapot out of my coat and checked it over to see if it had been broken. It had not. Then I took the shard of porcelain out of my pocket and compared it to the teapot. It didn't match. I thought for a moment about going back and giving the shard to the officer who had escorted me out but changed my mind.

How long had the shard been under the counter? *I'm sure something broke, and it was missed in the cleanup.* I deposited the small object in my jean pocket and took the teapot to its owner. Matt was relieved to see that one piece of his world was still intact.

CHAPTER THREE

The morning sun came out and warmed the cold January day. As I inhaled the fresh air trying to clear my lungs of the smoke, I checked the time on my phone and knew I needed to call Flora Smith-Jones my sixty-something assistant.

I didn't want her showing up for work and being caught off guard. Ha, like that would happen. Flora, who'd come with the bookshop knew all about inventory, ordering stock, and Pine Lake, Alabama. Of course, she'd know about the fire. I should've known better. You can't catch Flora off guard.

"Hi, Amy Kate, are you alright? I saw everything on the morning news. Do they know what caused the fire yet?" Flora rapidly pealed off her questions. "Is it true there was a death?"

"I'm not sure how the fire started. I didn't ask, and yes, I do believe Bryant Kendrick died in the fire, but I can't say for sure."

"That's too bad," her tone consoling.

I wasn't sure, though, if she meant it was too bad about Bryant's possible death or the fact, I was unable to confirm the rumors. After all, Flora loved her gossip and was a confirmed member of both the Pine Lake Community Church and the Pine Lake grapevine.

"I did get to check out the shop, though. The damage to our place is minimal considering what it could've been. We should be up and running soon, but the back door will need to be replaced pronto. The firemen made mincemeat of it. Which made me think about yesterday's deposit. I didn't make one. Did you?" I waited for Flora to go into one of her responsibility

lectures.
  Instead, she said, "I made the deposit on my way home yesterday afternoon." Flora was so dependable, and I was so appreciative. "I guess we'll have to cancel Tom Perkins' book signing at the end of the month." She sighed. "I was so looking forward to meeting him. He's my favorite mystery writer."
  "I hope not, but we might be able to have him come. We'll have to see what happens." We ended the call by agreeing to meet at the bookshop at eight. After I hung up with Flora, I sent a group text to my two sisters, Elizabeth and Alexia, and my roommate, Julia, all of whom watch the morning news.
  My text: *Hey guys, wanted to let you know I'm fine. Tell you about it later.*
  Elizabeth's text: *Sorry about your shop.*
  Alexia's text: *Great.*
  Julia's text: ☺ *Glad to hear you're alive and kicking.*
  Then I called my dad, Joe Anderson. I smiled at his gruff cop-like manner. Yet it was a cover for the quintessential protective father looking after his girls.
  His girls had included her mom, Maggie, until six years ago. That was before the accident, before the hit and run. She'd never forget that phone call. She'd been away at college in Jackson, Mississippi when it came.
  The other driver must've drifted into her lane, going way too fast. He'd wound up hitting the driver's side door, sending my mom's car careening down the wooded banks of the Tennessee River right around a point called Dead Man's Curve, or at least that's what I was told. The driver of the other car was never found. Since then, my dad has kept pretty close tabs on all us, girls. Today would be no exception.
  He answered his cell on the sixth ring. "Hey, Dad."
  "Hey, Amy Kate, are you okay? I saw the news." His voice carried a hint of worry.
  "I'm fine, and the shop isn't too bad either. If we can get all the insurance stuff straightened out, the actual repairs won't take too long."
  "That sounds promising. It might be a little tight for you if the shop is closed for a while. Remember, if you need anything, your old man is here to help."

"Dad," I said, "You know how I feel about your helping me. This is my business. I need to make it or break it myself."

"And you know old habits die hard. Taking care of my family is what I do. So, sue me." The gentleness in his voice touched me. He'd always been my rock.

"I know, Dad." I bent my head and closed my eyes, remembering some of the ways this man had taken care of my sisters and me in the years since Mom's death. "Listen, I'd better get going. I need to call the insurance agent and have the back door replaced. Just wanted to let you know I was okay."

"Thank you. Hey, be sure to say hi to Eddie for me."

"Too late, Dad, he's been and gone."

"Wow, Johnny-on-the-spot. Did you get the all clear from him to start the cleanup?" he asked.

"I don't know. I'll check with the lieutenant here on duty, but I'm glad you mentioned it."

"Happy to be of service, and sweetie—" he paused for a moment. "It's okay to need someone. Love you."

"Love you too, Dad."

As I put my phone back into my coat pocket, the thought of the insurance policy in the safe prompted me to risk entering my bookshop again. No one stopped me this time since most of the police and fire personnel had cleared out, along with most of the rubberneckers.

I made my way into the back-work area where I kept a small floor safe in a closet that doubled as the supply catch-all. As I was closing the door to the safe, someone cleared his throat behind me. I glanced over my shoulder from my squatting position to find Lieutenant Cooper, his face decorated in dimples.

"I see there's no keeping you out, Miss Anderson."

"No, I've never been easily deterred once I set my mind to something."

"Yes, I can tell. You know I never did get a chance to ask you any questions about the fire. Would it be all right if we talked now?" He pulled a notepad from his pocket.

I knew the question was a courtesy, so I sat on one of the swivel stools at my workstation, and he took the other one. The stools seemed clean enough, but I tried not to touch the soot-covered tables.

"Do you know of any reason why someone would want to set fire to the coffee house or your shop?"

"No."

"Can you think of any incident or event which might be connected to the fire?"

At that moment, Kirk's tale of the heated argument between Bryant and Matt popped into my mind. I guess it showed on my face because Lieutenant Cooper prompted me. "Tell anything, even the smallest thing you can remember. It might help."

Rats. I didn't want to be the one to place suspicion on Matt. If Matt loved his store too much to sell it, there was no way he'd burn it down. What would he gain? Then the body on the gurney came to mind. No partner, no pressure to sell.

"One of my employees, Kirk Woodard, went to the coffee house yesterday afternoon to interview Matt and Bryant for the college newspaper. He wanted to ask them about their business deal with the Benson Company. As I understand it, they wanted to buy them out. He said a heated argument had taken place between the two partners, and it ended up turning personal." I paused.

"How so?" asked the lieutenant.

"Kirk said that Bryant told Matt he shouldn't have married Lilly, that Matt wasn't good enough for her. Matt took a swing at Bryant—at least that's what Kirk said. Then Matt left to cool down. Kirk said Bryant and Matt wound up doing their interviews separately."

"Hmm, interesting. How long have you known Matt and Lilly?"

"Not long, I suppose. I used to go into the Beans and Leaves when I came home for a visit from Jackson, but I didn't get to know him well until I moved back and bought the bookshop. I see Lilly around, but I don't know her as well as I do him."

I found myself relaxing in Lieutenant Cooper's presence. His calm demeanor was influencing me.

"What was your impression of Matt and Lilly Murphy as a couple? Did they seem happy?"

"Yes, quite happy. As I understand it, they never had any children, but they seemed content with it being the two of them.

Matt said they had met in college. Lilly works at the antique shop across the square and helps occasionally at the coffee house. From what Matt said, Lilly spends a lot of time in her garden. He told me she even has a hothouse so she can garden in the winter. They seem happy." I shrugged.

"Do you think Matt could've started the fire?"

"There's no way he'd burn down his own store. He loves it too much. He even told me he thought he'd found his niche. No, he wouldn't."

"I understand you've owned this bookshop for about six months." He looked around him as if it were the first time he was taking in his surroundings.

"Yes, that's right."

A twinkle of mischief played in his chocolate brown eyes. "So, not long enough to make any enemies or enrage too many customers who might want to burn the place down?"

"Right," I said.

"One last thing. I need to verify your background information." He glanced down at his notepad. "Single, female, twenty-seven, and you reside at 207 Heartland, apartment 8A. Have I got it right?" He looked up and met my gaze.

"Yes," I said a little wary, "but where did you get all my personal information? You haven't asked to see my driver's license, and I doubt you're psychic."

"No, I'm not psychic, but I am a cop who has access to the DMV and other government agencies. I had my partner run your name through our database."

"Oh." I still wasn't sure what to think of this guy.

He placed his fingers to his temples and closed his eyes as if he were meditating. "My psychic vibe is telling me your favorite takeout is Chinese." He opened his eyes and gave me a lopsided grin.

"How did you know that?" I sat straighter on the stool. "Is it relevant?"

"Only to me," he answered, then winked.

He returned his notepad to his pocket and put his hands on his legs as he stretched them out in front of him. "It was an easy deduction," he said, "since you have the menus of three different Chinese restaurants pinned to your bulletin board." He pointed to them hanging over my desk. "Of course, the empty cartons in your trash can were a dead giveaway."

"Okay, I was a little flattered the good-looking lieutenant had noticed my penchant for Chinese food, but I was highly impressed with his skills of observation. He didn't look like he was watching, but he was. You don't make detective without those kinds of talents.

"Do you have a business card I could have? With a phone number where you can be reached, in case I have more questions?" he asked in a melt-your-butter tone.

"Does this have to do with the Chinese food or the investigation?" *Did I just say that?* I almost rolled my eyes. How lame.

"That depends." Before he responded, someone called my name from the sales floor.

It was Carter Cooper. The look on Lieutenant Cooper's face was priceless. Recognition registered in his eyes, then confusion since his father was somewhere, he shouldn't be, and then he smiled "Hey, Dad, is everything all right?"

"Oh, hey, I thought you guys would've wrapped things up by now, so I came to see if Amy Kate needed any help this morning," Carter said.

"Why are you checking on Miss Anderson, Dad?"

"I work for her." Carter announced with a grin. "Got the job yesterday, and I'm here ready to work." Carter Cooper scratched his silver hair with that easy manner he possessed. I had taken an instant liking to him.

"I'm not sure there's much to be done with the police tape up and everything so smoky," I said to Carter.

Lieutenant Cooper glanced around. "The crime scene investigators are finished with your shop, Miss Anderson, and the fire marshal gave the okay on the structural integrity. He also mentioned since the electrical is on two different circuits, yours is good to go. Both shops are safe for occupancy. But it's the Beans and Leaves that we'll need access to for a while since it's a scene of a homicide now and not just a fire."

"A homicide?" Carter asked.

"Yeah, we won't know for sure until we get the autopsy report, but it looks like Bryant Kendrick was dead before the fire was set."

"You mean he was murdered?" My mind reeled. Who would want Bryant Kendrick dead, and worse, who in my small town was a killer?

CHAPTER FOUR

"Murder." Flora arrived on time as usual. We sat in the club chairs, still wearing our coats and discussed the main topic of the day. To avoid the draft, we moved the chairs from the front by the full-length window to the kids' corner.

I sent Carter to the local hardware store to pick up a new back door, which he had offered to install. Hiring Carter Cooper was going to be a good thing.

"Yes," I shook my head in disbelief. "murder, right next door."

"Who do they think did it? Have they arrested anyone?" Flora asked.

"No, Lieutenant Cooper said they are waiting on the preliminary-autopsy report to make sure, but they think Bryant was dead before the fire started."

"Oh, then the fire was set by the murderer. It might be arson and murder." Excitement played on Flora's face.

I would've never believed this cuddly grandma could be the thrill-seeker type, but she had a point. Arson hadn't entered my mind. Someone could've set the fire.

I rose and made my way to the front counter where my purse sat, then thumbed through my contacts and found the number I wanted. "I'd better call the agent and get the insurance ball rolling. We can't afford to be closed for too long." I took a deep breath to settle my thoughts. Worry wouldn't solve anything. Might as well do something constructive.

I had met Theresa Thornton one time, when I went to her

office to arrange the insurance for Twisted Plots. She was very helpful and friendly, but at the time, I was giving her money. I wasn't sure how she would be now that I wanted money.

Our conversation went better than expected. Theresa gave me the information I needed and told me a fire investigator would be out later, sometime after two. His job, she explained, was to assess the damage and determine if the fire had been intentional or accidental. They had to make sure it wasn't insurance fraud.

Theresa also said I needed to take pictures of the damage and send them to her as soon as possible. On her end, she would work on the necessary forms to send to the insurer, All Care.

She explained the process to me. The insurer would send out an adjuster to take a look at the place. Once the adjuster had Theresa's forms, the fire investigator's report, and three estimates for the needed repairs, I would get the money.

Easy, right?

I began taking pictures with my cell phone the minute I ended the call, starting at the front door and working my way around the room clockwise. Then I did the same in the workroom. My phone captured every detail of the wall that joined my shop to the Beans and Leaves. I also photographed the pieces of wood and metal that used to be the back door.

I fought to keep my spirits up. The dark, charred wall and the soot-covered worktable and desk made my heart feel like a lead balloon. No amount of upbeat self-talk was going to lift them.

By the time I finished this chore, Carter returned. He replaced the door, shooting the temperature in the shop up to a balmy sixty degrees. We were able to take off our coats for the first time today.

After shedding mine, I noticed a nice black streak across the hem. *Nothing I can do about that now.* I threw it across one of the club chairs and then moved to the counter to turn on the computer. Once it warmed up, I downloaded the photos and sent them off to Theresa as she had requested. One item down, a few zillion more to go.

With the word *arson* floating around and the other word, *murder*, I decided to pay a visit to my sister, Elizabeth, the lawyer. She specialized in criminal law, but I figured she could give me some pointers on dealing with the insurance company. My bookshop was now my number-one priority since the banks insisted on being paid in a timely manner each month. At Elizabeth's office, Tilley Simmons, the receptionist, waved me through. I found Elizabeth at her desk on the phone. She nodded in my direction, then swiveled away from me.

I figured she needed some privacy, so I decided to hunt up the coffeemaker Elizabeth kept in the receptionist area. To be honest, I didn't know how I was functioning without my morning cup. The coffee here wouldn't be as good as the mocha I had grown accustomed to at the Beans and Leaves, but some caffeine was better than none.

I stepped into the reception area and located the burnt but still drinkable coffee. The smell reminded me of this morning's fire but not as pungent. I poured myself a cup of the dark sludge and added more sugar and creamer than usual. The first sip slid down my throat like oil, but I didn't care.

Tilley held a pen between her lips as she filed something away in her desk drawer. She caught sight of the face I made at the bitter mess and attempted a knowing smile in my direction. I caught her attempt and smiled back, nodding.

As Tilley disappeared into a separate filing room, Elizabeth stuck her head out of her office, looking for me. "Hey, heard all about the fire this morning on the news." She settled into her big leather desk chair and leaned back. "I want to thank you for the text. I was about to call you when I got it."

"Yeah, when I realized the time and knew the news media was covering it, I thought I'd better let everyone know I was okay, especially Dad."

"He told me you called him. That was a good move." Her eyes softened. "So, what can I do for you today?" She thumbed through some files on her desk. Elizabeth Anderson could be as fierce as a tiger in the courtroom, but as a sister, she was a pussycat. The two of us had become close since I moved back to Pine Lake, although she's five years older than me, making her an old-timer at thirty-two. Fending off our other sister's attempts at matchmaking had bonded us for life. I'd have to remember to tell her I'd signed up for the online dating site, Open Hearts, per

Alexia's directions. Whatever would keep her and Julia at bay.

"I was hoping you could give me some help with the insurance stuff. I talked with Theresa Thornton, and she gave me a kick-butt list to complete, but I'm afraid there might be a hitch."

"What is it?" Elizabeth asked. I had her complete attention now.

"Theresa said the fire may have been an attempt at insurance fraud. There's a chance the person who killed Bryant Kendrick might have also started the fire, but it can't be fraud because that would mean Matt Murphy was the murderer because it's only insurance fraud if the owner starts the fire or pays someone to start the fire, right?" I asked for clarification.

"Riiiight."

"So, if they think its fraud, it will slow down the whole process. They must think Matt did it, but I know Matt. He couldn't have done it. I'm starting to worry about him. He's going to need some legal help."

"I received a call from him earlier this morning. He retained me as his lawyer. Matt said some of the questions the police asked him concerned him, and when they told him not to leave town because he was a person of interest, he became nervous enough to call me."

"Good." It made me breathe a little easier knowing Elizabeth would be there for him. "I know Matt's not guilty, but I hope it doesn't take the police too long to figure it out as well. I need that insurance money."

"It shouldn't. I have to admit I feel a little overwhelmed with this case."

"Why?"

"I'm swamped right now. I have two other cases I'm right in the middle of, and with me in court and Matt's case needing immediate attention, I can't do it all. Plus, there's a two-week window before a case starts going cold. For Matt's sake, I can't afford to waste any time."

"Why not refer him to someone else then?" I asked.

"I've known Matt since he and Lilly moved here, and I don't want to let him down. Besides, I want to make sure he has the best representation possible, and the only way for me to do that is to represent him myself." Elizabeth didn't even give a hint of shame at being so self-assured.

She leaned forward with her chin in the palm of her hand and drummed her fingers on her cheek. It was her classic thinking pose. "I need someone to do the legwork for me, but I don't know who to retain. The two private investigators I use are in Chattanooga, and they're both booked for the next few weeks, which leaves me short on manpower."

"What about the guy here? The one with the ratty trench coat who thinks he's Colombo or something?" I couldn't remember his name.

Elizabeth shivered. "You mean The Creeper."

"Oh, how unprofessional of you, Sis. He can't help it if he's good at what he does, creeping around in the shadows, watching people with his beady little eyes."

Elizabeth rolled her own eyes. "Professional or not, the guy gives me the willies. I always feel like I need a shower after he leaves my office." She shuddered again. "I need someone local and dependable, but ever since my last good investigator, Danny, went out of business, I've been forced to hire from out of town. You have any ideas?"

We sat in silence for a few minutes—the question rolling around in both our minds. Then I broke the silence with what I thought was a brilliant idea. "How about me?"

"You're kidding, right? What makes you think you can do this job?"

"I like people." I grinned.

"Be serious." Elizabeth wasn't amused by my humor.

"I'm concerned about Matt. It's one of the reasons I'm here, and this would give me the opportunity to help him. Besides, the bookshop will be in the throes of repairs for at least a week or two, and I'm guessing this would be a paying job?"

"Yeah."

"Okay, this could help me pay salaries while the shop is closed. I view it as a win-win for both of us." I paused to check her reaction to my reasoning. She looked as though she were considering it, so I continued. "I need to earn some money to keep up with the bills, and I'll find the answers to the questions before the case goes cold." I paused again for dramatic flair.,

"Plus, you won't have to work with The Creeper. What do you say, Elizabeth? It's a perfect solution to both our problems."

"Amy Kate, you know I love you and would do anything for you, but sister, you are a walking trouble magnet. It seems to hunt you down. I don't mean to be discouraging, but you are trouble in high heels."

"I can't believe you said that. You know I've outgrown those antics. My word, Elizabeth, I'm not twelve anymore." I crossed my arms over my chest with a huff to prove my point. For a few minutes, I thought about the situation. I needed an income, and Elizabeth needed my legs. It was as simple as ABC. She was being paranoid. What could go wrong? Then for a split second, I let myself recall some of the instances in my life that should've been smooth sailing but wound up being more like a category-one hurricane.

Movement from Elizabeth's side of the desk brought me back to the present. She sat staring at me with her lips pursed.

Before I had a chance to stop myself, I blurted out, "You need me, and you know it."

With a courtroom lawyer, this argument, of course, ranked right up there with "I know you are, but what am I?" I was not helping my case, so I resorted to my last line of attack—begging. "Elizabeth, just give me a chance. A trial run, so to speak. If I don't work out or cause some major catastrophe, you can hire someone from an agency in Huntsville, but at least let me try."

Elizabeth was beginning to waver because she sat back in her chair with her hands folded together like she was considering her options. This was the exact pose our dad struck when he was about to cave.

"Oh, all right," she said, "even though it goes against my better judgment."

"Thank you, thank you." I clapped my hands in sheer delight. "You won't be sorry."

"I hope not," she said, "but at the first sign of difficulty, or if you find you can't handle it, you let me know. After all, this isn't a game. It's Matt's future, and it's riding on what you find out in your investigation."

As she finished her warning, my stomach rumbled. For some reason, it's hard to be serious when your stomach is gurgling its own tune. I giggled at the gurgle.

Elizabeth rolled her eyes and adjourned our meeting to the Deli on the Square where she answered my questions as best as she could about the arson and insurance issues. I was famished, so my mouth was too full to ask too many questions. As we finished our sandwiches, she pulled out the case file she'd started on Matt Murphy, and we began to make a list of people to contact.

We started with the obvious ones: Matt, employees of the Beans and Leaves, and those who had been there at the scene this morning like Mrs. Culpepper. I remembered the argument Kirk had witnessed and based on what he had told Flora and me, Elizabeth and I decided to include the employees at the corporate office of Java Vein Coffee Houses as well as Bryant's contacts at the Benson Company.

This was beginning to look like a full-time job, but I had to prove Matt's innocence. Sure, I needed the insurance money and the quicker the better, but that wasn't my only motivator. Matt Murphy was no killer.

Matt was the type of guy who would swerve his car and hit a tree rather than run over the dog in the middle of the road. He was the guy in charge of the committee at church collecting toys and personal-hygiene items for the kids at the local orphanage every Christmas. He was the guy who cut his elderly neighbor's grass because it was the right thing to do. No, Matt Murphy was no killer. Matt's one of the good guys, and we needed all of those we can get.

As I contemplated the names on the list, I checked my watch and realized I needed to get going. Flora and Carter might be looking for me, and the fire insurance agent was supposed to be at the shop by two o'clock. If I hurried, I might be able to get one or two repairmen called before everything closed for the day. I came to Elizabeth to help me with one kick-butt list, and now I was leaving here with two.

I said my good-byes and stood to retrieve my purse from the back of my chair when Elizabeth said, "Oh, I almost forgot to tell you, Matt is coming in today at four to give me his statement, so you can start then with your interviews. Also, I should've heard from Lieutenant Cooper by then about the autopsy report. I'm hoping I can persuade him to give us a clue about which direction the police are going with this case and see if they have any other leads or if Matt's their prime suspect."

"Lieutenant Cooper? I met him this morning. Do you know him?" I sat back down with my purse in my lap. I needed to hear what she had to say about the handsome lieutenant.

"We've worked together on a couple of cases, strictly business though. Why are you asking? Interested?" She smirked. "Did he make an impression on you?"

"No." I fumbled with my purse. "Yes, I don't know. He might have."

Amusement played in her eyes.

"Hey, I thought we weren't going to hound each other about this subject."

Undeterred by my reminder, she said, "Which is it, yes or no?" She knew she had me off balance.

"He's kind of hard to read. One minute he's all business and then, out of the blue, he seems personable, almost likable. Since I hired his dad to work for me, I have a feeling I'll be running into him more often. I thought maybe you could give me the scoop on him, so I'd know how to handle him."

"Oh, so he did make an impression on you. You think you need to handle him." Her brows furrowed. "You hired his dad?"

"Yep, yesterday. I needed the help. Even Flora agreed I needed an extra set of hands. His name is Carter. He and his wife, Maureen, moved here from Illinois about six months ago. His sons live here, and they wanted to be closer to them and as he put it, 'maybe someday our grandchildren.' So, what's the scoop? How long has the lieutenant been here?"

"Let me think. I believe he arrived here about a year ago. He came from Chicago. He's not married—no girlfriend from what I hear through the grapevine." She paused with raised eyebrows. I fiddled with my napkin. Then she continued, "As good-looking as he is, though, several ladies are vying for the position."

"Oh?" I tried to maintain an impassive expression.

She leaned forward. "They practically drool on themselves when he's around." She leaned back and continued, "I'm guessing he's somewhere between the age of thirty and thirty-five. When I've worked with him, he's been professional, fair and has gone out of his way to do what he could to help me without breaking the law. Does that give you the scoop?"

"Yes, it does. Thank you." I lifted my chin a hair. "We kind of got off on the wrong foot. I thought if I knew a little about him, it might help me to be better prepared—" My words trailed off when I caught sight of the look on my sister's face. There was no longer a teasing sparkle in her eyes, and her face had compressed into a series of deep lines.

"What do you mean you got off on the wrong foot? You have to work with him on this case. If he's not willing to work with you, or if your trouble magnet has been acting up again, it could make obtaining the information we need difficult."

"No," I said, "I didn't aggravate him, hound him with questions, or send him to the hospital, if that's what you mean."

"Then, what?"

"Well, I—" Hesitating, I took an immediate interest in the purse in my lap and fiddled with the magnetic clasp.

"What?" Elizabeth demanded.

"I fainted. There, happy?" I snapped.

Elizabeth looked surprised. "You fainted?"

As a lawyer, she's trained to anticipate the answers to her questions from those on the stand, and out of habit, she tends to anticipate the answers in everyday life. But she didn't anticipate this one.

"You fainted." This time it was not a question; it was a statement followed by an infectious giggle. Before I knew it, we were both giggling and trying hard not to fall into a full belly laugh. "You fainted. Now, I'm sure you made an impression on our handsome lieutenant."

I explained how he caught me, kept me from hitting the concrete, and called the paramedic over to look after me. This served to intensify the sparkle in her eyes. Now I'd done it. I supplied her with a good month's worth of teasing material, and she knew it.

"Now you know why I might be a bit hesitant to see him again." I glanced at my watch and knew if I didn't leave now, the insurance list would be on hold until tomorrow. "I've got to go. I have to find a repairman, so I can give him all the money

I'll make as your new investigator."

I stood and started to walk away, but Elizabeth, who always likes to get in the last word, called after me in a loud voice, "Amy Kate, try to keep your fainting spells to a minimum. I can't guarantee Lieutenant Cooper will always be around to catch you." There it was.

My cheeks turned a nice shade of red because I felt the heat of the blush rise from my neck and disperse onto my face.

Elizabeth was good at pinpointing the truth, and she nailed it. She knew there was a part of me that enjoyed a good-looking man rescuing me, even if it was from a knot on my head.

Answering in a similar spirit, I called over my shoulder, "Don't worry, Sis. I can catch myself. No knight in shining armor needed here." Then I made a beeline for the exit.

CHAPTER FIVE

"What do you mean the fire investigator can't get here until tomorrow? Has there been a rash of fires in Pine Lake I haven't heard about?" I asked after listening to Theresa Thornton on the other end of the line inform me of the delay. "I'm sorry, Theresa, this isn't your fault. I'm just anxious to get the store back up and running as soon as possible."

"Are you getting estimates?"

"Yes, I've started contacting repairmen to get the estimates. I have two lined up already, and one said the earliest he could be here was Friday, and the other is coming Monday. When do you think your adjuster will be here?"

"Monday." She carried on about the damage to the other stores.

I guess that would have to do. "Yes, you're right, Theresa. I should be thankful that the damage is minimal." At the end of our conversation, Theresa reassured me she would do everything she could to help.

By the time I finished with my phone calls, the third repair company was lined up for Friday as well. I did all I could do today toward my list of no return.

Actually, I hoped it had a great return, enough to return my semi-charred workroom back into my happy place.

I sighed and weaved my way through the piles of office supplies to the back for another look. My workroom. I brooded as I envisioned it pre-fire. The tall workstation equipped with sleek, thin computers that gave us plenty of room to work with our books, the swivel stools with padded seats and backs, set off by a floral china blue pattern that I adored. I loved it all.

In the corner, my overstuffed chair covered in the same china-blue pattern was surrounded by four end tables of various shapes and sizes. They had held a cascade of books that I pulled to read. A floor lamp sat beside my chair giving a warm glow to the area, but the item I most treasured was the second chair, covered in a bright blue material. It was where my friends and family would sit and talk about their lives.

Tears welled up in my eyes. Now the room sat empty.

Carter and Flora had moved the contents out while I was on the phone most of the afternoon. The main area overflowed with books, office supplies, reams of paper, and boxes of swag from our grand opening. The displays filled with bestsellers and staff recommendations sat adrift in the endless sea of objects.

The kids' corner now housed my personal desk next to the spindle rocking chair used during reading hour, and my overstuffed chairs looked lost poked in between the romance section and the large-print mysteries.

Everywhere I looked chaos and disorder reigned. I took a deep breath in through the nose and out through the mouth, then turned my attention to something more productive than the overwhelming feeling to cry, again.

Flora, Carter, and I discussed what needed to be done and what could be done during the rest of our week with the shop in its present condition. With a plan now in place, we decided to work on scanning last week's shipment into the computer to get rid of the clutter of boxes.

I was grateful the electrical system wasn't damaged. With it in place, we made some form of forward progress. I scanned the books into the computer, and Flora and Carter shelved them as best as they could. As we were finishing, Flora asked how it had gone with Elizabeth.

I caught both Flora's and Carter's attention with my answer. "It was rather a strange meeting." Intrigued, they turned from their work and joined me at the front counter.

"What do you mean, Amy Kate? Couldn't she answer your insurance questions? I know it's not her field of expertise, but I thought she might have some ideas," Flora said.

"Funny, I'm the one with the ideas, but not about the insurance stuff." My cryptic answer caused both their brows to crease.

"Oh, what were your ideas?" Carter seemed to catch on to my intentional vagueness and played along.

"I had the idea she needed to hire me."

"Hire you? For what?" Flora asked, her eyes widening.

"For my legs."

"What?" They said in unison.

I couldn't help myself but break out into a laugh.

"I guess I'd better explain." I said, showing mercy on them. "Elizabeth hired me to investigate Matt Murphy's case. She's swamped and needs someone to do the legwork. So, she hired my legs."

"What about her usual guys?" Flora had been around long enough to know what the usual was.

"They were busy." I shrugged. I didn't bother to tell them the details of how I had to beg Elizabeth to give me a shot, or the fact I needed the money to help out while I waited on the insurance claim. No, I kept all that to myself, though I had a feeling Flora already knew.

I spent the next fifteen minutes answering their flurry of questions and getting them as caught up as they should be. After all, this was my first and last case, and I wanted to do everything in a professional manner, as if it were a real job. I wanted to prove to Elizabeth I could do it.

"Hmm." Flora gave me a good once-over from head to toe. "I would've never figured you for a private investigator."

"Yeah, I know," I said. "I wouldn't have thought of myself as P.I. material either, although being a detective does run in the blood, you know."

"Yes, you're right. Your dad was a natural, and you have enough of him in you that I bet you'll be a natural too." This was Flora's way of giving me her vote of confidence.

Carter smiled and gave two thumbs-up. I loved my older employees. What would Kirk say? Knowing him, he'd want me to wear a trench coat and stalk around in the shadows like The Creeper.

Then it hit me. I'm an investigator, me. Since she was

paying me, it was a real job. I hoped I was doing the right thing. Before I let my imagination run in the direction of crime and murder and wind up with a full-blown panic attack, I decided to go ahead and send Carter and Flora home.

As Carter was leaving, he commented about this being the most unique first day on a job he had ever had in his thirty-seven years of employment. "I thought my job would be sorting and scanning books, but my first assignments were as a repairman and a mover. Who knows, tomorrow I might be a painter. Look at you, Amy Kate. This morning you were a bookshop owner. Now, you're also a P.I." He grinned, shaking his head. "Wait until I tell Maureen about all the excitement." He leaned forward. "I don't mean to make light of the situation. I know a man lost his life today."

"No, I believe in laughter. It's the best medicine for an aching heart, so if this craziness I call life will give someone a chuckle, have at it."

Carter Cooper was a thoughtful man, and if he had raised his son to be half as considerate as he was, I looked forward to getting to know Lieutenant Cooper better. The whole conversation with Elizabeth at lunch had set my mind thinking on things other than the two lists in front of me. I tried to work out a plan for finishing the insurance list and starting the suspects list, but my mind kept drifting.

As I pulled myself out of the daydream, I glanced at the clock. I needed to hustle if I was going to make it to Elizabeth's office in time for the four o'clock meeting with Matt. There was no way I was missing it.

I locked the door to Twisted Plots and headed toward Elizabeth's office. Lieutenant Cooper was striding toward the same destination. He was coming from the direction of the police station, which was on the same side of the square as Elizabeth's office on Lincoln Avenue, but it wasn't part of the town square.

When I reached her office, Lieutenant Cooper held the door open for me, and we entered together.

"I'm surprised to see you here, Lieutenant." I commented over my shoulder, trying to make casual conversation.

"I was thinking the same thing about you. Though I must

admit, it is a pleasant surprise." His breath brushed across my ear.

I turned to face him, a little startled by his nearness, then took a few steps backward to set up some boundaries, a little personal space. Lieutenant Cooper didn't strike me as a man who let personal space get in his way.

"Hi, Tilley," he called and took off his coat. He was now all business.

"Hi, she's waiting for you, Amy Kate. The two of you can go on in."

We proceeded into Elizabeth's office where we found her and Matt at a small conference table. They were deep in conversation, but the talk stopped when we entered.

"Hi, you two, come on in. Matt and I were going over his statement."

"Don't stop on my account," the lieutenant said.

"To be honest, Gabe, I wasn't expecting you this afternoon. Is there anything I can do for you?"

"Yeah, I came by because I found something in Mrs. Culpepper's statement that might interest you, so I thought I'd drop it off."

"Okay, her name is on the list of potential witnesses I gave to my investigator today." Elizabeth sat straight in her chair at the table and glanced my way.

"Oh, did you retain Osborn or Luther from Chattanooga to work this case with you?" The lieutenant leaned against her desk and faced the conference table.

"Neither."

"Don't tell me you hired Harvey Polosky."

"No." Elizabeth leaned back in her chair. "No, I didn't hire Harvey either."

At this point, my sister glanced at me, and the conversation stalled. The lieutenant's eyes darted from me back to Elizabeth, waiting for the answer to the great mystery of whom my sister had hired.

Then the light of understanding dawned in his no-nonsense eyes. "No, you're kidding. Right?"

"She hired me," I squeaked out like a teenage boy going through puberty.

Matt groaned. "You hired Amy Kate?"

Determined to show I was capable, I cleared my throat and tried again. "She hired me, Lieutenant. I thought you might be pleased. It means we'll get to spend some time together, and maybe we'll have time for a little Chinese takeout." Then to my surprise, I winked at him. I hadn't planned it, but if that's not confidence, I don't know what is.

The wink went unnoticed.

The lieutenant's calm demeanor vanished. He snapped his head toward Elizabeth. "Are you out of your mind? She has no training." He pointed his finger in my general direction. "She's your sister for goodness' sake. What if she gets hurt? We're dealing with a potential killer here—at the very least, an arsonist—and she's involved in the case." He sighed then dragged his hand down his face and collapsed into the chair behind him. "What were you thinking? She can't do this. It's unprofessional of you to hire your sister for this job."

Matt stood. "I agree. I'd feel terrible if Amy Kate was harmed while trying to help me. I don't like it."

Elizabeth didn't seem ruffled at all by the lieutenant's accusation of being unprofessional or by Matt's dislike of her choice. She waited for both to calm down.

Once Lieutenant Cooper took a second long, deep breath, and Matt reclaimed his seat, Elizabeth explained to them the benefits of, and the reasons for, her hiring me to work this case. She was kind enough to leave off the part about my begging.

The lieutenant was not pleased. His lips pulled into a straight thin line, and the muscle in his jaw clenched.

I did everything to contain my temper and not to let the overbearing ape rattle me. How dare he and Elizabeth talk about me as if I weren't in the room?

After a pause, the lieutenant glanced at me. "Can I speak to you alone, Elizabeth?"

"Yes." She circled the table to the door, and Lieutenant Cooper rose from the chair and followed her out into the front lobby.

As luck would have it, he didn't think to close the door behind him. When it cracked open by no fault of its own, Matt and I took complete advantage of the opportunity and moved

closer to the door so we could eavesdrop.
"Look, it's none of my business who you hire to do your legwork, but you're not going to make my job any harder. Do you understand?"
"Yes, I do, and I think you'll be surprised by Amy Kate's abilities to reach people. She can convince complete strangers to tell her their whole life stories within minutes of meeting them. Besides, she has a vested interest in seeing this case gets closed. She's Matt's friend and cares what happens to him. Plus, she needs her shop back up and running. Friendship and money are her motivators. What better ones could she have?"
Elizabeth had him there. It was wrong to listen to their private conversation, but Matt and I both agreed through silent nods it was the right thing to do. After all, it was our lives that had burned up, not theirs.
"All right, you do what you want, but I'm not responsible for her."
"Understood," Elizabeth said.
"Here's the statement from Mrs. Culpepper. You'll be interested in what she saw. It has the D.A. looking at a few other people as potential suspects. I thought knowing this might make you and your client breathe a little easier." He handed it over to her and then glanced at his watch. "I've got to go. Tell Amy Kate to be careful. This isn't a game."
He strode toward the front door and stopped.
"I'll tell her, but I think she already knows, thanks to you." She pointed at the door ajar. "My sister's capable, Gabe. She'll be fine."
With his hand on the doorknob, the lieutenant turned. "No, I don't think she will be. Your sister couldn't even handle the scene at the fire this morning. Did she tell you she wound up fainting? How is she going to handle it if someone gets rough with her, or worse, she finds a dead body?" He let go of the doorknob and ambled toward Elizabeth, placing his hands on her upper arms.
Startled, she glanced up from the report.
"Elizabeth, if anything happened to your sister and it was my fault, I wouldn't be able to forgive myself. Family is too important. You know I've lost a brother, and since you lost your

mother, I expected you—" His voice trailed off.

"I know, Gabe, but she has a good head on her shoulders. She'll be a natural at this, and I promise you we'll keep it to the interviews. If we find anything suspicious, we'll call you."

"Okay, if you say so."

I didn't miss the hesitation in his voice as if he didn't believe what she told him.

He let his hands fall away from her shoulders and stepped back.

Hmm, maybe the lieutenant did know a thing or two about personal space.

The scene in the outer lobby brought up more questions about the lieutenant than it answered. From what he said, he knew about the death of our mother. Elizabeth must've shared it with him, which indicated they had some type of personal relationship.

Gabe also mentioned a loss of his own, a brother. Since Carter Cooper worked for me, I was interested in knowing about this son he'd lost. I'm sure it had been painful for the whole family. I couldn't imagine being a parent burying a child. It wasn't the natural order of things.

I had spent time this afternoon daydreaming of a handsome, hunky detective. And now the detective had feelings, people he cared about, and a friendship with my sister.

The scene in the lobby also allowed me time to digest this new picture of Gabe.

True, I was upset about the exchange of words between my sister and the lieutenant. They both ignored my presence and treated me like the proverbial bump on a log, and the lieutenant acting like it was a huge imposition to work with me didn't help. My anger was working up to full pressure. That is, until the final exchange in the lobby.

It was then I saw the concern on his face and heard the genuine apprehension in his voice. His reaction gave me a glimpse into the heart of the man and showed the intensity with which he cared about the people around him. Being a cop wasn't his job. It was his mission.

I sighed. The daydreams had become complicated.

Once the lieutenant left, we made ourselves comfortable in

Elizabeth's office. I started the interview by asking about the argument between Matt and Bryant.

"I shouldn't have let Bryant get to me, but he knew how to work on my last nerve."

"Did you take a swing at him?"

"Yes, I did. We had started out talking about the deal with Benson and the contract Elizabeth had drawn up for me, then it got personal."

"How so?" Elizabeth asked.

"He started saying I was a loser who couldn't see the big picture and went on to say Lilly should've never married me." Matt flexed his hand. "He accused me of caring more about my own happiness than about her needs. Then he remarked about not being Lilly's biggest mistake, but I was."

"What did he mean by that?" Elizabeth asked.

"I don't know. Then he went on to say Lilly would've been better off without me. Said if I loved Lilly, I would sell the Beans and Leaves to Benson and quit whining about losing my shop on the square. He thought Lilly deserved the money to live in style."

"You love your shop," I patted his hand, knowing how he felt. It was killing me to see my own in such disarray. "Did Bryant say anything about the contract Elizabeth had drawn up for you?"

"As a matter of fact, he did." Matt moved forward in his chair. "Remember yesterday morning I told you I was afraid he would want me to sign a contract to blend flavors for their gain? Well, I was right. Bryant reworked the contract I had given him with the Benson lawyers."

"What did it say?" Elizabeth leaned toward him. Her brows furrowed.

"It stated that I could keep the Beans and Leaves on the square in exchange for three new flavors each year for the next three years." Matt flopped against the back of the chair and crossed his arms. "I figured he'd pull some kind of stunt like this, but once I read it, I was furious."

"How did the rest of your confrontation with Bryant go? Did Kirk see all of it?" Elizabeth asked.

"No, Kirk walked in at the end when everything wound up

being about Lilly. Bryant gave me a copy of the new-and-improved contract, and I laid it on my desk. He let it be known he wanted an answer by this morning."

"Were you going to sign it?" I asked out of curiosity.

"Since I kind of knew he'd pull something like this, yes, I was going to sign the contract and give them what they wanted. I'm ready to be done with it. He's been hounding me for months."

"So, you were willing to give them what they wanted in exchange for the store on the square. Of course," Elizabeth said, "you're going to make a killing by selling the other stores."

"All I want is my little piece of heaven. It was Bryant who wanted to make a killing. But once he started in about Lilly and me, I was determined to make him wait. I wasn't going to give him the satisfaction of thinking he'd won so easily." Matt sat up, leaning his elbows on the table. "Then he made a crack about me being Lilly's biggest mistake, and I rushed at him swinging. He ducked, and my fist hit the wall behind him. Kirk walked in, and I walked out."

"Was that the last time you saw Bryant?" I asked.

Matt sighed. "I came back about thirty minutes later to give Kirk the interview he wanted. Bryant was gone. I found the contract on my desk with a sticky note on it saying, 'I'll be here in the morning. Usual time. This had better be signed.' I signed it before I closed up." Matt tilted his head, and a faraway look came over him. "The funny thing about the contract was that Bryant didn't sign it. He'd acted like such a jerk, then didn't follow through."

"Did you kill Bryant Kendrick, Matt?" This was Elizabeth the lawyer asking, not Elizabeth the friend.

"No, I did not."

"Why were you meeting this morning if you had seen each other last night?"

"So Bryant could taste some of the new flavors I'd developed with a new bean. It worked well with a Jamaican bean we had been using. Amy Kate had a taste of it Tuesday. It's called Jamaica in the Morning." He turned and looked at me for confirmation.

"It was good too." I nodded and smiled at my sister. Her

expression was all business. I turned my attention back to Matt who continued.

"We tended to meet once a month on a Wednesday morning before the store opened in order to discuss business and try new flavors. Bryant was always impressed with what he called 'the magic' I could do with the beans and leaves. I'd brew them up and then Bryant would give them a try. It's hard to find the right flavor when you brew a single cup, so I always brewed a full pot. Then I could serve what was left in the shop once we opened at six and nothing would go to waste. The morning meetings made sense for what we needed to do."

"Who knew about these meetings?" I asked.

"Me, Bryant's administrative assistant, my employees, a couple of others."

"Lilly?" I asked.

"Yes, Lilly." Matt answered, unfolding his arms and placing his hands on the table.

"Was she at the shop after the incident with Bryant?"

"No, she wasn't there at all on Tuesday."

To clear her client of the suspicion that now hung over him, Elizabeth asked for his alibi. "Can anyone vouch for your whereabouts this morning? Was Lilly with you?"

"No, Lilly left to walk in the square as she does most mornings. She had to bundle up because it was in the low thirties. Of course, she checked on her flowers in the hothouse first. Her plants are her babies."

Elizabeth glanced at me, and I could read the concern in her eyes. She leaned forward in her seat. "You mean Lilly wasn't with you when you received the call about the fire?"

"No." Matt sat up straight, realizing the implications of what he said.

"Did Lilly know about the fight between you and Bryant? What he said about her?" I asked.

His body language said it all.

"You can't think Lilly would do such a thing." He shook his head. "No, she's not capable, not Lilly."

CHAPTER SIX

During the week and on Saturdays, my roommate, Julia, gets up before the rooster is even conscious. Without fail, she is faithfully at the Whispering Pines Bed and Breakfast by five o'clock for her head-chef duties.

But today when I rolled over to look at the clock for the hundredth time, I heard Julia moving around in the apartment. It was five thirty, so I got up to see if anything was wrong.

The noise was coming from the kitchen. I shuffled down the hall, my heart dragging on the carpeted floor. I entered the kitchen and stopped. She had two cups of coffee poured and was about to put cups, creamer, and sugar on a decorative tray.

"Amy Kate, you're awake." Her green eyes sparkled, and she greeted me with a warm smile. "I was just getting the coffee together to come wake you up. You were due some pampering after your day yesterday, and I thought coffee in bed would be the ticket."

I hadn't seen her the previous evening because I stayed late at Elizabeth's office and Julia works some evenings on her own business, Pure Sweetness. After the day I had yesterday, she was a welcomed sight. I needed a shoulder to cry on, and she had the appointed one.

I couldn't help myself but rush at my friend and hug her. Her thoughtfulness overwhelmed me. My heart was already starting to lift. "You, Julia Anne Jacobs, are my guardian angel, always taking care of me."

"You of all people know I'm no angel." She giggled and

headed for the living room with the tray. "I was so worried about you after I read your text and saw the news that I arranged for Miles, my sous chef, to cover for me. Told him I'd be in around seven. That should give us some time to catch up on what happened yesterday."

"I'm so glad you did." I followed her into the next room, plopping down in one of our overstuffed chairs. "What I need this morning is a big dose of venting, with a side order of please feel sorry for me. Then I expect you, my friend, to set me straight and put my feet back on the path to positive thinking."

"Will do." Julia nodded, causing her auburn curls to bounce.

For a moment, we both sat and savored the wonderful smell rising from the coffee and the comfort of our friendship.

"Is it true?" Julia asked in a small, gentle voice. "Was Bryant Kendrick murdered?"

"Yes, I believe so. Elizabeth is waiting on the preliminary autopsy report from the police to find out if he died in the fire or if he was already dead before the fire was set. But either way, it comes out to be murder." Gizmo, my black terrier, jumped up in the chair with me and found his favorite spot in my lap, jostling my cup.

"I can't believe something like that happened right next door to your shop." Julia sighed and shook her head. "How is Matt doing? Have you seen him?"

Julia's question highlighted how much I had to tell her. She knew nothing about Elizabeth hiring me, or the encounters I had yesterday with the handsome yet mysterious Lieutenant Cooper, nor did she know about me joining the dating service, Open Hearts.

I needed to pick a subject and dive in. After all, I had limited time to catch her up before she had to leave for work, and I wanted to hear her feedback on all of it.

When I was through, Julia sat stunned. "Wow, girl, you have a bad day, and you go all out. Me, if I have a bad day it's a flat tire, or an angry customer, but you—" She let out a low whistle. "No, you get tangled in a murder as both a l suspect and an investigator."

"I know." I let out a long, low sigh and ended with a "Hmm."

"What is it, Amy Kate? I know what it means when you start sighing like that. What are you thinking?"

"I'm concerned about what the lieutenant said. What if he's right? What if I am a liability? You, of all people, know how trouble can find me. It comes to me like steel to a magnet. What if I mess things up for Matt, or worse, get someone hurt? I begged Elizabeth for this job. What if I can't handle it?"

Julia shook her auburn curls again. "Elizabeth wouldn't have hired you if she thought you couldn't do the job even on a trial basis. Didn't you say she told the lieutenant you have a natural gift to persuade people to trust you? You're going to be a great help to both Elizabeth and Matt, an asset not a liability to the lieutenant."

"Thank you. You were just what I needed this morning. You and coffee."

Julia cut her eyes toward the big clock that hung over our fireplace, let out a gasp and jumped to her feet. "I've got to go." She dashed down the hall to her room. Ten minutes later she emerged dressed in her chef's uniform with her purse tucked under her arm and her keys jingling in her hand. She paused at the threshold. "Come by the Pines this afternoon so you can tell me all about the dating service."

"Okay, I will." I shrugged.

"No, promise. We didn't get to the good stuff. I need to know if you find your prince. It might tempt me to sign up too. I've been finding a lot of frogs in my pond, and a prince, even one not so charming, would be a nice change of pace."

With that, Julia left, inviting a burst of cold air into our warm home. Gizmo snuggled closer. It was time for a breakfast for two.

Gizmo gobbled up his scrambled egg, but I lingered over *the Pine Lake Daily News*. After a slow-paced breakfast, I went to my bedroom and started getting ready for the day.

My dirty clothes from yesterday lay in a pile on the floor. When I picked them up, the piece of porcelain I'd found in Matt's shop dropped from my pants pocket and landed at my feet. I leaned down and picked it up. I'd forgotten all about it. The shard of porcelain was white, and the unbroken edge was scalloped like a bird's wing or a border. I ran my finger along the edge. The shape intrigued me.

I started for the trash can in the corner of my room, then hesitated. I couldn't bring myself to throw it away without knowing what it went to, so I stashed it in my jewelry box instead and threw the pants in the laundry basket in my closet.

With time to kill before meeting Flora and Carter, I pulled out the insurance paperwork along with the lengthy to-do list and began working out my attack plan for the day.

First, I called Theresa. I had a feeling we'd either be good friends or die-hard enemies before this was over.

"Hi, Theresa," I said, trying to sound cheerful for eight o'clock in the morning.

"Hi." The tone of Theresa's voice matched mine. She must be a morning person.

"I was wondering what time I needed to be at the bookshop in order to meet the fire investigator. He is coming today, right?"

Theresa paused. "The fire investigator won't be able to be there until tomorrow."

I inhaled and exhaled letting the act clear my mind and tamped down my frustration.

"But," Theresa rushed on, "our insurance adjuster, Christine Templeton, will be there at ten. She was able to juggle her schedule and fit you in before Monday. Will that work for you?"

"Yes." I pushed to sound positive. "That will be great." At least something on the list was going to be completed today.

I ended the call and scanned the other items on my list. My plan for today also included working on the investigation. There were several people I needed to interview, and Elizabeth had stressed last night that time was of the essence.

After our discussion with Matt, I knew my first interview would be with Lilly Murphy, and I was keeping my fingers crossed that I'd like her answers.

~

On my way out the door, I received a text from Elizabeth asking me to pick up the preliminary autopsy report this morning at the police station since she was going to be in court.

I felt as though the stars were aligning. Theresa had given me good news about the insurance adjuster, and now I had a legitimate reason for going to the police station and speaking with the lieutenant. There were a few words I wanted to say to him about what had happened last night. I might have been a bump on a log then, but today, he needed to hear them. My irritation grew as I drove to the parking lot beside Twisted Plots.

I arrived at the police station a little after nine. Pulling the glass door open, I entered a waiting area and stopped to address the officer who was working the front desk. He had his head down, filling out some paperwork. "Is Lieutenant Cooper here?"

The older male officer glanced up and recognized me right off. "Amy Kate, long time no see. What brings you here?"

"Hey, Wallace." I smiled at my Dad's old buddy. "I came to see Lieutenant Cooper. Is he here?"

"Give me one sec. Okay, kiddo? And I'll check for you."

Three teenagers were milling around, and one slouched over an entire section of chairs like a king on his throne. He sneered in my direction when he caught my eye.

Officer Wallace made some gesture to one of the teens who decided to take a seat.

An older lady with a cane sat stiff and alert in an adjoining section of chairs, watching the teens and holding on to her purse with clenched fingers. From her body language, it was apparent there had been trouble between her and one or more of the teens, and she wasn't about to lower her guard just because they were in the police station. One of the young men sported handcuffs.

After a few phone calls and a stop to answer the squawking radio, Wallace cocked his head toward the door which led to a hallway. "You'll find Lieutenant Cooper on the second floor, homicide division. It's toward the end of the hall, big room, lots of desks, bad smell."

I smiled remembering the bad smell from Dad's days as a detective. All those people working together in a crowded room created a brew of cigar smoke, sweat and a myriad of aftershaves and colognes. Strange how some things never change.

I didn't need to ask where the elevators were because I was pretty sure their location hadn't changed either.

As I entered the large homicide room, the lieutenant was leaning against his desk with his back toward me. I neared his desk and stopped, waiting for the lieutenant to finish his conversation.

Just because I was going to give him an earful didn't mean I had to be rude. All good Southern women could give someone a stern scolding up one side and down the other without ever saying one impolite or unladylike word. Today, I intended to be a good Southern woman.

Gabe's buddy nodded toward me, which caused the lieutenant to turn to see who was behind him. His first look said it all. "Yes, Miss Anderson, what can I do for you?" His face radiated annoyance.

"My, Lieutenant, aren't we being formal today, Miss Anderson and all. Why don't we dispense with the formalities since we'll be working together on the Bryant Kendrick case? You can just call me Amy Kate, and what can I call you?"

"Incredibly busy, Miss Anderson."

"Well now, you're not going to be rude simply because you don't want to share your toys, are you? I mean you made it quite clear last night you didn't want me working on this case." At this comment, he rolled his eyes and crossed his arms.

"No, Miss Anderson. Now, what can I do for you?"

"Amy Kate, I insist." I plastered a polite smile on my lips. *Eat that.*

"Okay... Amy Kate... what can I do for you?"

From the edginess in his voice, I was getting to him. I figured I could get away with this southern charm baloney for about another ten seconds before he blew. This was going to be a fun ten seconds. *Ten...*

"Now, that wasn't so hard, was it?" My words dripped with sugar.

"No," I think I saw him grit his teeth. *Nine...*

"Now, what should I call you? And be sweet this time." I used my best Southern drawl as I patted his cheek for emphasis. One or two of his coworkers began to snicker. *Eight...*

"You may call me Lieutenant or Lieutenant Cooper since our relationship *is* a professional one." *Seven . . .* Then he repeated his question enunciating each word, so his frustration wouldn't be lost on me. "How . . . can . . . I . . . help . . . you?" *Six...*

"Aw, Gabe, now, I'm sure we will be great friends in no time. I see no reason for us to stand on all these little professional etiquettes. That might be how it's done up North, but there's no need to be so stuffy about it all here. After all, we're in the South."

Gabe let out a resounding, "Humph." *Five* . . .

Some of the other detectives in the squad room joined in our conversation with a little friendly ribbing.

"Gabe come on. Let her call you by your first name," one of his female coworkers called out to him, grinning from ear to ear. "What could be the harm in it?" *Four* . . .

One of the male detectives called out in *falsetto*, "Yeah, Gabe, no need to stand on these little professional etiquettes." *Three* . . .

Another chimed in with "That's right, Lieutenant, I mean, Gabe." He said it with a gentle tone and chuckled at his own joke. *Two* . . .

"You're just being difficult and now—" I looked at my watch for emphasis, "you're wasting my time." *One* . . .

"Me? Wasting *your* time?" Gabe lunged forward. "You're the one who started this stupid name game."

Boom.

Gabe Cooper, red-faced with neck veins bulging, grabbed my arm so quickly he about pulled me off my feet. He dragged me to the glass doors separating the detectives' squad room from the main hall and stuffed me through them.

Once he had me on the other side, he paced in circles, taking some deep breaths. I stood watching him mutter to himself, fighting to keep control of his temper. From the looks of it, he wasn't winning.

Gabe came to a standstill in front of me. Putting his hands on his hips, he leaned over me with his six-foot frame as if to intimidate me. "If you *ever* pull your Miss Southern-politeness bull on me again, I'll have you kicked out of here so fast it'll make your head spin. Do you know how hard I've worked to earn the respect of my coworkers? How challenging it's been to be accepted in such a tight-knit group? If it hadn't been for some advice your dad gave me, I would've never been accepted and trusted, and in law enforcement, trust can mean the difference between life and death for you or your partner." Lieutenant Cooper paused to catch his breath.

I had come to the station to give this guy a piece of my mind, and here I stood, again, letting him chastise me as if I were a child. As I started to say something, Gabe continued his tirade.

"I'm not going to let you waltz in here and make a monkey out of me so you can get some kind of weird satisfaction from working your feminine charms on me," he said straight-faced.

It took me a minute to register what he said. "Are you kidding me? Did you think I was flirting with you?"

"Yeah. What else could it be?"

"I wasn't flirting with you, you big moron." I swatted his arm. "I was trying to make you feel foolish like you made me feel last night when you told Elizabeth I was incompetent, and I'd probably get myself killed. I wanted to return the favor. See how you liked it."

The veins in his neck stopped pulsing. "Well, you probably will get yourself killed." His tone was much calmer. He rubbed the spot where I whacked him.

"What was all that 'Can I call you Gabe' nonsense then if you weren't trying to use your womanly wiles?" He wiggled his fingers in the air as if he was trying to cast a spell.

"I was just giving you the runaround. You don't strike me as a man who likes to have his time wasted." I crossed my arms over my chest. He thought I was flirting with him? What an oaf.

"That's not how I took it. It sounded like a blatant come-on to me, and it did to everyone else as well, given their comments." At this point, he gave me a sheepish grin. "Think about it, Amy Kate."

I closed my eyes taking a moment to replay the scene in the squad room in my mind. "Yes, Gabe, no need to stand on these little professional etiquettes," began to ring in my ears.

My eyes flew open. He was right. The detectives hadn't been egging him on to get a rise out of him. They were giving him a hard time because it looked like I was throwing myself at him.

That's why he became so red-faced and angry. He was mortified by my behavior. Here was Detective Anderson's daughter zipping into his realm to flirt with him, using business as a guise.

"You're right." I cringed. "I hate to imagine what everyone

in there must think. I should've talked to you as one professional to another instead of trying to even the score." I sighed. "I guess you wouldn't consider me embarrassing myself in front of all those detectives—many of whom are family friends, I might add—as my penance for trying to be so catty."

"Not on your life."

It took all I had to admit to him he was right. I was still sore about the things he said to Elizabeth, but if I was ever going to retain any sliver of dignity in this relationship, I had to make it right. That's one thing about us steel magnolias—when we make a royal mess of something, for honor's sake, we will apologize. I swallowed the lump of pride clogging my throat. "I'm sorry, Lieutenant, it won't happen again."

"Thank you, Amy Kate." His shoulders relaxed as his mild demeanor and natural face color returned. "You know, I'm glad we've had this talk because it's helped to improve my opinion of you." He gave me a lopsided grin. "I now no longer view you as the fainting floozy of Pine Lake, Alabama."

"I should hope not." I lifted my chin and stared down my nose a bit. "And for the record, if I ever did flirt with you, Gabe Cooper, you would know it. You wouldn't have to be a detective to figure it out."

"I'm sure I would, Miss Anderson." Gabe became serious. "Now, let's talk about why you're here."

"Okay, let's talk."

"I meant what I said to Elizabeth last night." At this point, he stepped closer to me and touched my shoulder. He was making sure he had my full attention, and he did. "Do not make my job any harder than it already is. If you find out anything of interest from your interviews, your first call is to me. You're not to go running off on your own following some lead. I won't stand for any foolishness. You are not—I repeat not—to put yourself in harm's way. Understood?"

Here was the detective I had met at first, the one in my bookshop, the one who wanted to save the world.

I took a step back. "For some reason you think you're responsible for my safety. I want to make it clear you're not. I am neither an imbecile nor a child. You will not dictate to me. If I'm to do my best for Matt, I must follow where the trail leads.

Do you understand, Gabe?" I added his name for emphasis.

"Yes, I understand. You are a stubborn, hardheaded woman who is playing at detective, and either you, or I, or both of us will wind up getting hurt because of it."

At this the lieutenant turned on his heels, whipped open the glass doors, and strode to his desk, with me following. I had come for the autopsy report, and after all this, there was no way I was going to leave without it. You could have knocked Gabe over with a feather when he turned around to find me again standing in front of his desk.

"You are one persistent lady. I'll give you that," he said.

"Yes, I am." I squared my shoulders. I didn't think my dignity could take any more potshots today. I had come to make the point with the lieutenant that I could take care of myself, and even though everyone in the room thought I was a desperate hussy, I had delivered my message. Determined to do my job and to do it well, I forged on. "I didn't want to forget the preliminary autopsy report, Lieutenant," I said with all the Southern iron I could muster, painfully aware everyone was listening.

He reached over, picked up a file and handed it to me with about the same enthusiasm as a child giving up his Halloween candy. "Here, take it. Tell Elizabeth this is her copy."

"I'll be sure to tell her, and as a professional courtesy, I'm letting you know I'm planning on interviewing Lilly Murphy sometime today if I can catch her at the antique shop."

"Fine, let me know if you find out anything worth sharing." Then, a gentleness invaded his dark brown eyes. "And Amy Kate, I know it's none of my business because you've made that clear but be careful. You never know whose attention you might attract when you start asking around about Bryant Kendrick."

"I will. Thanks for the report." I turned on my two-inch high heels and made a hasty retreat, ready to forget this whole encounter. Once outside the police station, I took a minute to review the autopsy results. What I found was not what I was expecting.

CHAPTER SEVEN

Bryant Kendrick hadn't died of smoke inhalation. No, he died from poisoning.

I was stunned. Poisoning? My mind raced. How? I couldn't wait to talk to Elizabeth and see what she thought about this. After replacing the report in the folder, I slipped it in my large shoulder bag.

Across the square, a woman stood by the front door of Twisted Plots. She was peering into the windows where the displays were still up from last week. The insurance adjuster.

I couldn't allow my foolishness to cause me to miss my appointment. She moved to her car and opened the door.

I jogged through the town square at full stride to the edge of the street. A car passed in front of me, forcing me to stop. This gave the lady, who had to be Christine Templeton, the time to start to pull away. She stopped half out of the parking space to let another car pass by.

This was it—I had one last chance to catch her before I lost this opportunity and was doomed to another day of waiting. I threw off my heels, the black ones I loved, tossed aside my bag, and in stocking feet, sprinted toward the shop. I waved my hands and yelled at the top of my lungs. My antics paid off. Ms. Templeton maneuvered her car back into the parking space in front of my shop.

I was too winded to speak when I arrived on the sidewalk next to her. I leaned over and tried to lower my heart and pulse rate. Once I could breathe through my nose again, I discovered an amused brunette with sharp green eyes staring at me.

"Are you gonna make it, girlfriend?"

"Yes—" I panted leaning over again. "I don't run. I'm a walker."

"Oh." She raised her eyebrows and nodded as if she understood. "I take it you're Miss Anderson?"

"I am." I stood up straight to shake her hand and noticed her hands were full of briefcases, gloves, papers, and purses. She didn't have a free hand to shake, but rather seemed to have been gifted with extras.

Remembering my manners, I stretched out my arms in order to take something. "Can I help you?"

"I think it would be better if you opened the door for me, then I could unload."

"Oh, yes." I patted down my coat pockets for the keys but came up empty. "Oh, I dropped my purse in my rush to catch you."

Christine Templeton's eyes sparkled with amusement. "Girl, you might want to go fetch your belongings before they walk off without you." Then she looked down at my wet, dirty, shoeless feet. "I take it your shoes were part of the left-behind group. Aren't your feet cold? Mine would be freezing."

"Now that you mention it. Yes, they are."

~

Carter and Flora arrived on time at one o'clock, and I excused myself to go conduct my first solo interview. The thought sent a little thrill through me, and I couldn't stop a smile from spreading across my face. A bit morbid, but true.

As I walked down the sidewalk to the corner and crossed to the north side of the square, I tried to remember Matt and Lilly would be in mourning for Bryant.

Lilly was in full view, arranging some pottery on a shelf when I entered the Junk in the Trunk Antique Shop. The bell didn't jingle because I held the clapper between my fingers. I wanted to see Lilly Murphy as she was when no one was looking. Her movements were graceful as she glided the knick-knacks from one spot to another.

Somewhere in her forties, her hair still held its natural color of brunette with a few strands of gray mixed in, which gave her an air of experience. She wasn't tall, maybe five foot four, and her figure was still intact, giving evidence she exercised. Lilly was no model, but she had poise and confidence—qualities that lend themselves to the concept of beauty.

I must've stood there a good fifteen seconds before she noticed me. When she did, she let out a little gasp.

"Oh, it's you, Amy Kate. I was so deep in thought I didn't hear you come in."

"Sorry, I didn't mean to startle you. I saw you were here alone, and I wanted to ask you a few questions about what happened yesterday."

"Matt told me you'd come by." She stopped working on the displays and gave me her full attention. Then she motioned for me to follow her to the counter where she handed me a stool.

"Here, have a seat," she said. "I've been on my feet all morning. It'll feel good to take a break." Lilly pulled out another stool for herself and sighed. "You know, Matt and I didn't get much sleep last night. We both tossed and turned. The bedcovers looked like there'd been a wrestling match." She took off her shoes and wiggled her toes.

"I know what you mean. I didn't sleep much after my mom's death either." I knew firsthand how stress robbed people of their sleep. It had evaded me those first few weeks until I fell out from pure exhaustion. It was months before I could lie down and drift off without a struggle.

I wanted to be sympathetic, but I had a job to do, so I started. "I wanted to ask you a few questions about yesterday."

"Go ahead, shoot."

"Matt said you weren't with him when he received the call about the fire."

"No, I had gone out for my morning walk."

"Do you always go so early?"

"Yeah, Matt gets up around that time anyway, and by doing it then, I don't have to worry about my exercise conflicting with my schedule here. I keep a routine. The walking is for my cholesterol, so consistency is important. At least, that's what my doctor says." Lilly smiled.

"Can you tell me what you saw yesterday? Was there anything unusual?"

"You mean besides the fire. You do know I'm the one who called it in, right?"

"You called it in? No, I didn't know that. How about you tell me what happened, starting from when you left your house."

"Let's see." She squinted as if she were visualizing the events. "I walked to the square. It's about a mile from the house. I do a couple of laps around the square and then go back to the house. It makes for about a three-mile walk."

I pulled my notebook from my bag and jotted down her account. "Three miles, got it." Since I was new at this, I didn't want to miss anything.

"I was starting on my first lap when I smelled burnt coffee. I used to waitress so I'm familiar with the smell." Lilly wrinkled her nose. "Anyway, I instinctively headed toward the Beans and Leaves. I suppose the smell made me go that way. I tried the front door, and it was locked as it should've been. I peeked in the windows, but it was so dark I couldn't see anything. So, I walked around to the alley. As I turned the corner of your shop, I thought I saw someone going around the corner at the other end, but I could've been mistaken. After all, once I reached the back, smoke was pouring out, and it was hard to see. I called 911, and they were there in seconds."

"Did you call Matt?"

Lilly looked surprised, as if I had asked her something she hadn't thought of. "No, I didn't, and to be honest, it never occurred to me. I was so sure he was already in the building my one thought was to get him out."

"What happened after the fire trucks and police showed up?"

"It wasn't but a few minutes later that Matt and you showed up, and the fire was out." As Lilly was talking, a sudden burst of noise, a car alarm, blared at us from outside. Someone must've pushed the wrong button on their key fob. Out of curiosity, we walked to the front of the store to see what was going on.

One of the employees from the hair salon across the street ran out, pointing a remote key at the offending vehicle.

"Those things are so loud. I know they're supposed to scare off the bad guys, but it's annoying." I turned from the window to glance at Lilly. She had gone stock still. "What is it, Lilly?"

"I think the stupid car alarm reminded me of something I forgot. You know I said I thought I saw someone leaving the alley behind the stores? I remembered while I was reporting the fire, I kept thinking how I wished the car alarm would stop blaring. Amy Kate, I heard a car alarm, and when it stopped not a second later, a black SUV flew by on Polk Street away from the square."

"Had you noticed a black SUV on the square while you were walking?"

"There're always a couple of cars parked on the square even in the wee hours of the morning. Owners like Matt coming in early or other walkers who drive here to use the area. Sometimes cars are even left overnight." Again, she squinted her eyes. "Hmm, now that I think about it, I do believe there was a black SUV." Excitement registered on her face. "You know who uses black SUVs?"

"Besides the FBI and every law enforcement agency portrayed on TV?"

At this remark, Lilly gave me a sour look. "Yes, besides them. Java Vein. They use them as company vehicles."

"You don't say." I wrote all this down and made sure I put in the part about Lilly *believing* she saw this car because one thing for sure, there is a big difference between believing and it being so.

"You didn't happen to see a company logo or any identifying marks on the SUV as it passed?" I asked with a degree of hope.

"No—" She frowned and shook her head. "Bryant drove one. It's why the SUV didn't stand out to me. I would've expected to see it there knowing Bryant was meeting Matt. I wonder what Bryant drove if he didn't drive the SUV?"

"Good question." And it was. I was going to have to go see the lieutenant about it. "Now, Matt said you guys had known Bryant since college. Is that right?"

"Yes, I met Bryant my junior year of college. He was outgoing and handsome too. Tons of friends and a different girl every month, a real player. I don't know how he managed to graduate, but he did."

"Where did he end up after college?"

"He went to work for his brother or uncle. I can't remember. I was in the middle of planning my wedding at the time. Then he struck out on his own. For a while we exchanged Christmas cards and an occasional email update. You know the sort of thing—weddings, births, the major events in life. For some reason, Matt had a soft spot for him."

Lilly leaned against the wall near the window. Having left her shoes by the counter, she stood in her stocking feet.

"Can you remember any of those major events?"

"I remember when he got married to his wife, Sarah Catherine. We received an invitation. It wasn't long after their wedding they arrived here. There weren't any birth announcements because he has no children—at least not to his knowledge." Lilly's remark sounded cold.

She continued, "I shouldn't say that, but you have to understand, Amy Kate, he was the kind of man who was in it for himself, but he excelled at hiding it. He reeked of sincerity, then took what he wanted while he was smiling at you. The man used people, plain and simple, either for money or for other things, and Matt and I didn't figure it out until it was too late."

"What do you mean too late?"

Lilly stared at the floor trying to regain her composure. I wasn't sure if what I was seeing was anger or regret, but the flash of emotion passed. "The business, of course. Matt made him a partner before we knew the full extent of what he planned for the business—our business." She paused and looked me full in the face. "Most would say Bryant was a godsend, taking one shop and building it into a statewide company, but as for me, the price was too high to pay."

The bell jingled, and Lilly stood to her full height and greeted the customer. She looked down at her shoeless feet and made her way back to the counter to amend the situation. I smiled at the customer and followed Lilly.

After Lilly slipped her shoes on her feet, she handed me my purse. "Is there anything else I can help you with?" She presented me with the smile of a saleswoman. I knew I was being dismissed.

A second customer entered the store, and it was time for me to leave. I so wanted to ask Lilly about the price she was paying—if she was referring to her husband's happiness or something else, but the moment didn't lend itself to anymore questions. I was left to ponder who had been driving the SUV and whether the business partnership was Lilly's only regret.

~

Flora and Carter had been holding down the shop all afternoon. They came in at one o'clock, and I slipped out to interview Lilly. I felt a twinge of guilt, but not as much as I would've had Flora been all alone—besides, the P.I. gig was going to pay some of their salaries this month.

When I entered the shop, I was pleased to find Carter and Flora had finished moving the rest of the furniture from the back, preparing for the parade of repairmen. "Wow, you did a great job getting everything out of the back workspace. Thanks." I hurried to my faithful friend and gave her a big hug, then patted Carter on the forearm. He placed his large hand over mine and gave it a squeeze.

"Our pleasure, kiddo."

"I guess we won't need Kirk tomorrow after all. I'll call him and let him know not to come in until Saturday. Can one of you come in tomorrow to help with the shipment that's due? I'm not sure how busy I'll be with the repair guy."

"Tell you what," Carter said, "let's give Flora tomorrow off, and I'll come in. I'm sure she can find something to keep her occupied at home." He winked at Flora, who grinned and swatted at him. "And I might be of some help with the repairmen. A man's presence might keep 'em honest."

"I don't think there'll be a problem, but thanks for your thoughtfulness. You remind me of my dad, looking out for other people all the time."

"Yes, I've heard about your dad. He made a lasting impression on my Gabe. Your dad helped him out when he first came to town. Gabe has a great deal of respect for him."

"Yeah, Gabe mentioned something about it to me this morning." I didn't want to go into the details of our encounter after the way I made such a mess of things. I wasn't looking forward to my next conversation with Gabe Cooper. Obviously, he didn't hold the same respect for the daughter as he did for the father of the Anderson crew.

"Speaking of detectives, I received the autopsy report this morning from Gabe."

Flora zeroed into this tidbit. "What did it say?"

I dug the report out of my purse and handed it to Carter.

"Should you be showing this to us?" He asked.

I reached out and grabbed the folder in his hand. "If you're not interested—"

"I didn't say that." Carter smiled and pulled the folder toward him. He opened it and read the paper inside. "Poisoned, really? I didn't think it would come down to a murder. I figured they would find some sign of an accident. A bump on the head or something."

"No, it was murder." I tried to sound casual about it, but I felt like Carter—a little mystified at what was happening.

"What kind of poison was used?" Flora asked, not a bit ashamed of her morbid curiosity.

"Let me look." The three of us gathered around the report and tried to read it at the same time. "It says here *digitalis purpurea*."

Flora frowned and drew her head back. "What's that?"

"I have no idea." I glanced at Carter.

"Google it."

We moved to the computer located on the front counter. I drew out the stool and typed *digitalis purpurea* into the search bar of the Google site.

Flora planted herself in front of me on the other side of the counter, and Carter stood at the end leaning up against it.

"Well, I'll be," I said without thinking.

"What is it?" Flora grabbed the computer and shifted it to face her. "Oh, my."

Carter, who had shown he was a patient man, was on the verge of snatching the computer away from Flora. "What is it? Tell me."

"Foxglove." I said.

"Hmm." Flora gave me a knowing look.

"Okay, ladies, I'm missing something. What is foxglove, and what does it have to do with the case?"

"Foxglove," Flora said in a lecturing tone, "is a flower, a poisonous flower, which grows to be about three feet high and comes in purple, pink, and white blossoms. It droops, giving it the appearance of little bells. It says here it causes heart problems if any part of the flower is consumed."

"Ooh, wicked stuff. That explains why things were knocked off the work counter close to where they found the body." I turned the computer back to me to study the picture of the plant.

"Okay, I agree it's not good, but why the grave faces?" Carter shrugged. "I still don't get it."

Flora looked across the counter at me again, waiting for me to fill in the blanks for Carter.

"Foxglove is a flower. For someone to grow foxglove this time of year, they would need a hothouse. Lilly and Matt have a hothouse. Matt told me the other day Lilly loves to garden, and she spent time in the hothouse before she left for her walk. Meaning if Lilly grows foxglove, Matt had easy access to the murder weapon." This was bad news. I was supposed to be proving Matt's innocence, but with every turn, I provided the prosecutor with new fodder for his case.

"I see," said Carter, as grave now as the two of us. "We are, however, taking some pretty big leaps here. Your theory is filled with ifs and maybes. If she grows foxglove—If they used it to poison Bryant, if they even know it's a poisonous flower—lots of ifs going on here."

"Carter's right. We need proof, not what-ifs. And the fact Lilly and Matt had each gone their own way yesterday morning doesn't help. That leaves neither one of them with an alibi and leaves me with the hard job of trying to clear them. I'll need to go ask the lieutenant about how Bryant traveled to the Beans and Leaves yesterday since Lilly was sure there was only one black SUV in the square, and I'll also need to ask if they've searched the Murphy's house yet."

"I'm sure they would've, since they received the preliminary autopsy report this morning. Gabe won't waste any time. He says with each day the trail of a murder becomes harder and harder to follow. So, he'll have to move on the information. No time to waste." Carter leaned his forearms on the counter.

"I'll have to check in with him and see what he found," I said.

After we made the final decision that Carter would be the

one to help me the next day, he and Flora went home for the evening. I called Kirk to let him know he wasn't needed until Saturday at noon, and I'd have a work schedule made out for the following week.

I still needed to get in touch with Tom Perkins, the mystery writer, and his agent to verify the date of his upcoming book signing. We had decided on January twenty-sixth as the target date, with a few others picked out in case it fell through. Of course, that was pre-fire.

I prayed the shop would be ready by that date and the book signing could coincide with the grand opening of the new Twisted Plots post-fire.

With a few minutes before I needed to go to the Pines to keep my promise to Julia, I checked my Open Hearts listing to see if anyone had shown any interest in my posting.

When I opened the site, I was nervous. It was like putting on a bikini the first day of summer, a little too much exposure all at once. I was encouraged to find I didn't have one request but two, so I decided to play the field. I responded to both gentlemen through the private chat room and set up two separate dates for Saturday.

One was for an afternoon of hiking around our beautiful lake, and the other was for dessert and coffee at one of my favorite seafood restaurants in town.

Pleased with my planning, I couldn't wait to go to the Whispering Pines and tell Julia all about it. So, I grabbed my coat and purse, then spotted the autopsy report poking out from the top and decided to run it over to Elizabeth on my way. I was anxious to see Julia's expression when she heard I had two dates.

The reception I received from Julia was not what I expected.

"You have two dates for Saturday?" Julia shook her head. "Have you lost your mind?"

A little put off by her response, I refused to let her hang a gray cloud over my excitement. "No, I thought if I could consolidate my dating, I might find my Prince Charming a little faster."

"Really? Are you sure Lieutenant Cooper caught you before you hit your head? Because I think you're suffering from a concussion."

We settled ourselves at a table by the window and were indulging in one of Julia's famous pastries left over from this morning's breakfast run.

"Julia, I thought you would be all for me trying to find my Prince Charming out there among the frogs."

"I am." Her tone softened. "But I've known you too long to think planning two dates on the same day isn't inviting trouble."

"Me, get into trouble? Never." I shook my head. "No way."

At this point, Julia couldn't help but smile. She was well acquainted with the trouble I've been in through the years, because she'd been in most of it with me.

She leaned back in her chair and let out a sigh. "I guess I'll prepare for another famous Amy Kate-dating disaster. Will I need one, two, or three stretchers? One for you and one for each of those poor unsuspecting frogs—I mean men."

CHAPTER EIGHT

Gizmo's furry face and sandpapery tongue tickled me awake as my phone vibrated on the bedside table.

"Happy Friday, Gizmo." I scratched him between his ears before rolling over to grab the phone. It's amazing what a good night's sleep can do for one's outlook. Of course, having a date or two can't hurt either.

"Hello."

"Hi, Amy Kate, I hope I'm not disturbing you?"

"Oh, no." I recognized the voice on the other end of the phone—my new best friend, Theresa, the insurance agent. "I'm not busy at all. What can I do for you?"

"The fire investigator just got in touch with me, and he's available this morning. Can you meet him at the store?"

"Yes. When?"

"He said he could be there by nine thirty. Does that work for you?"

"Sure does. Thanks." I was making headway, and the day held great promise.

When I rolled over and looked at the clock, my hopes fell. Ugh, I had twenty minutes to get ready. I didn't even try for beautiful; I settled for presentable.

The trip to the bookshop wasn't long. Parking, though, added a couple of extra minutes. I made better time when I walked to work. My daily runs to the post office meant I needed to take the van.

I was able to park in front of my own shop, which is not

always the case. The fire investigator sat in his car next to the parking space I snagged. I identified him from the magnetic logo on the side of his vehicle and waved to him, letting him know it was me.

He grinned and waved back. then turned his head away.

While he was occupied, I jumped out of the van and dashed ahead to open the door and turn on the lights. I didn't want to leave him stranded on the sidewalk holding a mountain of things the way I had with Christina, the insurance adjuster.

The rather round fire investigator shook my hand after he entered the shop. His left hand held a single clipboard over the mountain of his stomach.

With great efficiency, he started his investigation. First, he took his own set of pictures, which I thought was overkill, since so many had already been taken of the scene. Then he began to write notes.

After he'd checked things out for about thirty minutes, he called to me from the back room, "You know this is just procedure, since the fire marshal over at the fire station has turned in his report."

"Did you say the fire marshal has turned in his report?"

"Yeah, you should be good to go for cleanup and repairs, since there's no suspicion of insurance fraud on your part."

"Really?"

The fire investigator stuck his head out the doorway, looking a little like a turtle peeking out of its shell. "Yeah, if it's proven to be insurance fraud on your neighbor's part, the insurance company will handle it from within, since you both have the same insurance. At least, that's how I think it works." He pulled his head back into his shell.

"Who receives a copy of this report?" Why had no one contacted me with the good news?

Again, he poked his head out. "Umm, the fire marshal gives a copy to the police officers who are handling the investigation, and they distribute it to the attorneys if need be, and of course, the insurance agent." Quick as a flash, his head retracted into his shell.

"Of course, the insurance agent." I stood with my elbow propped on the front counter, resting my head on my hand, trying to decide which one I should be upset with—Theresa, Elizabeth, or the lieutenant.

Theresa called so early she couldn't have seen the report, and if she was like me, coffee first, report later. I let her off the hook. She at least told the fire investigator who had now told me. Elizabeth, too, might not have seen the report yet, and if it was dependent upon Lieutenant Cooper for its delivery, he might not have sent it to her. Hm, He should've told me. Ding, ding, ding. I have a winner.

When the fire investigator was finished and I had signed all the necessary paperwork, I fished out my phone to check my calendar. I love purple, so I use purple dots on my smart-phone calendar for my business appointments. I also like green, which I use to designate my personal engagements. Trust me, there are a lot more purple dots than green.

I checked on the times when the repairmen were scheduled to come today, and I had two thoughts.

The first—it was time to go catch the lieutenant to ask my questions about the SUV and see what they found at the Murphy's' house. And the second—how thankful I was the fire investigator had come this morning with his good tidings.

This way the repairmen weren't only giving quotes for the insurance company's use. They were submitting actual bids for the job as well. My day looked brighter still.

I set my sights on Lieutenant Gabe Cooper. Someone needed to pay for the lack of communication going on here, and it seemed natural it should be him. It was now around ten-thirty. I'd pop into the police station to see if I could catch the lieutenant.

After the scene I made yesterday, I was not looking forward to prancing into the squad room unannounced, but I needed answers. I wanted to see if the Murphy's hothouse harbored any foxglove, and I also wanted to know why I hadn't been told about the fire marshal's report.

I bypassed the front desk and pushed the elevator button for the second floor, figuring it would save time to head on up. When I reached the glass doors, I hesitated. I remembered the faces of everyone who had been there yesterday, smirking, laughing, and giving Gabe a hard time on what I thought was my behalf. I could only imagine what transpired once I left. Dad had told me the other detectives could be merciless in their pursuit of a good laugh, and I gave them an ample supply of ammo to use on Gabe.

Well, today's a new day. I have the chance to redeem myself from the curse of the fainting blond floozy. I will be professional, courteous, and will get to the point, like the twenty-seven-year-old adult woman I am. Rats. I knew at that moment I must remove the target from Lieutenant Cooper's chest and keep my temper in check, no matter what. "Okay, I need to keep it together. I have no idea why he brings out the weird in me—first the fainting, then the yelling, but he does. So, I need to be on my guard."

I stood there afraid to walk through those doors, not knowing what might happen in the lieutenant's presence today and being a little terrified to find out.

"Have you decided to go in or are you going to stay out here in the hall?"

That voice, the husky quality. I inhaled, put on my game face, and turned with a cheery smile plastered on my lips. "How long have you been standing there?" I hoped he hadn't overheard me talking to myself.

"Long enough."

"You're the very person I was looking for."

"Did you have some information for me today, Miss Anderson?" He exaggerated the emphasis on my name. "Or did you drop by to do a little more flirting?"

I grinned though I didn't appreciate his humor and swallowed the urge to call him something a little nastier than his name. "I was hoping we could sit and go over a few things. Your dad thought you would've gone to investigate the Murphy's' home by now, and I wanted to see what you found there."

"Miss Anderson," again with an overemphatic drawl, "I do have work to do on other cases, but I guess I can squeeze you into my busy schedule."

He reached over my shoulder, drawing ever closer to me and peered into my eyes. His brown ones turned warm like hot chocolate. He grabbed the handle of the door that was behind me to open it.

Somewhat flustered, I stepped back out of the way.

"Ladies first." He smiled revealing every dimple. Then with a twinkle of mischief in his eyes, he bowed his head and extended his hand to show the way.

Once we entered, I headed between the rows of desks toward the one I thought was his. When I glanced up, he was crossing over to a room with windows—a conference/interrogation room of sorts, and he stood by the door, holding it open for me.

"I thought we could meet over there." I pointed to the chairs at his desk.

"Here would be better," he said. "Quieter."

"Oh, yeah," I understood his meaning. He was unwilling to risk a repeat performance of yesterday. Better to keep me out of earshot of the other detectives. I guess that makes him handsome and smart.

I took a seat at the end of the table, not paying attention to where I sat until I noticed he had taken the seat at the other end of the table. From the other side of the window, we looked like two opponents preparing to square off in some deranged tennis match. I decided distance might be a good thing, so after taking out my notebook and slinging my purse over the back of the chair, I asked my questions. "So, did you get a chance to go to the Murphy house and check out what was there?"

"Yes, I did. I wanted to have a look in the hothouse. It turns out Lilly does have some foxglove growing there. She was forthright with me when I asked about it and perplexed by my questions about her gardening."

"I just don't see her or Matt as a killer."

"You'd be surprised. When caught in peculiar circumstances, it's the most unlikely people who do the most extreme things."

"Yeah, I guess you're right. You sound like you know this from experience. How long have you been working in law enforcement?"

"For about six or seven years. I was with the Chicago P.D. until about a year ago when my parents moved here to be closer to my brother. That's why I moved here—family. But I got my start in the military. I enlisted when I was eighteen."

"What branch?"

"The Marines."

This meeting sounded more like a date than a murder investigation, so I directed my next question to the topic at hand. "The fire investigator from my insurance company was able to meet with me this morning. He said the fire marshal had turned in a report to you?"

"Yes, I saw it this morning. He must've brought it over yesterday afternoon while I was over at Java Vein Corporate interviewing the administrative assistant, Samantha Holiday. She worked with Mr. Kendrick."

"Did you find out anything useful from her?"

"Yes, she's worked for Bryant Kendrick for the last six years, so she knew a lot. She gave me his schedule for the week before the murder. One thing of interest—Kendrick had met with his wife, Sarah Catherine, and their attorneys the afternoon before the murder to renegotiate the divorce papers."

"They were getting a divorce. That puts a new spin on the case. Why were they renegotiating? What was the problem?"

"From what Samantha gathered, Sarah Catherine didn't know anything about the national deal until a news story came out earlier this month in one of the business magazines. Samantha said he went to great pains to keep it from her. Apparently, Kendrick didn't think he should have to share whatever he made on the deal with his soon-to-be ex-wife."

"Hm, not good."

"No, Samantha said Mrs. Kendrick was, and I quote, 'livid.' They had met at around three o'clock and stayed behind closed doors until close to four-thirty. She said Bryant had refused to sign the new papers from Sarah Catherine's lawyers."

"Wow."

"A lot of yelling went on behind those closed doors, and when they opened, nobody was happy."

"Which means Bryant was already keyed up before he reached the Beans and Leaves for the interview with Kirk." I thought about this for a minute. "That might explain why he was so belligerent to Matt."

"Yeah, it might. It also gives the wife a motive. If she was disgruntled with the way the divorce was going, murder might have seemed a better route. This way, she gets everything."

"Do you know if she does get everything?" I hoped the answer was yes. She would make a great prime suspect, and right now, my job was to give Elizabeth someone else to offer up to the D.A.

"No, I haven't talked with her since my initial interview. She was grieving, and as the victim's wife, I went easy on her." He sighed. "Maybe I shouldn't have, but that's the part of the job I hate most, having to tell someone a person they cared about has died."

Taken aback, I glanced up from my notes to see Gabe with his eyes turned down, staring at his hands. The man at the other end of the table wasn't the at-ease-in-a-crisis lieutenant nor the save-the-world-cop. No, he was a man who was haunted by his own losses.

I couldn't help staring for a moment at the emotion he wore. When he looked up, I continued the conversation with the next question that popped into my mind.

"Did you interview anyone else while you were there?" I regretted asking such a novice question, knowing it must have sounded absurd to Gabe. He had interviewed several of the people who worked with or for Bryant Kendrick. After all, this was a murder investigation, and he was a detective.

"Yes, I did." He named off the people.

This list included Samantha Holiday and Casey Russell, the marketing agent. He had also asked about any disgruntled employees and hit the jackpot with a guy named Ed Philips.

By this time, I had filled a page and a half with names, titles and addresses, figuring I would need to speak to some of them myself.

"Okay, Miss P.I." A mischievous glint shone in his eyes. "What do you have for me?"

"You won't believe what I found out. In the middle of my interview with Lilly, a car alarm went off."

"And this is important, how?" Gabe's eyebrows rose.

"The car alarm going off made Lilly remember something she had forgotten. The morning of the murder she had heard a car alarm, and moments after the alarm was silenced, a black SUV drove past the back alley of the Beans and Leaves. It could've been the murderer getting away."

"Could've been." Gabe showed no excitement whatsoever.

"Well, it could have been." I crossed my arms, fighting the irritation that threatened to poke a hole in my bubble.

"What's wrong?"

"I bring you what I consider a lead in the case, and you act like it's nothing. I'm a little insulted." I pushed my chair away from the table. "This is my first case, and I am giving you, the police, information I uncovered on my own at my first interview, and all you can say is, 'Could be.'" I stood trying to bite back the angry words.

I promised myself not to let the weird happen. *Professional, professional, professional*, the mantra played in my head. But he seemed to draw it out of me. I vacillate between being mad and being weird when in his presence. It's like being Dr. Jekyll and Mr. Hyde, never knowing which personality will show up around this guy, fainting, flirting, or fuming.

"What should I have said? We don't have enough information to know if it was the killer leaving the scene. It could be a potential witness, or it could've just been a car passing by. We don't know." Gabe sighed and shrugged.

I stuffed my notebook and pen into my purse.

He was right, but for some reason after yesterday's run-in, my ego needed an "Atta-girl" from the lieutenant. My lips trembled. No, I refused to cry in front of the lieutenant over something as small as this. I wasn't sure why it mattered to me anyway. Maybe it was because he didn't want me working this case. Maybe it was because of the things he had said to Elizabeth.

All I knew was that I needed to leave, or I would do or say something to add to my growing list of embarrassments. My composure trembled, threatening to crumble.

The lieutenant's chair made a horrific scratching noise as the legs scraped across the brown tile. He reached my side before I knew what was happening. His hand moved toward my shoulder, but he pulled it back and let it fall onto the back of one of the chairs in front of him.

When he met my gaze, his face held a hint of concern. "Amy Kate, you're right. You've brought in a solid lead, and I should've acknowledged that fact." His voice was surprisingly full of kindness. "Please, I didn't mean to insult you."

His tenderness caught me off guard. "It's not your fault, Lieutenant. I tend to tear up when I get angry." I shrugged. "Or embarrassed or stressed out or sad." I chuckled through the tears. It was one of those 'I'm uncomfortable' laughs. "It seems to be my go-to coping mechanism."

I brushed the treacherous tear away, took a deep breath, and resumed the business at hand. "I wanted to tell you something else. Lilly said that Java Vein uses black SUVs as company cars. That brings me to one of my other questions I had for you. How did Bryant get to the meeting that morning?"

"We found his personal vehicle parked on the square. It was a silver Camaro, a newer model."

"Then if the black SUV was one of the Java Vein cars, someone else from the company was there."

"Again, not to be insulting, we have a lot of ifs here."

"Your dad said the same thing to me yesterday about the foxglove, and you're both right. We need answers, not ifs." I clenched my lips together. By the look on his face I'd said too much.

"You told my dad about the foxglove?" The kindness in his voice faded. "Amy Kate, I'm allowing you access to police information only as a favor to Elizabeth and because I don't want to see Matt get railroaded by an over-eager D.A., but there is only so much I can share, and what I do share needs to be kept in strict confidence."

Rats. The veins in his neck were bulging again.

"I don't need the whole town talking about this case."

I scowled. "It's too late for that. It's what everyone in town is talking about." I crossed my arms. "But you're right. I'll try to be more discreet."

His lips thinned into a straight line. "All right, but if this happens again, you're on your own."

"Fine." I went to the door and not wanting to end on such a sour note, I said, "I am thankful you're letting me tag along on this. It's helping me get the shop back up and running. The sooner we catch the killer—"

"We all want to catch the killer." Gabe said. "Plus, this way if we're together, I can keep an eye on you."

I pulled the door open before I said anything else, I might regret. "I'll go over to Elizabeth's office and see if she has a minute. Fill her in on what we've talked about."

"I'll join you. She may have some information for me, and besides, I want to make sure she knows about our understanding. No more sharing information. Okay, Amy Kate?"

I held my chin higher. I didn't like the fact that he thought I gossiped. "Sure."

He closed the door to the interrogation room with a thud.

As we moved into the squad room, Gabe stopped. "Let me grab a file off my desk and get my coat. Then, I'll be ready to go."

I phoned Elizabeth to see if this was a good time. She was at the Pines having lunch and invited us to join her.

Perfect. Now I was locked into spending the next hour with the handsome detective who caused me to act like anything but a thinking adult woman.

CHAPTER NINE

I'm not sure how, but we made it to the Pines in one piece. I willed my feet to move while Gabe carried on some form of a conversation.

Elizabeth waved to us from the table she had procured by the window. The sunlight bathed the area with warmth, and after our short brisk walk, I was glad to take the seat washed in its rays.

"I'm glad you came, Gabe," Elizabeth said. "It'll give us a chance to come up with a game plan, so we aren't duplicating work."

"You read my mind." Gabe graced me with a wink as he pulled out my chair.

The waitress came and took our drink orders.

As hungry as I was earlier, the sheer shock of how I had acted curbed my appetite.

The waitress returned with drinks and asked if we were ready to order. Tony, the lunch chef, made a mean meatball sub, and today, that's what I wanted—comfort food.

We made small talk until lunch was served, and then everybody but me pulled out a manila file folder.

Elizabeth opened the discussion. "Matt called me this morning to tell me about the police search and the contents of the hothouse. I let him know about the autopsy findings. He sounded shocked it was poison. When I asked him about the foxglove, he said it didn't prove anything. Anyone could've done it if they knew anything about plants."

"Why is that?" Gabe asked.

"Because," Elizabeth said with a little dramatic flair, "the foxglove was in the coffee shop. Matt often brought in some of Lilly's flowers to put on the counter and to use as centerpieces on the tables. So, anyone with the knowledge of plants could've been our killer."

"True, but what better way to have the murder weapon in place than to bring it in days ahead of time? It still could've been either Matt or Lilly, and Lilly seems the more likely one."

"Why?" I asked.

"Because I'd bet my next doughnut Lilly's the one who picked out the flowers to send to the shop. Men don't have a preference when it comes to those types of things. Women do," the lieutenant said.

"It doesn't help either that Mrs. Culpepper said in her statement she saw Lilly out in front of the coffee shop making a phone call," Elizabeth added.

"Hm, I never did get to read her interview, but Lilly told me yesterday she called 911 from the alley to report the fire. Maybe she was mistaken. Maybe she called from the front," I said.

"That's why Mrs. Culpepper's statement stood out to me. Lilly had given me the same account."

"Maybe she was calling Matt." Elizabeth sipped her tea, then patted her lips with her napkin.

"No, I asked her that yesterday when I interviewed her, and she'd seemed put off, like it had never occurred to her to call Matt. She said she'd assumed he was in the shop." I took a bite of my meatball sub. The flavor of the Italian sausage burst on my taste buds.

"Interesting, I guess I need to get Lilly's phone records, as well as Kendrick's, and see who's been calling whom." The lieutenant jotted down some notes on a sheet inside the folder. "I also should have some feedback from Bryant's computer. We went ahead and brought it into the station for our tech guys to look over. His office didn't give us any insights into the man. He didn't have any personal belongings there, other than a photo of his wife I found tucked away in a drawer. His office was professional and sterile."

"Matt did say Bryant had gone through several mom-and-pop companies, building them up and then selling them. If you move around, you don't get attached to places or people." Elizabeth dipped a french fry into a glob of ketchup. "Matt said the six years Bryant had been here in Pine Lake were the longest he'd been anywhere."

"Yeah." The lieutenant bit into his roast beef sub, and after swallowing, he said, "that would be true."

"Something keeps bothering me." I leaned back in my chair. "Wednesday evening when we interviewed Matt, he said Bryant had talked about Lilly. They knew each other in college, but Bryant claimed Lilly thought he was her biggest mistake. Bryant was referring to Matt when he said that."

"What do you think Bryant could've meant?" Elizabeth wiped her mouth clean of the crumbs from her hamburger bun.

I flipped through my notepad, searching for my interview notes. "When I talked with Lilly, she referred to some regrets she had, which centered around Bryant. She said Bryant used people, and she and Matt hadn't figured it out until it was too late. When I asked her what she meant, she said she was referring to the business deal, but I got the impression it was something else."

"All right, it sounds like you need to follow up on your hunch, and Gabe, you need to see if the phone records or Bryant's computer gives us any new leads you can share." She smiled at Gabe. "I appreciate all the help you're giving us. Matt is appreciative as well."

"I'll do what I can, but I can't make any promises." Gabe looked directly at me.

I thought for a moment he was going to tell Elizabeth about my sharing information with others, but he didn't. Instead, he worked on his sub.

"And I, as Matt's lawyer, want to compile a list of other suspects while you two are here to help." Elizabeth pointed a french fry at the lieutenant. "Especially you."

I rummaged through the pages in my notepad, and Elizabeth thumbed through sheets in her file, both of us searching for the list we made together. Elizabeth was rather clever getting the "enemy" to help. Gabe was only doing his job by following the leads that suited the D.A., but he didn't strike me as one to overlook a sound lead even if it ran in a different direction. That was going to work to our advantage.

Elizabeth finished her last bite of burger, wiped her hands clean, and picked up her pen ready for action. "The killer had to know about the morning meetings, so the question is who knew?"

I started the list. "Of course, I hate to say it, but Matt and Lilly did."

"We can add Samantha Holiday, the administrative assistant. She would've known about the meeting," Gabe said.

"We've put them down on our original list of the employees at Java Vein Corporate. We also wanted to talk to some of Bryant's contacts at Benson, the company buying out Java Vein. I thought it might give us a different perspective on the victim." Elizabeth said.

"I wouldn't waste too much time on the general employees. We sent some uniformed officers over to do preliminary interviews with those who might've had any direct contact with Kendrick, but we came up dry. But Casey Russell, the marketing agent, would know when Kendrick was meeting with Matt since it was her job to distribute the new flavors to the other stores. Her knowing would be crucial."

Elizabeth and I jotted down some notes.

"Hey—" I hesitated for a moment to decide how to address the lieutenant. It struck me as being silly to call him Lieutenant since he knew such personal things about me. And Elizabeth seemed comfortable calling him Gabe, but then there was the whole mess with the name game leaving me unsure. In all my born days, I've never had this much trouble calling someone by their name. I'm an emotional train wreck around this guy. "Sorry," I said. "Didn't you say you had a name of a disgruntled employee, Gabe?"

"Yes, Ed Philips. He's not exactly an employee, but he was with the advertising company who previously had the Java Vein account. I was told he was dismissed from the company when Kendrick moved the account to a larger firm."

"Oh, that doesn't make any sense. Does that mean Casey Russell, the marketing agent, works for Java Vein or does it mean she works for some other firm but has this account? Or is she the marketing agent for Java Vein but works with the other firm?"

"Sorry, I wasn't very clear. She is a marketing agent with the advertising firm of—" It was Gabe's turn to rifle through paperwork. "Inkster, but she's over the Java Vein account."

"Great," Elizabeth said. "I'll add Mr. Philips to my list and scratch off the general employees."

"We should also look at the wife who was soon to be the ex-wife until Bryant's death. Gabe said she was mad when she left the meeting with Bryant and their lawyers yesterday." I glanced at Gabe who met my gaze and smiled.

"*Livid*, I said *livid*," Gabe corrected and then winked at me from across the table. "But I don't expect you to hang on my every word."

He had the cutest lopsided grin.

"Miss Holiday, who told me about the meeting, also made a point to tell me she had caught Mrs. Kendrick looking through her desk calendar. If that's the case, then Mrs. Kendrick knew about the morning meeting as well." Gabe glanced at his watch. "As delightful as this has been, ladies, I must leave. Duty calls, and the city can't afford too many of these long lunches."

"Thanks, Gabe, for all your help. I owe you one," Elizabeth said.

"And one day I intend to collect, but right now, I'd better hustle back before they fire me. You'd have little use for me if I wasn't your inside man." He gave her a dimpled grin as he donned his coat and scarf, then left a generous tip for the waitress whose table we had monopolized for over an hour.

Once Gabe left, I released a pent-up sigh and slipped down into my seat, letting my head fall against the back cushion.

Julia chose that moment to walk out of the kitchen. Upon seeing me in such a state, she shot a questioning look to Elizabeth, who lifted her shoulders. "You look like you've seen better days," she said.

"Hmm."

"All right, Miss Drama Queen, what is it?" Elizabeth asked.

I pulled myself up from my slumped position and patted the chair beside me. "You got a minute?" I asked the two of them.

"Yes," Elizabeth answered, her eyes wide.

Julia nodded and took the chair offered her.

"I am an emotional klutz."

They glanced at me and then at each other.

My faithful friend, Julia, scowled. "Okay, I'll bite. What exactly do you mean by an emotional klutz?"

"When I'm around Lieutenant Gabe Cooper, I become an emotional klutz. I'm worse than Dr. Jekyll and Mr. Hyde. I never know what I'm going to do."

"It can't be that bad, Sis. So, you fainted in front of him. He's already forgotten about it, and it doesn't seem to have affected your working relationship with him. Everything seemed fine."

Elizabeth didn't have the whole story. She had witnessed the one interaction between Gabe and me when something weird, crazy, or explosive didn't happen.

I sat a little straighter in my chair, leaned forward, and shook my head. "You have no idea."

"Okay, enlighten us," Julia said.

"This lunch was the first time in forty-eight hours of having met Lieutenant Gabe Cooper that I haven't made a complete and utter idiot of myself in his presence."

"What do you mean?" Julia asked.

"Yeah, explain yourself, girl." Elizabeth leaned her forearms on the table.

"Okay, you both know at the fire I fainted in front of him and then the EMT asked me if I was pregnant."

Their shameless grins weren't lost on me. It became apparent I hadn't told them that part.

"Then, at Elizabeth's office, he lays down the law about me working on this case, and though I was furious with him, I seemed to have gone mute. I sat there taking it like a helpless little cream puff, which you both know I am not."

"All right, I see you may have something to be concerned about, but—"

"I'm not finished. Then, yesterday, I decided I needed to tell him how I felt about his behavior at your office. Since we were going to be talking to the same people, I wanted to clear the air and make sure he knew he didn't have to take care of me. That I'm a full-grown woman and capable of taking care of myself." I paused and rested my forehead on the palm of my

hand, horrified by the memory. "When I went to confront him, I may have inadvertently . . . come across . . . as flirting with him."
"What?" They asked in unison.
"How could someone confuse being lectured and being flirted with?" Julia's eyebrows pulled into a tight V.
"I was trying to be catty about it, and anyway, as I said, it turned into a disaster. He got mad and pulled me into the hall. From the things I said, some of the detectives might've thought I was throwing myself at him because I insisted, he let me call him by his given name." The heat of embarrassment washed over me. Where is a hole when you need one?
"You've got to be kidding. Amy Kate, you are one of the brightest women I know. How could you have thrown yourself at some guy without realizing it—and not just any guy, but Gabe?" Elizabeth groaned.
"Imagine my surprise." Sarcasm dripped from my words. "But, that's not the worst of it."
"There's more?" This time it was Julia with the astonished look. "I'm afraid to ask. Did you humiliate the poor man in front of his mother, or did you kick his dog?"
"Neither. Today, we were working on the case, and he said something I took as an insult. I don't think he meant it that way, but I got so mad. And I had promised myself I wasn't going to lose my temper. Instead of yelling at him or stomping out, I wound up crying in front of him."
"Oh no. How could you? You used to be a schoolteacher. You know all about being professional." I could see Elizabeth trying her best not to lose her temper. She warned me the first day about keeping a good relationship with the lieutenant because we needed his cooperation.
"Let me finish," I said.
"No, there can't be anything else. You haven't known the poor fellow long enough for there to be more," Elizabeth shook her head.
"Well, there is, so let me get it out. Today, on our way here, he started teasing me, and I elbowed him in the ribs. It was a knee jerk reaction."
"More like an elbow-jerk reaction." Julia said.

At this point, neither Julia nor Elizabeth could keep a straight face. I could see they were fighting the urge to laugh but lost. The giggles poured out, and I couldn't help but join them.

After hearing my own tale, I could scarcely believe it myself. It sounded so ridiculous, yet it was true. I had lived it—the harrowing tale of the emotionally inept.

"You sure have been busy," Elizabeth said, once she was able to speak again.

"Yeah, I know."

We sat there grinning at one another, shaking our heads, when Julia said what I was thinking, "Poor, poor, Gabe."

CHAPTER TEN

When I arrived at Twisted Plots the next morning, Carter was in the shop unpacking the Friday shipment. I was so glad he had remembered to ask for a key yesterday when he decided to come in to help because—well, I was late.

I was also grateful he would be around while the repairmen were there. I didn't expect there to be any issues, but to be honest, I wouldn't know a lug nut from a peanut. His understanding of carpenter lingo might come in handy.

The bell on the door jingled, and a tall, rather lanky man of about forty entered the store. He stooped a bit to clear the doorframe. His hair looked like salt and pepper mixed together, a little heavier on the salt. When he reached the counter, he stuck his hands deep into his pockets and rocked back and forth from his toes to his heels as he waited for me to address him.

"You must be from Sonshine Home Repairs. Are you Albert Shine?"

"Yes, ma'am, I am. It's mighty good to meet you." We shook hands.

"Mr. Shine, I'm so glad you could come today on such short notice."

"Yes, ma'am, January is one of our slower months. Lucky for us there are the occasional accidents. You know, broken windows, busted pipes, and of course, the occasional home fire from unattended heaters. Keeps the bills paid." At this, he beamed, revealing his crooked top teeth.

I couldn't help myself. I liked Mr. Shine and hoped he

would give me a reasonable quote.

"I'll show you the damage. It's not as extensive as it could've been, and I'm grateful for that." I don't know if I was trying to convince him or myself, but if I downplayed the severity of the damage, he might downplay the cost of the repairs.

Whistling while he worked, Mr. Shine shared his cheery disposition. Once he was done with his inspection of the needed work, he came out to where I stood. He laid his work order on the counter and hunched over to write down some numbers. When he was done, he straightened to his full height. "I was looking through the room and noticed there isn't much damage to the one side, but the other is going to need a lot of work."

He rocked back and forth on his heels again. "Of course, we'll have to check the structure between the walls of the two businesses, but I think they're alright. The fire marshal would've said something otherwise. Then, we will have to tear out the water-damaged Sheetrock, dry the area, and put in the new Sheetrock. Once all that's in place, the ceiling will need to be scraped and sprayed again with ceiling popcorn, and then of course, the whole room will need to be painted."

I lowered myself into a club chair.

"I see the back door has been replaced," Mr. Shine continued. "Are you going to want it painted to match the room?"

I didn't answer. Shock had set in. "That does sound like a lot," I said, more to myself than to him.

"Here's the numbers. As far as I can tell, the studs in the wall should be all right, but if we get in there and find they need work, it'll have to be added to the estimate."

"I understand," I said. Snapping out of my stupor, I thought to ask, "I also need to know a start date and how long you think it'll take to complete the work. I have a guest author coming for a book signing in about two weeks and would like things to be back to normal if possible."

"Miss Anderson, like I said earlier, January is a slow month so starting isn't a problem, but I'm not sure two weeks will be enough time to finish. However, it should be close enough to finished for you to have your book signing if we get started soon."

As Mr. Shine peeled the estimate from the other copies, I reached out my hand and took the nasty itemized list. I wanted to hold it like one holds a dirty diaper, extending my arms while holding my breath, but instead, I studied the numbers. It would be two hundred for this and four hundred for that. I couldn't believe the figures I saw. Deep in thought, I was scrutinizing the numbers when I remembered I wasn't alone.

I glanced up, and there stood Mr. Albert Shine, smiling his crooked-tooth smile at me and rocking on his heels. "Well, ma'am, it's been a pleasure meeting you. I hope we hear from you soon to set up a start day. Our number is at the top of the estimate. My wife mans the phones during the day, so don't think you dialed a wrong number when a woman answers." I thanked him as he ducked to exit.

The total was a whopping five thousand dollars, which reminded me I hadn't asked Elizabeth about payday. I needed to ask her about it soon because I needed every single penny, including the loose change from under the couch cushions for this restoration.

Carter, who had been listening to the exchange, came over to eyeball the estimate. He perused the piece of paper and then took it with him into the back workroom. I sprang up and followed him. He reviewed each item one at a time over his reading glasses.

In the short time I had known him, Carter Cooper had shown himself to be a man of great character. He was honest and open in his interview, wise when it came to advice, and father like when it came to protecting people. And now, he was being thorough to make sure that Mr. Shine was honest. Surely his sons inherited some of his moral fiber.

The thought of sons made me think about what Gabe had said about the Cooper family having experienced a loss of a son, a brother. This mystery danced around in my mind as I watched Carter work, but I didn't know how to broach the subject. I didn't want my curiosity to put Carter in an awkward position or bring up a painful memory.

My phone buzzed with a text, distracting me from these thoughts. It was Gabe. How did he get my number? Oh, yeah, I remembered. I gave him my business card the day of the fire in case he had any more questions.

Gabe: *Going to Java Vein Monday morning to interview Samantha and Casey again. Thought you might want to tag along.*

Me: *Yes, I would. What time?*

Gabe: *How about ten?*

Me: *Sounds good.*

Gabe: *;)*

Oh, my word, he just winked at me via text. Honestly, I think this guy has a winking disorder.

"As far as I can tell, Mr. Shine has given you a pretty fair estimate." Carter said, bringing me back to the task before us.

"Awesome." I silently thanked the Lord for an honest appraisal and hoped the next guy would do the same.

I didn't hear the bell jingle when Mr. Juniper arrived later in the afternoon. I was stooped behind the counter cleaning, with my head stuck between the shelves trying to reach the back corners. Startled, I gasped when I emerged to find a short man in overalls standing near the front of the counter. I smiled, trying to hide my embarrassment at being caught in such an awkward position by a stranger.

Mr. Juniper was about five foot five, which for a man is short and for a handyman a disadvantage. But Mr. Juniper's size was not what was so astonishing about the man.

"Hi, I'm Wesley Juniper of Juniper and Mosley. I came about the estimate you needed."

I stood dumbfounded for a moment. The sheer thump, thump, thump of the man's bass voice caused my heart to pick up the rhythm. His body was small, but his volume was huge. I had expected perhaps an oboe or a clarinet. I would've never expected the bass drum from this piccolo.

"Miss?" He scowled.

I cleared my throat. "Oh, yes, Mr. Juniper, I was expecting you."

I cut my eyes toward Carter, who was dusting the books in the mystery section, and caught a smile playing on his lips before he turned his back to our guest. At least Carter was polite enough to keep his amusement to himself. I, on the other hand, was having a difficult time keeping a straight face as I listened to Mr. Juniper's spiel about his company.

I was relieved when it came time to show Mr. Juniper to the back workroom and excuse myself. At least behind the counter, I wouldn't be tempted to make any unnecessary comments to the man about his stature or voice.

Mr. Juniper's estimate was a tad higher than Mr. Shine's, and I was grateful for this stroke of luck because it gave me the excuse I needed not to hire him. I know myself too well. I would've never made it weeks on end without saying something regrettable. Plus, with my most recent behavior around Gabe Cooper, my tongue was not to be trusted.

Carter emerged from among the bookshelves, stretching his back as if he needed a breather. "All done," he said.

I was amazed. "Wow and in record time too. I think you're going to work out fine here at the Twisted Plots."

He chuckled. "The Twisted Plots is exactly what I needed, but if truth be told, I think Maureen needed it more."

"You mean she needed you out from underfoot, I take it?"

"Yeah, she was more pleased than I was about me finding a part-time job. Once the boxes had been unloaded, she didn't know what to do with me. My retirement's getting in her way. She has her job, and I guess she thought I might feel lost." He grinned. "But after forty years of marriage, I still go out of my way to be in the way, if you know what I mean."

Having never been married, I didn't know what he meant, but from the smile on his face and the warmth spilling from his eyes, I could guess it involved a great deal of happiness. His present mood gave me courage, and I forged ahead before I lost it.

"Carter?"

"Yes, Amy Kate."

"I was wondering, when you interviewed for this job, you said you had three sons. I've heard you speak about Gabe and about his brother who's an English teacher, but I haven't heard you say much about your other son." I left the unasked question hanging in the air.

Carter looked down, and I could tell he was mulling over what to say. I didn't notice any pain in his eyes. He seemed calm and at peace with the subject. "How 'bout we sit down for a minute? My back is telling me it's time to get off my feet."

We sat in the soft leather chairs by the window and watched the sun struggling to release its final rays before it set for the day. Carter turned his focus to me and searched my eyes as if he were about to reveal a prized treasure and wasn't sure I could be trusted with it. "My son, Seth, was the youngest of my three boys. He was a doer, always in motion. And he loved people. He could make everyone smile and laugh no matter what the situation. Seth brought a great deal of joy to his mother and me."

"He sounds wonderful." I slipped off my shoes and pulled my feet up under me.

"He was."

"I'm sorry, Carter. We don't have to talk about this if you don't want to. I was just wondering."

"No, it's all right. It happened back in 2003. He was killed in the Iraq war. He had gone into the military before college like I did, and Gabe did. He was following in our footsteps. Seth thought he wanted a military career and was so excited to join. Then after he'd been in the Marines for about a year, the war started. His unit was one of the first ones to be called up. It wasn't but a few months into his deployment when we were contacted." Carter exhaled and studied his hand as he rubbed the leather on the arm of the chair.

"How terrible for you and Maureen. She must've been devastated." I laid my hand on his forearm.

Carter reached over and patted my hand. "It's all right. He died with honor serving his country. I must say this move has been good for his mother and me. We feel closer to him now being here in Pine Lake."

"Why?" I asked, not following him.

"Because Seth is buried here next to his grandparents. You see, this is where I grew up back in the 50s and 60s. Then my parents moved away. Once they retired, they returned here, and the boys spent some of their summer vacations here with them. When Mich—"

The door flung open, and I jumped as Flora rushed in with her arms full. She trotted across the shop, making a dive for the counter. Her packages spilled out of her hands.

From the looks of things, Flora had used her day off to do some shopping on the square.

"Flora, what are you doing here?" I leapt from my seat and ran to the counter in time to catch the tumbling packages that threatened to end up on the floor.

"I was shopping and saw you two were still here. I couldn't pass by and not stop in. That would be rude." Flora's green eyes flashed with mischief. "Besides," she said as she tried to smother a smile, "I need an update on the case."

"Flora Smith-Jones, you are incorrigible."

"Yes, that's true, but—" She waited for me to start talking, so I did.

An hour later, I slipped my shoes back on, and the three of us left the shop heading in different directions. Flora scurried home to her sweet husband, Herman, bursting with the latest on the case. She had been concerned about Matt and Lilly as well and was glad to hear they were holding their own. Carter went home for a back rub from Maureen, and I headed to my apartment to read the newest Tom Perkins novel before the book signing.

In the course of our conversation, Carter reminded me a killer was out there, one who had used poison, which indicated Bryant had known the culprit. When he said this, it struck me that I might know the killer too. After all, it is a small town. This revelation sent a chill up my spine. I locked the car doors on the way home even though the ride was a short one.

CHAPTER ELEVEN

Two dates in one day, what on earth was I thinking?

I could hear Julia's remark ringing in my ear about the poor frogs. It's not like I don't have a track record of dating disasters: Jeff and the wrecked truck (to be fair, not my fault), Carl and the broken leg (snow is slippery), and Ted (prom night at the emergency room with his disjointed shoulder). Julia's ambulance comment wasn't too far off the mark, and here I was about to expose not one but two unsuspecting men to my tried-and-true first-date debacles.

It was Saturday afternoon around one o'clock, and I was standing in my walk-in closet deciding what to wear for a hike in January. I wanted to look feminine but not freeze to death.

My first date of the day, Chet Baker, had planned a quiet get-to-know-you hike around our beautiful Pine Lake.

I had spent a large portion of the morning rummaging through my notes from the Murphy case from the past week. Then I pored over the police interviews Elizabeth had given me at our lunch on Friday.

Carter's warning kept playing in my mind. The fact Bryant knew his killer seemed to act as a button on my warning alarm. If Bryant knew him or her, then I probably did too. This thought had unnerved me last night and had hung with me throughout the day.

What I gleaned from my notes was the list of real suspects wasn't as long as I had thought. Gabe was right. It had to be someone who knew Bryant's routine, his schedule.

There was Lilly. Yes, she had grown foxglove, but anyone with gardening knowledge could've used it since there was some on each table in the coffee shop. She also knew about the early meetings.

Then, there was the wife, Sarah Catherine. According to the administrative assistant, she knew about the early meeting. She also had a strong motive—greed. With Bryant dead, I suspected she stood to make a killing—bad choice of words—from the sale of Java Vein.

Of course, there was the administrative assistant, but in her case, there was no clear motive.

And what about the marketing agent? From what Gabe had said about her, she was young and rather pretty. And then we had Ed Philips, the disgruntled ex-employee.

Gabe's offer to tag along Monday was a good one. I needed to meet these people for myself and ask my questions my way. With all these thoughts whirling around in my head, I had to force myself to focus on the task at hand, getting ready for Chet Baker, potential Prince Charming Number One.

~

As we headed from the parking lot to the trail, our footsteps left deep indentions in the earth. It had rained earlier in the week, and with it being as cold as it was, the ground remained damp.

Chet was a gentleman—opening the car door for me when he picked me up and making sure the car was the right temperature for me with my heavy attire.

I had decided to wear jeans and hiking boots, along with my thickest pair of socks and my long johns. Practicality over beauty.

Chet, however, had chosen beauty over practicality. He was a handsome man somewhere in his thirties and looked as though he had stepped off the cover of *GQ*. He stood outside the passenger side door, dressed in the latest trendy clothes—straight leg jeans, a pink and orange sweater, and a pair of boating shoes as if we were going out for a sail. He had enough product in his blond hair to keep the manufacturer in business for a while. Chet looked good, that was for sure, but I feared he'd be frozen before we got too far.

After he opened the door for me, he pulled a heavy jacket from the backseat but left it unzipped.

The conversation started out like any average first date.

"So, how long have you owned the bookshop?"

"About six months. To tell you the truth, if it weren't for Flora, my assistant, I'd be lost. She came with the shop and keeps me straight with the bookkeeping and the inventory. I didn't know how much of a learning curve there would be."

"Nice she came with the store," Chet said.

"Yeah, I've come to depend on her for several things. She mothers me at times."

"I can see how that might be the case with her being older."

I decided to direct the focus of the conversation back on him. "Yes, so are you originally from here or are you a transplant?"

"I've lived here all my life except when I went to college. I'm sure you don't remember me, but I was a class below your sister Elizabeth in high school."

"Oh, you were the one voted friendliest guy on campus your senior year. Now I remember you. It was my freshman year, and I asked you to sign my yearbook."

"Really? What did I say?"

"I believe it went something like 'roses are red, violets are blue, you may know me, but I don't know you.'"

"And with all that charm I got voted friendliest? Now that's democracy for you." He chuckled.

As we rounded the bend that starts down the backside of the lake, Chet brought up the fire at my shop. He asked me how long I would be closed.

I answered him. He was sweet and caring, showing interest in the drama going on in my life, which, thanks to the news media, everyone knew about.

Then he asked if I knew how much it was going to cost to repair the damage. This question was a little too personal. I wasn't going to talk about my business finances with someone I hardly knew.

Then the questions became weirder. They started sounding rehearsed, like he had planned what he wanted to ask. "Is it true Bryant Kendrick was dead before the fire started?"

I stopped. I was overcome with a sense of déjà vu. Then it hit me, the crowd of reporters at the fire Wednesday morning, the questions being shot at me in rapid succession. Chet Baker's questions were sounding a lot like those. "Is it true . . . do you believe . . . could it be possible . . ." The phrases stood out like firecrackers against a night sky.

"You sorry, no-good phony. You're not an Open Hearts client. You're a reporter. I knew I recognized you from somewhere other than high school. You're the 'Around Town' guy." My temper rose like hot lava. The rat.

Chet squirmed. "No, I am a client, but you're right, I'm a reporter too. When I saw your name Wednesday night on my list of potential interests, I had to meet you. Your name had been floating around the newsroom all day. I didn't know you were Elizabeth's sister until now. Figured if I asked you out, I might get a scoop on the others and land the promotion I've been working on getting." He shrugged. "They got me doing fluff. But if I could get an exclusive with you—the inside story about one of the biggest crimes to happen in Pine Lake in the last few years—it might prove my worth to my boss." Here Chet Baker made his fatal mistake. He thought I would care.

"So, you were willing to lie to me and set up this charade of a date to pump me for information with no thought about my feelings? This was all about you and what you could get out of it. How long were you going to pretend this was a real date? The whole time? Would I find out tomorrow on the evening news you were a two-faced dirty—" My rage hit its boiling point. I leaned over and filled both my hands with the squishy mud under our feet.

"Now, Amy Kate, don't do anything rash," Chet pleaded as I charged toward him.

He stepped back, but since he was too afraid to take his eyes off me, he backed himself up against a stump and without warning found himself seated.

I took both hands and smeared the entire clump of muddy goo down the front of Mr. GQ, then for kicks, I pushed him off the stump, ensuring his backside would match his front. I would hate it if his outfit clashed.

Feeling quite satisfied, I spun and strode away.

Perhaps I did have the detective gene in me. I had figured out the liar was a reporter. No sooner had this thought passed through my mind than I heard the loud crunch of leaves followed by the breaking of limbs.

When I turned to see what Chet was up to, I discovered a very large, very angry raccoon.

I screamed.

The raccoon hissed at me.

An angry, aggressive man I could handle, but I knew nothing about rabid raccoons.

So, I ran.

No surprise to anyone but me, the raccoon gave chase. Angry his sleep had been disturbed, he pursued me with unrelenting focus. How speedy and agile this animal was! The faster I ran the quicker he seemed to go until the inevitable happened.

Glancing behind me instead watching where I was going, I stumbled, hit my knees, then my butt, then my knees, then my butt, and landed in the lake with a splat.

Chet ran to the bank, panting and found me sitting in the coldest water I have ever had the pleasure of meeting, drenched from my waist down.

My screams must've scared him, but when he found me in the lake and saw the raccoon lumbering off to find new entertainment, he doubled over with laughter.

"You dirty rotten—"

"Now, Amy Kate," Chet interrupted, "I thought since you've had a nice swim, your temper might've cooled down. I see I was wrong." He stood above me with his hands behind his back, grinning from ear to ear.

"Help me out of here," I demanded and reached my hand out to him.

"Not until you agree to give me the interview and apologize for ruining my sweater." He peered down at his mud-crusted apparel. I must admit Chet had guts.

"Fat chance, b-b-b-buster."

Chet's resolve gave way. He reached out his hand and pulled me out. "I never could watch a damsel in distress."

"Thank you, even a pig has its moment in the sun."

Chet smiled an amiable one and helped me up the side of the lake to the trail. "We'll need to hurry, Amy Kate. If you get too cold, it could be bad, and keeping up a brisk pace will help to keep you warm."

I hated thinking we had a whole hour's worth of walking in front of us. As we rounded the bend of the trail, we saw one of the marina's employees in a golf cart collecting trash from the receptacles.

Hallelujah, I thought.

George was happy to give us a ride back to the parking lot. Chet took off his jacket and wrapped it around my frigid legs. Its warmth helped ease the pain of the chill.

"Now you're going to be cold. We don't both need to be frozen solid. Who'll drive us back to my apartment?" I asked.

Chet ignored my protests. He placed his arm around my shoulders and pulled me close to his side. I let him. The cold was winning, and I was too tired to fight with him. He, the dirty rotten scoundrel of a newsman, was being gallant, and it irritated me to no end.

Chet settled me in the car, still wrapped in his coat, and turned the heat up to blazing. While it warmed, he leaned over and pulled me back into his arms. "I owe you an apology. It was rotten of me to trick you. The opportunity presented itself, and I took it. I'm sorry."

I leaned my head against his shoulder. "The Christian thing to do is to forgive you, but it might take me a day or two to get there." Sarcasm colored my words.

"I can accept that," he said.

The heater warmed the car, and I began to thaw. I raised my head from his shoulder and slid over to my side of the car. Chet removed his arm from around me and cleared his throat. "Amy Kate, I would like us to be friends." He gave me a sideways glance.

I gave him a withering look, but he continued, "This was a terrible start, but—" His face broke into a sweet, innocent smile. He locked eyes with mine. "I had a good time."

I couldn't decide between "you conniving, low-down dog, you lied to me" or "I had a good time too." I decided to play it safe and kept quiet.

Chet had proven to be a good sport and found the humor in the situation. I liked a guy with a sense of humor, but he lied. That's a hard one to accept.

Ever the Southern gentleman, Chet walked me to the door of my apartment and planted a kiss on my cheek.

It was the cleanest spot he could find.

Once inside, I went straight for the shower. The hot water beat down on my cold body and felt like heaven. My toes tingled from the heat when the water hit them. They had been trapped in my hiking boots with a thick layer of lake ooze and my heavy, wet camping socks as company.

So much for choosing practicality over beauty. I almost froze to death.

~

Date number two was coffee and dessert at Hooks, the restaurant at the marina. I didn't want to do dinner in case I wasn't comfortable. It's easy enough to down a piece of pie in an emergency and take a couple of swigs of coffee. I figured it might take all of five minutes if I was in a rush. But if everything was going well, I could make coffee and dessert last for a good hour. It seemed like a safe choice.

Michael Cooper was the one who had decided on Hooks. I wasn't too thrilled about returning to the marina as I had seen all I wanted of the lake for one day, but we made the arrangements before I met the raccoon. Besides, the restaurant offered great ambiance. White lights illuminated the outside of the old cabin that had been transformed into an elegant seafood spot. The lights gave it an ethereal aura.

It was close to six, and the date was set for seven, so I decided to go to the Open Hearts site and rate my first date while it was fresh on my mind. I thought this would be easy, but it wasn't.

Though I was still steamed about Chet tricking me, his candor about enjoying the date charmed me. The fact he walked me to my door even though neither one of us was fit to be seen in public also left a lasting impression. He hadn't once complained about the mud or worried about the interior of his car, though I knew it would smell like wet fish for a good month even with those little pine trees hanging from the rearview mirror. He was a gentleman through and through, even down to the peck on the cheek.

I considered maybe Chet and I could be friends—but only friends. I've had all the lying, cheating, egotistical males I cared to deal with stomp through my love life. This time I wanted a keeper.

While I was perusing the Open Hearts site, I went to Michael Cooper's information to see what he looked like, so I could recognize him. Seemed he was an English teacher and worked at the local high school. He must be Carter's other son. Carter hadn't mentioned his name, but I bet it was Michael. I did remember Carter—or was it Gabe—saying he was a teacher.

The picture I found posted was a school faculty picture. They tended to be bad to begin with, but this one was the worse. I couldn't make out any of his features except for the fact he had dark wavy hair that looked like Gabe's. *This must be his brother.*

I arrived at the restaurant a little tardy and asked to be seated. Since the guy's picture was blurred, he'd have to come to me.

"Hi, Amy Kate?" I heard a deep strong voice rumble. I turned around in my chair to find a familiar face.

"Hi, yourself. What're you doing here, Gabe?" Curious. Was he meeting someone here for an interview or maybe a date? This last thought bothered me.

"Did you call me Gabe?"

"Yes, and please, don't tell me we're starting the whole name-game business again." I held my hand up, palm side out. "I thought we'd settled that since I apologized. And since we're off the clock, I thought Gabe would be all right."

"Gabe's fine whenever." He shrugged. "May I join you?"

I scanned the room. "I'm waiting for a date."

"Oh, I see," Gabe said. "Who is he? I might know him."

"Actually, you might at that. His name is Michael Cooper. Are you related?" I asked, a little worried by the look that came over Gabe's face. His eyes danced with playfulness.

"You're right, I do know him. Very well, I might add."

"Is he your brother?" I wondered what the connection was

that would bring on such an impish smile.

"No, I can honestly say he's not my brother." The fun Gabe was having with this conversation confused me. What could be so amusing about Michael Cooper?

Gabe took a minute. He was thinking something over by the way he cocked one of his eyebrows. "I tell you what, let's give this Michael a few more minutes, say fifteen, and if he's a no-show, have dessert with me." He pointed to himself.

"Well—" I glanced at my watch and discovered it was past the agreed-upon time. "Okay, we'll give him another fifteen minutes, and if he's not here, I'll be happy to have dessert with you."

Gabe sat down at another table.

I drank some of the water my waitress had brought me. I played with the silverware, tapping the butter knife in time with the music. I periodically checked my watch.

After the fifteen minutes were up, Gabe moved over to my table, and we ordered the most decadent chocolate goo to ever pass between my lips. It was mind-blowing.

Between bites, I brought up the case since it was something we had in common. I was surprised when he asked if we could talk about something else.

"All right, if you don't want to discuss the case, what do you want to talk about?"

"I understand you own a bookshop. What kind of books do you like to read?" He understood I owned a bookshop. He first met me because of the bookshop. For some reason, something didn't add up. "Murder mysteries are my favorite. I guess that's no shock." I chuckled. "I also like historical fiction—the kind of books that transport you back in time, and I like to read the authors who've done their homework, so the major events of the time are presented well. I always learn something new about whatever era they've written about."

"I've read some great ones about the French Revolution and World War II. It always amazes me the way the authors work their characters into the heart of major world events and give the readers such an insider's view. It pops the history to life."

Okay, this looked like Gabe and the voice sounded like Gabe, but the words, this was a different Gabe.

The conversation was delightful, and I was immersed in the various topics. We covered books, dream vacations, and we even touched on our faith. Then as we were in the middle of discussing some of the other local restaurants and our favorite foods, Lilly Murphy and another woman entered and waited to be seated.

I ducked and drew my chair closer to the table. Gabe noticed the abrupt change in my behavior and leaned forward. "Are you hiding?"

"Yes, Lilly Murphy just walked in with another woman, and I don't want her to see me. It might scare her away. If she stays, it'll give me the chance to see who she's with. Maybe even have a chat and see what she knows. Don't you want to know who she's with?"

CHAPTER TWELVE

Gabe scanned the room as if he didn't know what Lilly Murphy looked like. I watched his expression. Never did I see any signs of recognition light his eyes.

With his head turned, I noticed a star-shaped birthmark behind his right ear. Unique, almost hidden by his wavy brown hair.

"She's going toward the kitchen. Do you see her?"

Gabe nodded and made a grunting noise. I turned to watch Lilly being seated. When my gaze returned to Gabe, he was checking his watch. He laid his napkin on the table and pushed his chair back.

"You're leaving? I can't believe you're going to miss this great opportunity to talk to her while her guard is down. She'll be freer with her answers. You're not going to leave, are you?"

"Yes, I am," Gabe said. "I'm leaving the situation in your capable hands."

Right. Now, I knew something is up.

"My capable hands, my eye. What's going on?"

"If you must know, I—" he stammered. "I have another appointment this evening, so I need to get going."

"Is it something to do with this case?"

"No, it's a personal matter."

"Oh." I said disheartened by the fact Gabe had a personal matter late on a Saturday night. I couldn't help but wonder if it was with one of those women Elizabeth had told me about at lunch, the ones vying for his attention, the drooling ones.

Gabe walked to my side of the table and placed my hand between his two rather large ones. "I had a nice time tonight. I'm sorry your date didn't show."

"I'm not." I smiled up at him.

"Me either." He grinned. "His loss was my gain." Then Gabe lifted my hand to his lips and kissed it.

As I watched Gabe leave the restaurant, it came to my attention the restaurant was still standing. I spent two hours with him, and I neither fainted nor fumed. I didn't make a spectacle of myself in any way. We had quietly enjoyed our dessert and coffee. Neither Dr. Jekyll nor Mr. Hyde showed up. The only two people here this evening were Amy Kate Anderson and Gabe Cooper.

Come to think of it, I never did find out why Gabe was here in the first place. It seemed too coincidental that he happened to be here and even odder that he left when we had a suspect to interrogate, I mean interview.

The mystery of the appearance of Gabe Cooper and the even bigger mystery of his departure would have to wait.

I grabbed my purse and made my way toward the back of the restaurant to the tables near the kitchen, nodding at Lilly as I approached her table. "Hi, Lilly, how are you this evening?"

"All right, I guess, considering Bryant's funeral was today." She paused and peered at the woman sitting beside her. "You know Sarah Catherine, his wife, don't you?" Sarah Catherine was in her late thirties with short brown hair and hard green eyes. She was well-groomed and gave me the impression she liked nice things.

"No, I don't think we've ever met. I'm Amy Kate Anderson. I own the bookshop next to the Beans and Leaves."

"Oh, sorry about your shop." She motioned to one of the empty chairs. "Would you like to join us? We were going to get something to eat, but it seems neither one of us has an appetite. So we decided drinking would be better." She shook her glass, making the ice clink.

"I understand. The stress of the situation must be weighing on you both." I slid into one of the vacant chairs at their table for four.

"Dealing with all those people at the funeral was draining,"

Lilly said, her swollen, red-rimmed eyes telling the whole story.

I turned my attention toward Sarah Catherine, who as the wife seemed less upset by the day's events than Lilly. "I'm so sorry for both of you."

"No need for sympathy. Bryant and I were over a long time ago." Sarah Catherine lifted her drink to her lips and took a long swallow. Then she placed the glass on the table. "Today was about doing my duty."

The cool remark halted the conversation until Lilly asked, "Do you want something to drink? I'll be glad to call the waitress over for you. Sarah Catherine and I agreed we'd earned this little indulgence after the fiasco with the newspaper reporters." Lilly took a sip of the Long Island Iced Tea in her hand.

At this rate, they both should be very relaxed, very soon, and I hoped very cooperative. Sidestepping the question, I asked, "What happened with the reporters?" Had Chet made it home and cleaned up in time to get in on the action?

"There were five or six of them outside the funeral home trying to interview people as they were coming and going from the visitation this morning," answered Lilly.

Hmm, I bet Chet had gone to the visitation before our date. Wonder what he found out? Maybe a friendship with a reporter might be beneficial. "How did you handle it, Sarah Catherine? Was it painful to hear people talking about how he passed? It couldn't have been easy."

"No, but life with Bryant hasn't ever been what you would call easy. I didn't expect his funeral to be any different. He was always attracting attention." Sarah Catherine took another sip of her Tom Collins, then continued, "He was the type of man you either loved or you hated. There wasn't any in between with him. In my case, I loved him at first, but once he started cheating, all I had left was hate."

"He cheated on you?" Her openness surprised me.

"Yes, but I couldn't prove it. I would find makeup on his sleeve, or his clothes would smell of a woman's perfume. At first, he said I was paranoid and tried to smooth things over, but then it got to the point where he didn't even bother."

"Why didn't you hire someone to look into it for you?" I

asked.

"I did. I hired that local guy."

"Ah, the creeper."

"Is that what everybody calls him? I don't know. I guess that's the one. All he did, was take my money. He did find something, but Bryant got to him first and paid him off. By the time I hired the guy, we were already headed for divorce court, so it really didn't matter."

"Now, he's gone. I guess there's no divorce, which means no settlement. Everything will come to you. I'm sure there's a life insurance policy, too."

Sarah Catherine stared at me for a moment. Her eyes searching my face, then answered, "Yes, there was a policy."

"Oh, I hope it's enough. I had an uncle once who died without warning, and everybody thought he had a policy large enough to cover the funeral and to take care of his estate, but he didn't. It left my aunt in a tight financial situation. We all felt so bad for her." I placed my hand over my heart and leaned forward a bit as if it this were confidential information.

"Let's just say I should be comfortable for many years to come. Besides, Bryant was a brilliant businessman, and I'm expecting to see some cash flow from some of his deals. Lord knows, I didn't see as much as I should've when he was around."

Lilly patted Sarah Catherine's forearm. "You do have your own money, dear."

"Did would be a better description. Thanks to Bryant." Sarah Catherine drained her glass and looked around for the waitress. "But I don't want to get into that today."

I leaned back and redirected the conversation. "You said earlier people either loved him or hated him." Sarah Catherine's eyes drifted back to me. "How did that work with him as the chief financial officer of Java Vein?"

"The women either loved him or hated him because of his attentions toward them, and the men hated him because they all wanted to be him." A grin played on her lips.

The waitress stopped at the table, and the ladies asked for another round of drinks and ordered some appetizers. I was hoping the food would help absorb the alcohol. Otherwise, it looked like I'd be the designated driver for this little party.

The ladies described both the visitation and the funeral to me and commented on some of the people who had attended. "The reverend did such a lovely job, and the hymn we sang at the end of the service was perfect." Lily touched her napkin to her eyes.

Then Sarah Catherine mentioned seeing Ed Philips there, and I zoomed in on the topic. "Ed Philips was at the visitation? Isn't that a little odd? I thought he was a disgruntled employee, at least according to Samantha Holiday."

The waitress returned with their second round and the appetizers.

"You can't depend on what she tells you. She was as loyal as a wife to Bryant." After she realized what she said, she giggled at her choice of words. "Actually, she was more so." Her comment dripped with insinuation. "Always faithful, always there. Like a golden retriever."

Sarah Catherine's focus seemed to be drifting a bit now that she was halfway into her second drink, and Lilly seemed to be sliding down the slippery slope of melancholy as well.

To redirect the conversation to the crime, I asked, "What do you know about Mr. Philips, if he's not an ex-employee?"

Lilly propped her elbow on the table. "Mr. Philips worked for a local ad agency who handled the Java Vein account. He's a wonderful man. The way he took care of his wife during her illness was commendable." Lilly's face clouded. "He was at the hospital every day for weeks, and when she was sent home with little to no hope, Ed went back to work to find out he'd been fired." She shook her head.

"Fired? Isn't that a bit harsh?"

"I thought so," Sarah Catherine said. "Come to find out, it was Bryant's doing. He called and complained several times during Ed's absence that things weren't being handled for his account. Bryant used this as an excuse to move the Java Vein account to a bigger firm, which I later found out he was planning to do anyway."

"Ed got fired for losing one of the firm's biggest accounts." Lilly's mouth pulled tight. "He's been doing odd jobs trying to start his own advertising agency ever since."

"That was about a year ago," Sarah Catherine said, "and

with his wife's passing about six month later, Ed has just about become a ghost. There's almost nothing left of the poor man, bless his heart." She tried to lean her chin in her hand but missed, causing her head to bob.

"So, let me get this straight. Bryant accused Ed of dropping the ball with his account and moved the account to a larger firm. And then Ed was fired although he'd been out taking care of his sick wife." Shock and outrage rose in me. I sat straighter. "Unbelievable."

"That was Bryant, unbelievable," Sarah Catherine said. "Once something became about someone other than himself, Bryant was quick to move on. I'll give him that. You always knew where you stood with the man, which was right behind him. I think he loved someone once, but it wasn't me." She hiccupped. "He made that crystal clear."

Lilly sat quiet, her gaze on her hands in her lap.

Sarah Catherine rattled the ice in her now-empty glass.

"Are you about ready to go?" Lilly asked as she picked up her purse from the table.

With all the alcohol gone and some of the appetizers nibbled on, Sarah Catherine nodded and pulled her purse from the back of the chair. It had been a long day for both. One had buried a cheating no-good husband and the other a lifelong friend.

As the ladies called the waitress over to take care of the check, I needed to take this opportunity to ask Sarah Catherine where she'd been Wednesday morning around five o'clock. I wasn't sure I'd get another chance.

"Where else?" she asked in mock surprise. "I was home alone, tossing and turning, trying to figure out how to get every last penny I could out of my no-account husband."

Her candor puzzled me. Even if she were a little skunked, she wasn't even trying to fake any emotion over her dearly departed husband.

"Look, Tuesday night I confronted him about the national deal with Benson. He tried to hide it until after the divorce. I wanted him to know he wasn't taking any more money from me. We fought in his office, but my lawyers, who were present, were working on getting me my cut." She shook her head. "For being so savvy, you would've thought he was smarter about giving interviews to business magazines. I wouldn't have found out except he subscribes to a few, and his mail still comes to the house. What irritated me was after seven years of cheating on me, the guy was still trying to pull a fast one on me."

"Did you know about the meeting Wednesday morning?"

Sarah Catherine squirmed in her chair before she answered. She decided the truth would be the best route. "Yes. But so did anyone who worked for him." She hesitated. "Like I said, I wanted out with money and my lawyers were making sure that happened."

"So, you knew about the meeting, and you'd spent a restless night plotting your revenge over the money. How far were you willing to go with your revenge? Would you have done anything?"

"I guess that about covers it," Sarah Catherine answered with no hesitation and no remorse.

"Anything, including murder?" The words slipped out before I knew it.

But I shouldn't have worried. Sarah Catherine replied without batting an eye, "Your words, honey, not mine."

As the ladies meandered toward the door, wobbling every few steps, I followed them out and asked if they needed a ride. Because of my dad being a retired detective and the accident involving my mom, I didn't mind being their taxi.

Both declined my offer and headed for a nice-looking Buick. They had drunk enough to loosen their tongues, but not enough to end up in a ditch. At least, I hoped not.

Lilly walked to the driver's side of the car while Sarah Catherine dug out her keys and handed them to her. As I watched them pull out of the parking lot onto the highway, I thought about Lilly's red-rimmed eyes. Obviously, she'd been crying, but of the two women, I would've expected the wife to be the one with the red eyes, not the friend.

Sarah Catherine had confessed the only emotion she had left for him was hate. She didn't even seem able to muster any tears for the poor dead guy. Hate could be a strong motive for murder, added to the fact he was trying to hose her out of what could've been millions. She looked like a prime suspect to me.

On top of that, there was the insurance money that would leave her comfortable for years to come. What kind of woman lives with a man for seven years—even a lying, cheating man—and sheds no tears on the day she buries him? The coldhearted kind, but if her lawyers were working to get her share for her, then killing Bryant wasn't necessary.

Then my thoughts turned back to Lilly and her tearful, mournful eyes—the eyes of a woman who cared about the man who was buried.

Lilly cared about Bryant.

The thought struck me as odd since she was the one who said he used people. Had he used Lilly somehow? Why would saying good-bye to a scoundrel like Bryant Kendrick bring tears to Lilly Murphy's eyes?

My gut told me Lilly wasn't being entirely forthcoming. It was more than the business deal and more than Matt's happiness. Something significant lay right beneath the surface, and I could tell she wanted to let it out. All I needed to do was dig a little deeper and give her the chance to share her dormant secret.

~

The quietness of church felt good after the long, unusual week. The soft singing of the choir and the giggles of the children during the children's sermon refreshed my soul after dealing with fires and death.

Although I had not been a regular church attendee when I was in Jackson, as Christians, Dad and Mom had raised us to go to church. It was so easy to slide back into bed and sleep away those Sunday mornings. But here in Pine Lake, the people of First Community Church had become like a second family. They wrapped me in their welcoming arms and made me feel at home. That the majority of my actual family attended the church made it that much sweeter. Elizabeth and I would meet Dad and Alexia, Cole, and baby Grant in the third pew to the left of the middle aisle almost every Sunday. Sometimes, Julia joined us.

After services, we always met at Dad's house and cooked lunch together. Our usual was a pot roast, but sometimes when we were celebrating a birthday or something special happened, we'd make chicken and dumplings. To be sure, there were never any leftovers.

Today, because of the hideous week that had been my life, we needed comfort food. The chicken and dumplings simmered on the stove as I entered the kitchen. Dad stood over the pot stirring when I took the opportunity to talk to him alone.

I leaned against the counter and placed the bread on the cookie sheet he had laid out for me. My job was to make the garlic bread.

"That smells divine." I inhaled the sweet savor. "Guess what? I met someone new this week whom you know."

"Oh yeah, who? I figured you pretty much knew everybody I know."

"His name is Gabe Cooper. In fact, I've met several of the Coopers this last week. I even hired Mr. Cooper to work at Twisted Plots. He said his son, Gabe, speaks highly of you."

"That's nice to hear." He grinned and stirred the dumplings.

"Gabe told me you had given him some advice when he first arrived in town. It sounds like you two were close during your last few months with the department." I wanted more information on Gabe. Last night's date had been so pleasant. I enjoyed hearing him talk about other topics besides the case. It showed me he had outside interests, that he wasn't all work. He seemed so different during those two hours.

"Gabe is a great guy. He's easygoing and nothing rattles him much, but when he first arrived here from Chicago, it took him a while to power down from the hectic pace he was used to in the big city. Pine Lake was an adjustment for him. I helped him along a bit, that's all. What's your take on him?"

"Who?" Elizabeth asked as she entered the kitchen with Grant in her arms.

"Gabe Cooper. You know him, right, Elizabeth?" Dad asked.

"Yes, I do. I take it Amy Kate is asking after her knight in shining armor?" Mischief twinkled in Elizabeth's deep blue eyes.

"Knight in shining armor, huh?" Dad shifted his attention from Elizabeth and the baby back to me. "Is there anything I should know?"

"She didn't tell you about her fainting spell—" Elizabeth placed her free hand on her brow acting the part of a swooning

Southern belle. "—and how Gabe came to her rescue?"

"No." Dad leaned his elbows on the counter. "Do tell." He wiggled his eyebrows at the suggestion there was more to the story.

"Elizabeth, I'm going to kick your butt." I tore off after her. Still holding the baby, she wisely ran from the kitchen. The baby squealed with every step.

"Now, Amy Kate, you can't hurt a defenseless woman with a baby."

"Wanna bet?" I made a dive at Elizabeth and Grant, pushing them onto the couch. With her hands full of Grant, I started tickling the two of them. Grant giggled and drooled.

"Stop, I surrender," Elizabeth said between laughs.

"I'll stop on one condition. If you hand over the baby." I playfully lifted Grant over my head and twirled him. He loved to be twirled, and we all indulged his passion.

Dad was still in the kitchen when I returned holding Grant. He had taken over the job of buttering the bread and sprinkling garlic on it since I abandoned the task. "So, Gabe helped you out."

"Yes," I answered and changed the subject. "I'm sure you know, Elizabeth hired me to do some leg work for her, and Gabe wasn't too happy about having to work with a newbie. He thought it might be too dangerous for me." There was no way I was telling any of these people, especially Elizabeth, that one of my dates had ended up being a no-show and I had spent the evening with Gabe.

My dad glanced up from the tray of bread. "He's right. It is dangerous work. Don't ignore his warnings. He knows what he's talking about." Then a smile tugged at his lips while he shook the garlic over the slices. "He'll warm up to the idea of working with you. All you have to do is unleash the Anderson Southern charm on him, and he'll be glad he got to know you better."

"I think I've unleashed all the Anderson Southern charm on him he can tolerate for the moment. But I'm sure you're right. Once he gets to know me and sees what I can do, he'll be happy I'm around." At least, that's what I hoped for after our wonderful time together at Hooks.

"Soup's on," Dad called to the troops.

We gathered around the dining room table. Dad sat at the head with his back to the window and Alexia's husband, Cole, sat at the other end with baby Grant. The rest of us filled in the space and bowed our heads to say a word of thanksgiving to the Creator of all.

CHAPTER THIRTEEN

At ten o'clock Monday morning, I entered the elevator and pushed the third-floor button for the Java Vein offices. Though I had to travel to the fringe of the city limits to their building, I made it on time. Gabe stood, waiting by the double glass doors as I stepped off the elevator.

The glass doors opened into a receptionist area decorated in a hip modern style. Some of the chairs were so curvy I wasn't sure if they were chairs or art. The receptionist told us to have a seat, and she'd see if Samantha Holiday, Bryant's administrative assistant, was available.

I hesitated, determining the best way to approach sitting in this architectural achievement that was a 'chair.' I envisioned it in an art museum with the label "chair in motion.". After a few moments of contemplation, I opted to stand.

The receptionist returned saying Miss Holiday would be with us in a moment. A few seconds later, a tall, long-legged beauty emerged from behind a wooden door. She was in her late thirties with dark brown hair. For her age, she was in great shape—not one ounce of flab anywhere to be seen.

She wore a dark green wrap dress that clung to her shape. It wasn't meant to be showy, but anything would hang right on this woman. I looked down at my skirt and blouse and felt like something the cat had dragged in.

I rolled my shoulders and stood straighter.

She greeted us coolly, and we followed her down the paneled hallway to the corner office. Miss Holiday's area, with her desk, chair and filing cabinets, was in as good a shape as the lady herself. Everything was tidy and in its place. There was no waste here in this tip-top, efficient office. How did she get anything done?

The desk calendar was out for everyone to see. I remembered what Gabe had said about Sarah Catherine, the wife, being caught by Miss Holiday looking at her husband's upcoming schedule. It didn't seem like it would've taken much effort to obtain the information since the calendar was in plain sight.

Gabe thanked Miss Holiday for seeing us and gave her some information. Meanwhile, I did a sweep of the room and took note of three plants in her office--one on her desk and two large plants near the window.

They all looked healthy. Curious if Miss Holiday gardened, I wandered over to one of the plants and touched it to make sure it was real. It was.

One personal picture sat on the top shelf of the bookcase behind her desk. An older couple. Probably, her parents.

Her desk sat across from two doors. One was open, and I saw a long table with ten chairs positioned around it—a conference room. I figured the other door had to be Bryant's office.

As Gabe took a seat in one of the chairs in front of her desk, I walked toward the unopened door in order to take a quick peek inside. I hoped Miss Holiday would be distracted by Gabe and his rugged good looks, so I'd go unnoticed.

I turned the knob, and the door swung partway open. The window in the room let in enough light for me to tell the room needed straightening. Several file drawers hung open, and papers covered the desk. A round indention appeared in the carpet where something heavy had sat at one time. The indention was the right size for a potted plant. If I had to guess, I'd say it probably matched the two pots in Miss Holiday's office.

I was about to step into the room when Miss Holiday caught sight of me. "Don't go in there."

Gabe stopped mid-sentence. "Why can't she go in the office?"

"Because I haven't had time to put things away from when

you and your men were here the other day." She walked over to where I stood and closed the door.

"Miss Holiday, you do understand this is a murder investigation. Because of the circumstances under which your employer died, we need to know everything, personal or private that might help us catch his killer."

"I know," she said curtly.

"Do you mind if I take a look?" I asked.

"Who are you again?" She crossed her arms.

"Miss Anderson is working for the attorney representing Matt Murphy. She has some questions she wants to ask you about Bryant and Matt."

I don't like people answering for me, but Gabe's explanation lent an air of authenticity to my presence. Gabe gave me a warning look, and I moved away from the door, trying to take the tension level down a few notches.

I sat in one of the two chairs in front of Miss Holiday's desk and took out my notepad. Miss Holiday moved from the door and slid into her seat behind the desk.

Gabe resumed the interview by asking, "Miss Holiday, I am curious. Who knew about the morning meeting on Wednesday?"

"Hmm, let me think. Of course, Matt and Bryant, Bryant's wife, I believe, knew because I caught her looking at my desk calendar Tuesday afternoon before her meeting with Bryant and their lawyers. I'm kind of old school. Of course, I keep everything on the computer, but I also keep a calendar for quick references and as a backup."

"Yes, I'm aware of those individuals. Can you think of anyone else?"

"Yes, the marketing agent, Casey Russell. She would've known. Bryant kept her in the loop about those meetings because it meant an influx of work for her. There was always a new flavor to introduce to the public after one of those meetings." Samantha leaned back in her chair and crossed her legs.

"Matt has a natural ability to combine those flavors. He's like the Ben and Jerry's of the coffee and tea world." Miss Holiday said.

I doubted this woman had ever tasted any flavor offered by Ben and Jerry.

"It's funny, though, Bryant didn't appreciate the flavored coffees at all. He always took his black and was happy with whatever was on sale. He told me once he always had a small pot of coffee brewed to clean his pallet after all those flavor tastings," she said. "Anyway, Casey took over the account about a year ago when Bryant moved it from Tidwell to Inkster. He needed someone besides himself to oversee the advertisements and marketing campaigns. It had become too big of a job for the people at Tidwell, and Bryant, being as aggressive as he was, needed a firm who could give him the kind of attention he wanted."

"I took her statement Thursday down at the station, but we'll want to speak to her, again. Is she here today?" Gabe asked.

"She's here often enough," Miss Holiday said with a slight snicker. "We set up an office for her to use when she's here, but she does most of her work from her own office at Inkster. As she said on numerous occasions to Bryant, we aren't her only clients."

Wow, even I picked up on the temperature drop as Miss Holiday gave us the number and address of Inkster. There was no love lost between the two women. I couldn't imagine what Bryant's assistant could have against an employee from the advertising agency.

Gabe took the information down in his notebook. "You had mentioned Thursday Ed Philips was the advertising agent for Tidwell who had the Java Vein account, and that he had become disgruntled with Mr. Kendrick. Can you think of any other reason why he would be angry with Mr. Kendrick other than being removed from the account?"

"Ed Philips blamed Bryant, I mean Mr. Kendrick, for losing his job. Mr. Philips' wife had been terminally ill and in the hospital for months. Whenever Bryant called, he was never available. Bryant started complaining to Mr. Philips' bosses, and when he returned to work, he was handed his notice of termination."

"Yes, I heard he had been fired," I said.

Gabe gave me a strange look but continued with the questioning.

"Anything else?" Gabe prompted Miss Holiday.

"There were a few nasty calls to Bryant here and some emails sent both here and to his house. When Bryant didn't reply, Mr. Philips showed up in the parking lot one evening waiting for him. Bryant threatened to get a restraining order, but he didn't need to because Mr. Philips never came back. I heard Mr. Philips' wife had died around that time. After that, the phone calls and harassment stopped."

"When was it?" I asked.

"About six months ago, and we haven't heard from him since," Miss Holiday said.

"Do you have any idea what Ed Philips wanted to talk about with Mr. Kendrick?" Gabe asked.

Miss Holiday shifted in her chair. "Mr. Philips blamed Mr. Kendrick for his wife's death. With the loss of his job, their health insurance was cancelled, and it made things hard for them. Mr. Philips wanted Bryant to help out somehow with the medical bills."

"Thank you, Miss Holiday, you've been very helpful." Gabe closed his notebook.

"Oh, I have one last question," I said as I stood. "I understand Java Vein uses SUVs as company vehicles. Do you have any way of finding out who used those vehicles on Tuesday and Wednesday of last week?"

"Hmm, I'll have to look for the log, since Bryant was the one who kept up with it. We have four SUVs, though, and Bryant used one of them on a permanent basis. So, there were three to keep tabs on. One was left for me and the other administrative assistants to use for running company errands. Of the other two, I believe one was available to Matt, and one was sometimes used by Casey Russell when she had to make out-of-town trips for Java Vein business. Inkster didn't provide a company car, so Bryant would let her use one of ours."

"Do these company vehicles have any logos or identifying marks on them?" I asked.

"They have our logo on it, but they're magnetic and can come off pretty easy. I'll see if I can find the log, and I'll be sure to get it to the lieutenant when I do."

Miss Holiday stood. "Lieutenant, Miss Anderson, if there

isn't anything else, I need to get back to work. So, if you can see yourselves out, I would appreciate it." With this dismissal, we started down the hall.

When we reached the door to the receptionist area, I said, "Shoot. I forgot my purse. You go ahead, and I'll meet you in front of the building."

I trekked down the hall but stopped short of knocking on Miss Holiday's door when I heard what sounded like a woman crying coming from inside. I tapped on the door and opened it in increments. To my surprise, I found Miss Holiday sitting behind her desk with her face in her hands, dissolved in tears.

I cleared my throat not wanting to intrude. She looked up, and embarrassment washed over her face. She sniffled and pulled a tissue from a box on her desk.

"I'm so sorry, Miss Holiday, but I forgot my purse." I crept into the room and tiptoed over to the chair where I left it.

As I picked up my purse, I chanced a glance at Miss Holiday. Her eyes were closed, and her head leaned against the chair. Fresh tears glistened on her cheeks.

"I know it's none of my business," I said, my need to set things right took a hold of me, "but I can only imagine after working with someone for six years that you must have grown very fond of him."

Miss Holiday opened her eyes casting a cold, hard stare through her tears at me. She straightened in her seat. "You're right, it is none of your business, and I'll thank you to keep your comments to yourself. Good day." Miss Holiday pulled her chair closer to the desk and opened the file in front of her.

I marched to the door, but as I was about to step out, Miss Holiday said, "You do learn a lot about a man when you work for him. You learn what kind of a man he is. What drives him, and what his dreams are." She looked up from the file, her eyes now sedate. "So, yes, after working with someone for so long, you would've had some sort of feelings for him, wouldn't you?"

"Yes, I think you would," I said, waiting to see what would happen next.

"Good day," she said.

I entered the parking lot and spotted Gabe leaning against a bright red Corvette that I assumed was his.

I must admit, Gabe cut a striking figure in his suit and tie, and the sparkling, cherry-red Corvette in the background put the image over the top. I was surprised, though. I didn't think detectives made much in the way of salary.

He stood to his full height and opened the car door for me. I tilted my head to the side, trying to figure out what he was up to. We had arrived in separate vehicles. He must've read my facial expression because he said, "I figured we could ride together to interview Casey Russell."

"Can you have me back here by noon? I have a repairman coming later to give me an estimate, and I'll need to be back to the shop in time to meet him."

Gabe checked his watch. "Yeah, it shouldn't take longer than an hour to interview Miss Russell. I can have you back here by noon. So, do you want to go for a spin?" He wiggled his eyebrows at me.

"Sure."

Once we were on the road, Gabe asked, "Okay, rookie, how did you know about Ed Philips?"

"Oh, that's why you wanted to ride together." I nodded my understanding.

He winked at me with a grin. "Maybe."

"Okay, Saturday night after you left, I went over and talked to Lilly, who was having dinner with Sarah Catherine Kendrick. Sarah Catherine told me all about Ed Philips and how Bryant was responsible for getting him fired. I swear Bryant Kendrick was heartless. I'm surprised he lived as long as he did without his heart."

"When I left, you went over to talk to them?" Gabe repeated as his brow furrowed.

"Yes, I told you I was going to. Don't you remember?"

"Not all of it. Could you refresh my memory? We had dinner and talked about—" Gabe left the thought hanging in the air, waiting for me to fill in the missing pieces. It was as if he hadn't even been there.

"First, we didn't have dinner, just dessert, and we talked about books and hobbies. You know, the usual get-to-know-you stuff." What was this guy up to? I had so enjoyed the date, and now he can't remember it? Something didn't compute.

"Was I charming?" His lopsided grin appeared, and a herd of butterflies came alive in my stomach.

I wasn't sure how to answer, but I decided I'd play along. "Yes, very. And you even picked up the check."

"Really? You mean we didn't go dutch? Since I'm not responsible for you, and you can take care of yourself and all." A sparkle danced in his eyes.

He was trying to stir up trouble, but I'd sworn to myself I would be one hundred-percent professional today with Lieutenant Gabe the Babe. "Nope, you paid for both desserts and coffees at Hooks, and I have to say it was one of the yummiest desserts I've ever had, and I live with a pastry chef. So, that's saying something."

"Can you remind me why you were there?"

"Yeah, I was supposed to meet a guy named Michael, whom I met through an online-dating service. But he never showed, and you did."

"Ah, Michael." I could see Gabe's wheels churning as his jaw tightened. "His loss was my gain."

"Yes, so you said Saturday night." I leaned back on the leather seat.

"What else did you learn from Lilly and Sarah Catherine after I left?"

"I learned Sarah Catherine is receiving enough from a life insurance policy to live comfortably for years to come." I raised my eyebrows for effect. "What do you think about that?"

"I think it's a good piece of detective work on your part, and I believe it proves Mrs. Kendrick has a motive besides the business deal with Benson. I'll have to make a point of going by and seeing her again today."

"Thank you, Lieutenant, I appreciate the encouragement." I was rather pleased with the compliment from the man who thought I would be a liability. I suppose he didn't want me crying on him again. "What did you think about the interview with Miss Holiday?"

"I think she's good at her job. Her office was immaculate, everything in its place," Gabe said.

"Yes, it was. Did you notice the nice, healthy plants?"

"Yes, I did, but they could've been fake," Gabe said and

made a right turn."

"They weren't. I checked."

Gabe chuckled. "I should've known you would be thorough. It's a quality that goes hand in hand with persistence."

"I also have another bit you might be interested in," I said.

"What's that?"

"When I went back to get my purse, I found our very professional administrative assistant in tears. She was sitting at her desk sobbing. I could hear her through the closed door."

"What did you do?"

"I knocked and went in to get my purse." I shrugged.

"You know what else stands out about our interview with Miss Holiday? She tried several times to refer to her boss as Mr. Kendrick but kept going back to Bryant out of habit. She seems to have been very familiar with her boss." Gabe glanced at me from the corner of his eye.

"Maybe everyone is on a first-name basis within the company."

"But she didn't call Miss Russell, Casey."

"No, she didn't. But Miss Holiday worked for Bryant for almost six years and only knew Miss Russell for less than a year, and as I told Miss Holiday when I returned to get my purse, after knowing someone for that amount of time, you have to have some kind of feelings for them."

"My point exactly," Gabe said.

"I don't follow."

"Miss Holiday worked for Bryant for almost six years. That's almost as long as he was married to Sarah Catherine. When you spend a lot of time with someone working on projects, in close quarters, sometimes lines become blurred and you find yourself having feelings for someone you shouldn't."

"Are you implying Miss Holiday was his mistress?" I wasn't shocked by the idea.

"She is a beautiful woman who's loyal to her boss."

Gabe had noticed how attractive she was. I frowned, not happy with this new revelation. "Sarah Catherine did say she thought Bryant was cheating on her, but she could never prove it. She said she found makeup on his shirt a few times, and he'd come home late after his Wednesday night business meetings smelling of perfume."

"Then, Miss Holiday could've been that woman." Gabe's brow furrowed.

"She doesn't strike me as the type for a one-night stand." For some reason, I felt the need to defend her.

"No, she doesn't. But what if she didn't think it was a one-night stand?"

"Then she might have viewed the affair differently. She wouldn't have thought of it as a fling but rather as her finding love at an inopportune time," I said, presenting a woman's perspective. "And for some people, that's enough to justify doing the wrong thing."

"Like cheating." Gabe turned into the Inkster parking lot and parked the Corvette in a spot near the entrance.

CHAPTER FOURTEEN

Casey Russell's office reminded me of mine, littered with papers and file folders. A mug of this morning's coffee sat near her computer. Pictures of products for ad campaigns lined a large board behind her design table, and a whiteboard hung on the wall to the right of the entrance. This was more like it.

When she heard the light knock on her door, she answered without looking up. "There you are, Tim. I've been waiting on those proofs."

When Gabe cleared his throat, Casey, whose back was to the door, swiveled her chair. "Oh, Lieutenant Cooper, it's nice to see you again so soon." She was a slim woman, well dressed, with long dark hair and big brown eyes.

She rose and came toward me with her hand held out. "And who is this with you?"

I shook her hand. "I'm Amy Kate Anderson. I work for Matt Murphy's lawyer, and I've a few questions to ask you. Would you mind?"

"No, not at all." Casey directed us to the two seats near her design table and then returned to her own chair. "I already spoke with someone from the department, but I don't mind answering your questions."

"Thanks." I dug in my purse for my notepad. Flipping to a clean page, I began. "I understand because of your connection with Java Vein you were aware of the Wednesday meetings they had once a month."

"Yes, Bryant kept me in the loop. He was very particular. The instant we secured the new flavors, we were to start work on the campaigns to promote them in the stores statewide. Bryant was rather aggressive and didn't tolerate any—shall we say—hesitations on the part of his employees. He expected Inkster to be at his beck and call."

"So, would you say Mr. Kendrick was hard to work for?" I asked, fishing a little for her feelings for Bryant Kendrick. After all, his own wife said women either loved him or hated him.

"Not particularly. I have several clients who think we should be available twenty-four-seven. Bryant wasn't much different."

"Did you know about the meeting last Wednesday morning?"

"Yes, I did. Bryant called me Monday to let me know to clear my schedule. He was pretty sure Mr. Murphy would have a new flavor or two for us this month."

"You referred to Matt Murphy as Mister. Do you know him well?"

"No, we've met a handful of times over the past year since Inkster took over the account for Java Vein. I understood from Bryant he handled the business end and that Mr. Murphy was the mastermind behind the flavors."

"So, I take it since you referred to Mr. Kendrick as Bryant, you knew him well enough to be on a first-name basis."

"Yes, I did."

Because of the conversation in the car about mistresses and one-night stands, and the fact Bryant wasn't the most upstanding of men, I decided to take a shot and see what I hit. "How well did you know Bryant?" I asked. "Was it a business relationship or were you two … friends?"

Casey sighed and stared down at her hands in her lap. When she raised her head, she locked eyes with me. "I knew him quite well. We had been seeing each other." She didn't flinch as she said the words.

I was surprised my arrow hit its mark so quickly. "You were having an affair with Bryant?"

"Had been, those are the key words. He'd become

possessive and acted like it was more than it was. We didn't view our arrangement in the same light. He wanted a commitment, and I didn't, so I broke it off with him."

Had I heard her right? Bryant Kendrick wanted a commitment. The man who used women like they were cheap perfume—a dab here, then on to the next one?

"Yes, he'd mentioned leaving his wife. I had no interest in a long-term relationship."

"When did this happen?" I asked.

"Back in the fall." Casey said.

"How did Bryant take the breakup?" Gabe asked.

"Not well. For a while, he kept after me. He would show up at my apartment, call at odd hours. He swore he was in love with me. I wound up telling him I had a job to do, that we were through, and if we couldn't work together, I would give the account to one of my male coworkers, or better yet, I would have a little talk with his wife."

"Did he leave you alone after that?" Gabe asked.

"For the most part, he'd give it the ole-college try every now and then, but I wasn't interested. I like my freedom too much to be tied down to one man." Here, she smiled and batted her eyelashes at Gabe who sat a little straighter in his chair. She crossed her legs and a knee peeked out from under the hem of her black skirt. "I thought Bryant would've understood, but he didn't. He was the type of man who wanted whatever it was he couldn't have."

I didn't like the look she was giving Gabe, so I intervened on his behalf. "What made you think he was more invested in the relationship than you had originally perceived?"

"The thing that grabbed my attention was the fact he filed for divorce. Bryant did it without discussing it with me and thought I would be overjoyed at his surprise announcement. When I became irate, he was shocked. He couldn't understand why I wouldn't agree to marry him after his divorce went through."

"He asked you to marry him while he was still married?" I groaned, disgusted by Bryant Kendrick's lack of marital fidelity.

"Why didn't you tell me all this on Thursday when I was taking your statement?" Gabe asked.

"Honestly, I was scared. The murder had just happened, and I was terrified how it would look. Then over the weekend, I was able to think it through and decided to tell you everything if given the opportunity. It would come out anyway, and at least this way, you heard my side of the story before jumping to any conclusions," Casey said.

"So, let me get this straight." I tried to fit these new pieces of the puzzle into place. "You and Bryant had an affair lasting a couple of months. While you two were seeing each other, he files for divorce, and this action causes you to break it off with him," I paused for emphasis. "Because it was getting too serious." I cut my eyes to Gabe to see what his reaction was to this information.

He had crossed his arms over his chest, and his face held no noticeable expression, a good poker bluff.

"Since you're being so honest," I said, not meaning to sound as catty as I did, "Would you mind telling us where you were Wednesday morning around five?"

"I was home."

"Alone?" Gabe asked.

Casey at least had the decency to turn a little pink. "No."

"I thought you said in your statement you were at your gym that morning," Gabe said.

"I said that because the guy I'm seeing I met at my gym and thought it would be better for him if everyone thought he'd seen me there Wednesday morning, since he's my alibi. We spent the night together."

"I take it he's married."

"About to be, and I don't want to ruin it for him."

My mouth gaped open at the sheer absurdity of her last statement. I wouldn't have believed it if I hadn't heard it with my own ears. What a piece of work. She didn't want to hurt this guy's future marriage, but she was still seeing him. I swear there are some things in this world I'll never understand, and women like Casey Russell were at the top of the list.

Finished with questioning Casey, we left her office to return to Java Vein for my car.

As Gabe's sleek red Corvette stopped at a light, I asked him if Casey's alibi checked out. He told me the guy had said they were together, but of course, it was at the gym.

His cell phone played the Marine Corps Hymn. All I heard were a lot of "hm's" and "yeah's" on Gabe's end of the conversation.

Once we were going again, he filled me in on what the phone call from his partner, Floyd Simms, was about.

It seems Floyd had received word from the fire marshal that the fire was ruled accidental. They believed Bryant had knocked over a coffeemaker as he'd fallen to the floor with heart palpitations. That's why the fire damage wasn't too extensive. This was good news for Matt and me. It meant nothing stood in the way of our insurance claims.

Floyd had also gone through Bryant's phone records and found them to be an interesting read.

Gabe was quiet on the drive back. I could tell he was mulling over this new information about the phone records, which he chose not to share with me. It was noon when we pulled into the parking space in front of my minivan. Gabe climbed out and came over to my side of the car.

I sighed and ran my hand along the leather seat and across the dashboard. He opened the door for me, and I stepped from the vehicle. My eyes roamed over this beautiful ride. Is it coveting if you love something that's not yours? Because I love Gabe's red Corvette. It's splashy, and everything my blue minivan is not.

Gabe was already headed to the driver's side door on my van. I turned and reached down to retrieve my purse from the floorboard. As I closed the Corvette door, my purse strap got caught on the inside door handle, and I was pulled back with a quick yank.

Gabe hadn't seen what happened before he locked the door with his key fob. Once he looked back, he found me wrestling with my purse strap.

"Do you mind?" I shifted my weight from one hip to the other.

"Hold on," he said. "I'll unlock it for you." He chuckled as he walked back my way.

With the click of the lock, I opened the door to pull my purse strap free of its entrapment, then slid the strap over my shoulder, making sure it was clear of the car. I turned and swung the door closed. My skirt cut me at the knees, preventing me from moving. Apparently, Gabe had again clicked the remote before I had shut the door.

I mumbled something under my breath and turned to find my hem mashed between two pieces of metal, sure that there would be a grease spot. All this from the simple act of getting out of a car. Frustrated because I needed to get to my appointment with the repairman, I said, "A little help, please."

When Gabe turned and found me still attached to his car, he crossed his arms over his broad chest and let out a hardy laugh. "My car doesn't seem to want you to leave."

"No." I smiled back at him. "It doesn't."

He approached, then stopped about a foot away. "At least it has good taste in women." He leaned his hip up against the side of his car, twirling his keys on his index finger. "If it had to trap someone, you're a good choice." A lopsided grin spread across his face.

My heart skipped a single beat at his compliment and three from the look in his eye.

A loud group of ladies on their way to their car passed by, breaking the moment.

"Would you mind releasing me?" I felt a little self-conscious. "I'd rather not be on public display." I tugged at the hem of my skirt, but it didn't budge.

"I don't know." A spark of mischief zipped into his eyes. "These kinds of opportunities don't come along every day, at least, not as often as they have since I've been working with you." He rubbed his chin with his pointer finger and thumb. "You ever read *Ivanhoe*?"

"Give me a break. Of course, I've read *Ivanhoe*. I was a high-school English teacher for six years, so I've read most of the classics. What's your point?" I checked my watch. I didn't have time for this.

He ignored my actions. "Then as a retired English teacher and a reader of *Ivanhoe*, you should know that in medieval times, when someone was captured and wanted to be released, they would negotiate a ransom—a payoff—with their captor."

"Yes, that's true." I squinted, locking my laser glare on him.

"What're you getting at?"

"I want to know, what you're willing to give me, Lady Anderson, for your release?"

"Are you serious?" I shifted my weight from one foot to the other and plopped my fist on my hip.

Gabe leaned against his car and crossed both his arms and his legs. He was settling in for the long haul.

"Don't you have somewhere to be? Some important police work to be doing?"

"No, but I believe you do." The dimples appeared framing his firm lips.

"That's right. I do." I tugged on my skirt to get loose.

Gabe appeared unaffected by my panic. "You're going to rip it."

I gave it one more good tug. "Gabe, if you don't let me out of—" I hesitated, not sure what to call this particular state of existence. Trapped by a car door and a handsome cop who wanted a ransom, I was a little nervous to ask what he might want. I stopped tugging on my skirt, straightened myself to my full five foot-two inches, and slung my purse over my shoulder. "Okay, Lieutenant Cooper, what do you want for a ransom?"

"Lieutenant Cooper, are we back to that?" Gabe sounded a little hurt.

"I thought this was business," I said, lifting my chin a little higher, unmoved by his tone.

"I thought this was pleasure." Gabe pulled himself up to his full six feet to face me. "At least, I'm having fun." He wiggled his eyebrows.

I attempted to take charge. "Yes, I can tell. However, I do have an appointment to keep, so let's get to it, shall we?"

His grin widened. "Do you know how to bake?"

"Bake?" I scowled, surprised. I thought he might have asked for a kiss or another date. But no, the prize was food. I should've known.

I rolled my eyes, a bit disappointed. "Yes, I can bake. What's the demand?"

"You see, I love oatmeal raisin cookies, and the only person who can make them like I like them is my mom, because she makes them from scratch."

"Uh-huh, I'm listening," I said a little less snippy as my steel-magnolia resolve melted into a puddle of gray goo. Who could be annoyed with a man who loved cookies and his mom? It would be un-American of me to refuse his request now.

"I'll let you go on the condition you bake me a batch of oatmeal raisin cookies within the next forty-eight hours."

"What happens if I agree in order to make my meeting but fail to produce said cookies?" I fought to keep a serious face.

He took two steps closer to me, his cologne wafting in subtle waves. "Then, in medieval times, the captor would have the right to pillage and burn your house, but in your case, I'll make sure you get a couple of unexpected parking tickets."

"You are insufferable." My smile spread across my lips, and I couldn't keep the tingles from fluttering in my heart.

"Yes, but I would kill for a good oatmeal raisin cookie. My mom's been so busy with her new job at the hospital she doesn't have any time to bake, and the lack of her baked goodies is about to do me in. As you can see, I'm a desperate man willing to stoop to desperate measures."

"Okay, but I need until Sunday. I'm kind of busy trying to solve a murder and repair my business, so the soonest I can bake them for you is Sunday afternoon. Is it a deal or not?"

"Yes, I can wait until Sunday, but remember there will be a price to pay if you don't have the cookies," he said. "Plundering and tickets."

I shook my head. "You're hopeless."

"Ivanhoe is not hopeless." Gabe clicked the remote lock in order to free my skirt. This time he waited before relocking the door, checking to make sure no part of my outfit was left encased in metal.

"No, but you're no Ivanhoe. You're a bandit robbing helpless women of their baked goods." I strode past him to my vehicle.

"Oh, that's better, Robin Hood. I like it. Steal from the rich and give to those destitute of baked goods. A real hero." Gabe followed me to my car.

I unlocked the door with my key. It felt so old-fashioned.

Gabe opened my door for me, which was the reason he got out of his car in the first place. Now I owed him cookies and a polite thank-you for his courtesy.

"Hope you make it in time," he said.

I looked at my watch. "I should if I hurry. Of course, I would've had plenty of time if you had unlocked the door earlier instead of playing around." I wanted to make him feel a little guilty, but it didn't work.

He shrugged and smiled at me. "It was worth it for the cookies."

I put the car in gear, rolled down the window and yelled, "Hey, Gabe, thanks for letting me go with you today."

He turned and waved at the door to the building.

I waved back, looked behind me, and stepped on the gas, unaware that I had put the car in D for drive. I cringed when I heard the thud. Luckily, I wasn't going fast, but I saw the look on Gabe's face from across the parking lot. His eyes were closed, and he looked like he had eaten a raw lemon.

I eased back as slowly as possible and peeked with one eye over the dash, then I let out the breath I'd been holding when no visible damage showed from where I sat. I jumped out for a better look. By the time I got to the front of the minivan, Gabe was crouched down, giving the front end of his sleek sports car a good once-over. He ran his hand along the edge of the hood and then along the bumper.

I watched in agony. "How is she?" I asked, afraid to hear the answer. I could imagine the look on Theresa Thornton's face if I went in with another claim.

"She seems to be fine." Gabe peered up at me. "You know, if you didn't want to bake those cookies, all you had to do was say so. You didn't have to take it out on my baby." He patted the bumper of his car and stood.

"Oh, Gabe, I am so sorry. I can't begin to tell you how bad I feel."

Gabe took me by my shoulders. "It's okay, Amy Kate, no harm, no foul. But if you feel the need to make restitution, two batches of cookies sound about right." Now his dimples framed a warm smile.

The genuine gratitude radiating from his face took me aback. I melted, squish, squish, goo. I had a sneaking suspicion I had just become Lieutenant Cooper's new source of oatmeal raisin cookies. I wasn't quite sure how I felt about it, but unable to resist his hopeful look, I said, "Two batches, it is."

CHAPTER FIFTEEN

"Well, well, well. Not good. No, not good at all." Words you never want to hear from two types of professionals: doctors and repairmen.

I knew before Mr. Doomsayer ever handed me the estimate it was going to be out of my price range. He pointed out so many problems I considered breaking his pointer finger in hopes that it would keep the estimate within reason. He also told me he couldn't even start the job until February because he and his wife take a Caribbean cruise during part of January in order to melt away some of those winter blues.

From the estimate he handed me, I knew exactly how he could afford those yearly meltdowns, and I fought the urge to have one of my own. How dare this guy charge these kinds of prices for wood, nails, and paint? I glared at him over the estimate and swallowed the words I wanted to say. Fortunately, Flora walked in from the front of the shop to tell me we had a customer.

"Oh, I thought we were closed for repairs."

Flora's smile widened. "This customer you'll want to see."

As I walked from the workroom into the main area, I could hear the jabbering of a one-year-old. "If it isn't my favorite little man in the whole wide world and his mom." I scooped up my nephew, Grant, and planted a big sloppy kiss on his chubby red cheek. "To what do I owe this pleasure, Alexia?"

"Grant woke up from his nap today and demanded to go see his Auntie Amy Kate and his Auntie Elizabeth so he could get in some good snuggles. And I decided I needed to get out of the house before I went stir crazy. I decided a few turns around the town square would do us both some good. So, here we are."

Grant squirmed in my arms, trying to get to the floor in order to continue his inspection of the room's contents—at least the items three feet from the floor or lower. I set him down, and Flora came out from behind the counter carrying a small tub of baby toys I kept handy for little guests. The tub of baby toys had been Flora's idea. She had pulled the suggestion from her bag of grandma tricks, and it came in handy many times.

She placed the tub on the carpet. Grant wasted no time in going over to investigate its contents. He found the squeaky hammer, which was a favorite, and hit it on one of the bookshelves, filling the room with squeaks and happy jabbering.

"I was wondering if you wanted to take a few turns around the square with me. You could catch me up on your new exciting career. There was so much going on yesterday at Dad's we didn't get a chance to talk about it, and I'm dying of curiosity," Alexia said.

"Me too," Flora said. "The last juicy details I heard were Friday night when I forced you to spill the beans."

"I did go today with the lieutenant to interview Samantha Holiday, who was Bryant's administrative assistant." I looked at Alexia. "Nobody's a secretary anymore. Why is that?"

"I know, right?" Alexia shrugged.

"And we also went to Inkster to interview Casey Russell, the marketing agent who was handling the Java Vein account."

"Wow, it sounds so exciting," Alexia's eyes widened with childlike curiosity.

"Girl, you've got to get out once in a while," I said, a little concerned about my sister's well-being but thrilled she was intrigued.

"What did you find out? Anything worth repeating?" Flora asked without any shame.

Before I could answer, Mr. Doomsayer emerged from the back, stopping at the counter where Flora stood. "I've finished my estimate of the needed work. I added a few items to it after you left. So, I wanted to give you the final copy with the added costs."

My head spun. I tried to imagine what new tasks he added to the already massive list. He walked over to the bookshelves and handed me the new numbers.

I folded the piece of paper in half without looking at it. "Thank you for coming out and giving me your estimate. Since you can't start until February, I'll have to go with one of the other two contractors, but I do appreciate your time."

"I understand, Miss Anderson." Mr. Doomsayer spotted Grant and smiled down at him. "Cute baby," he said and pointed at Grant.

I wanted to yank his finger off. After all the pointing he'd done in the workroom, adding this and that to my estimate, I half expected him to say, "Cute baby, that'll be another four-hundred-dollars," but thankfully, he turned and left.

Not letting a little interruption detour her from the hunt for good gossip, Flora asked, "So, what did you and that good-looking lieutenant find out?"

"A couple of things. One, Bryant definitely had an affair. At least one we can prove."

"No way," Alexia said. "I knew Sarah Catherine and Bryant weren't happy together, but I didn't think he was cheating on her."

"What Lilly told you about him being a player was right on the money then," Flora said.

"Looks that way." The thought struck me if Lilly was right about him still being a player, was Casey Russell his only affair? From what Casey said, he seemed to enjoy the pursuit. From Lilly's description of Bryant's college days, he put his needs above everyone else's. And what about what Sarah Catherine had said? She made it sound like he had been cheating on her for a lot longer than a couple of months in the late summer.

"What was your take on them?" Alexia asked, pulling me back to the conversation.

"Casey Russell was pretty enough, but she came off as self-absorbed." I gave myself credit for being kind.

"What about Samantha, the secretary?" Alexia made air quotes when she said the word *secretary*.

"She struck me as a caring, loyal person. Which is kind of funny because Casey is the one who gave us a warm welcome and Samantha was the one who started off as cold and distant. In fact, from first impressions, you'd have thought Samantha was untouchable and Casey was friendly and charming, but the exact opposite is true. It just goes to show you—pardon the pun—you can't judge a book by its cover."

Alexia and Flora groaned.

"Imagine book humor in a bookshop." Alexia rolled her eyes for effect, yet a little smile played on her lips. "okay, oh punny one, what did Samantha look like? You said Casey was pretty, but what about Samantha?"

"She was a natural beauty. Model material."

"Really? Do you think Bryant kept her around for her looks?"

"Maybe, but I don't think so. You should've seen how tidy her office was. Everything was just so. Her attention to detail tells me she's good at her job. She gave me the impression of being a professional, not some babe biding her time."

Grant had moved on from the bookshelves and sat at Alexia's feet trying to scale her pant leg and fussing for attention.

Alexia leaned down and picked up her sweet baby, holding him close to her. "Someone is getting antsy. It's time for us to make another lap or two around the square and then drop in on Auntie Elizabeth. Can you come?"

"No, I wish I could, but I still have to make the deliveries to the post office and call Tom Perkin's agent about the book signing."

"Do you think he'll come? Wouldn't that be so exciting, Flora. Can you imagine the crowd he'd draw?"

"I know." Flora said. "It would be great for business. It might even help us make up what we've lost being closed this past week."

"That's what I'm hoping for—a big crowd."

"I'll say a little prayer for you that the call goes well." Alexia placed Grant in the stroller and snapped the straps around him. They waved before they left. I watched them cross the street to the town green.

By the time three o'clock rolled around, I had made my delivery to the post office, called Tom Perkins' agent, who had agreed to the book signing on the twenty-sixth, and contacted Albert Shine to let him know he'd gotten the job.

Mrs. Shine had answered the phone and taken the message, but Mr. Shine returned my call within the hour and announced to my most grateful ears he would be at Twisted Plots first thing the next morning.

Relief flooded over me. Only another week or two, and life would be back to some semblance of normalcy. Then it hit me. Only two weeks until the book signing. I must be nuts to think that this charred-to-a-crisp shop would be ready. That wasn't a lot of time to pull together the book signing. I decided we needed a staff meeting pronto. So, I texted Carter and Kirk to let them know we would meet the next day at nine o'clock to shore up plans.

Tom Perkins would be spending the weekend in our humble town in just two weeks. I was filled with excitement at how everything was falling into place. I'd have to thank Alexia for her prayers. They seemed to be working. But I couldn't help the little pit of worry in my stomach that Mr. Shine wouldn't have the shop done in time.

Flora and I sat side by side, hunched over the worktable, looking over my checklist for the insurance company. This was my last big item on today's to-do list. I was having Flora, who is a stickler for details, make sure I had all my *t*'s crossed and *i*'s dotted.

"Did you send in the requested pictures?" Flora asked.

"Check."

"You met with the insurance adjuster?" she asked.

"Check."

"Does Theresa have the fire investigator's report as well as the report from the insurance adjuster?"

"Check."

"Okay, sweetie, it sounds like the next step is to take Theresa your quotes from the repairmen."

"Check." I grinned. "And then my last step is getting the big fat check."

We giggled, leaning into one another for a hug. I was glad to finish the insurance list. Now, I needed to make progress on the suspect list. The D.A. was still looking at Matt, though Gabe had come up with other suspects.

It was Monday, and the clock on the case was ticking at a rapid pace. The two-week window was sliding shut, and I didn't feel any closer to having the suspect list whittled down than I did on Thursday, the day after the murder. I needed to get busy.

With thoughts of the window, suspects, and poor Matt swirling around in my head, I asked Flora if she would mind closing the bookshop so I could go to Elizabeth's office after I dropped off the quotes to Theresa. I wanted to take a peek at Bryant's phone records.

If Floyd Simms, Gabe's partner, had found them interesting, I figured I might too. Plus, I wanted to run a hunch by Elizabeth, one I had come across while talking with Gabe and then again with Alexia.

CHAPTER SIXTEEN

Tilley, Elizabeth's receptionist, was nowhere in sight when I entered the office, so I headed back on my own. Elizabeth sat with her unshod feet propped on her desk, engrossed in a file sitting in her lap. I didn't want to startle her, so I tapped on her door, which stood ajar.

She grunted something but didn't look up.

"Elizabeth." I stepped over the threshold but waited for her to acknowledge my presence.

Her brows furrowed into a tight V shape. "Hmm?" she said.

"Elizabeth." My voice sounded sharp, but it caught her attention.

"Oh, I'm sorry, Amy Kate." She pulled her feet from off her desk. "I was looking over some of the statements from the witnesses in Matt's case."

I took a seat across from her, setting my purse on the floor by the chair leg.

"Mrs. Culpepper stated that she saw Lilly out front making a phone call. I was comparing the estimated time of that call to Bryant's phone records."

"That's why I came by. I was with Gabe when he received the call from Floyd Simms telling him they had the phone records. I figured they would've given you a copy by now."

"You figured right."

"What've you found?" I leaned forward in my seat placing my elbows on my knees.

"Only that Lilly made the call to Bryant."

"She didn't call Matt, but she called Bryant. That's weird, don't you think?" I was surprised to know she had phoned Bryant the morning of the murder but had told me herself that she hadn't checked on Matt.

"Yes, I do think it's weird."

"Why do you think she called Bryant?"

"I don't know. But I think we need to ask her." I had the feeling that by "we," she meant me, so I offered to go speak with Lilly at the Junk in the Trunk once we were done, if the store was still open.

"You'll have to let me know how it goes, Sis," Elizabeth said.

"If I find out anything, I'll call you later. There's something else I wanted to talk to you about."

"Okay, shoot." She leaned back in her leather chair.

"Today, I went with Gabe to interview Samantha Holiday and Casey Russell. He let me tag along," I said.

"That's a good sign. I see you're still in one piece. You must be making progress."

"Yes." I ignored the sarcasm. "Anyway, during the interview with Casey, she confessed to having an affair with Bryant. She was actually upfront about it all."

"Really? I guess an affair doesn't surprise me, not after hearing what Lilly told you about Bryant."

"No, it doesn't, but Casey said the affair took place during the late part of the summer into the fall and then she broke it off. Sarah Catherine, though, led me to believe she thought Bryant had been having an affair for some time even before he had met Casey."

"Okay, let's assume Sarah Catherine is right. That would mean he's had at least two affairs, but from the stuff we're learning about Bryant, I bet he's had several over the years. Are you thinking there are more suspects?"

"No, I was thinking about Samantha Holiday. What if she was involved in one of those affairs? It would give her motive, right?"

"Maybe, it would depend upon whether she still had feelings for him or not." Elizabeth rolled her chair out from her desk and pressed her fingertips together as she swiveled her chair back and forth.

"Sarah Catherine did say Saturday night at the restaurant that women either loved him or hated him. So, let's say Samantha hates him. They were together. He dumped her for the next pretty face." I stood and paced.

"She would've felt betrayed, but she had to know his reputation. Samantha worked for the man for six years. She shouldn't have been surprised when he dumped her."

"That may have been the problem." I moved from one end of the desk to the other. "Let's say she knows his reputation, but in working with him, she grows to care about him anyway. She finds herself attracted to him, and she succumbs to his charms. Lilly mentioned he had tons of friends in college and a different girl each month. He had to have been a first-class manipulator to pull that off," I said.

"Yes, several of the employees the police interviewed remarked on his charisma."

"Today, Casey said Bryant always wanted what he couldn't have. So, let's say he runs after Samantha for a while. She says no for the first couple of months or years. He makes promises. Maybe he even promises to leave his wife and their loveless marriage, and after years of him chasing her, she says yes."

"Then, she wouldn't be expecting to be another one-night stand. She would be expecting to be the next Mrs. Kendrick," Elizabeth said.

"That makes sense. Gabe and I talked about this possibility this morning after meeting Samantha, and I made the observation then that she didn't strike me as a one-night-stand kind of woman. She's too loyal. Even Sarah Catherine commented on her loyalty to Bryant." I stopped. My mind whirled with the possibility of Samantha Holiday as the killer. I couldn't shake the sight of the woman dissolved into tears.

"Then she must've thought it was more. She would've never become involved in a relationship with Bryant if she thought it was purely physical." Elizabeth leaned forward with her elbows on her desk.

"That's the conclusion I came to while I was talking with Alexia. I told her Samantha wasn't some babe biding her time," I said. "She was loyal to Bryant. We also know she's not the type to be a one-night stand. She has too much pride to allow herself to be used. So, if she were one of his mistresses, then he had to have promised her something more lasting than a fling, and when he didn't deliver, she was heartbroken. Wouldn't you say that's a motive for murder?"

"Yes, it is, but we can't prove any of this." Elizabeth sighed and stretched her hands above her head before rolling her chair back under the desk.

"No, not yet. Then I also found out that Bryant asked for the divorce while he was seeing Casey Russell. And from Samantha's attitude when we asked her about Casey, I can guarantee you she knows the reason for Bryant's pending divorce. If he made promises to Samantha and broke them but was willing to leave his wife for Casey, Samantha must have not only felt used but also betrayed."

"'Hell, hath no fury like a woman scorned,'" Elizabeth said.

"Shakespeare must have known a thing or two about women." I nodded.

"Now all you have to do is prove it."

I sat back down, still turning these thoughts over in my mind.

"What about Casey as the killer? She admitted to an affair with Bryant. Maybe she's the scorned lover," Elizabeth said.

"No, she has an alibi Gabe says checks out, and besides, she broke it off with Bryant, not the other way around. She's already moved on," I said, confident Casey Russell, though a somewhat morally-loose woman, was not our killer.

Elizabeth turned her attention back to the phone records and scanned the sheets littered on her desk. "I'm noticing Bryant made and received several calls from both Samantha and Lilly. I think if I were you, I would follow up on your scorned-lover hunch with Samantha."

"Any calls involving Sarah Catherine or Ed Philips?" I asked, thinking through our list of suspects.

"None from Ed Philips, but Sarah Catherine had made a few to him. But the times of the calls all seem to be during working hours. She could've been calling about meetings with the divorce lawyers. Nothing stands out to me."

"Okay, so we have Samantha as a possible scorned lover,

and Sarah Catherine a soon-to-be ex-wife as well as the woman Bryant was cheating out of a huge sum of money. We also have Ed Philips, who according to Samantha, blamed Bryant for his financial woes, and we have Matt and Lilly who were less than happy about Bryant trying to sell the Beans and Leaves out from under them."

"And don't forget Lilly's phone call to Bryant the morning of the murder."

"That too." I still felt I was missing something where Lilly was concerned.

"If Samantha is an ex-lover, then every one of our potential suspects has a motive."

I nodded my agreement with Elizabeth's observation. "And my job is to eliminate them one by one until we find the one who killed Bryant Kendrick."

"I have to tell you it's starting to look much better for Matt. The police are now looking at some of the same leads we are, which is taking their focus off Matt. Since Bryant and Matt had both signed the contract giving the original Beans and Leaves to Matt, the D.A. figured he has no motive."

"Good for the D.A.," I said. "Now if we can hand him the murderer, Matt can get on with his life."

"You sound pretty confident, rookie." A male voice rumbled from behind me.

I whirled with my hand over my heart. "You shouldn't sneak up on people, Gabe. It's bad manners."

Elizabeth, of course, giggled at my reaction to Gabe's sudden appearance. I gave her one of the famous Anderson scowls, but it didn't keep her from relishing the moment.

"I'm glad you are both here. It saves me a trip to the bookshop."

"What'cha got for us?" Elizabeth propped her feet back up on her desk. She seemed very comfortable around Gabe the Babe.

"I went by today to talk with Mrs. Kendrick. The fact Bryant died before the divorce did leave her in a better financial position. Of course, she didn't want to go into how much better, but I might enlist Floyd to do some digging. She has an alibi for the time in question."

"I'm finding it hard to believe all these people have alibis for five-thirty in the morning," I blurted out.

"It seems just those who knew Bryant Kendrick have alibis." Gabe chuckled.

"So, what was her alibi? The President of the United States dropped by for breakfast?"

"No." Gabe smothered a grin. "Wednesday morning was covered by her lawn service."

"Her lawn service? It's January." I leaned back in my chair with a huff. "Really?"

"I know, but the Kendricks' own about ten acres, and according to Mrs. Kendrick, she has a lawn service come out even during the winter to keep the grounds in tiptop shape. She said she got a call Wednesday morning at a little after five from the service to let her know they would be on her property earlier than usual. They had tried to reach her Tuesday evening to let her know, but they were unsuccessful."

"The lawn service couldn't reach her Tuesday evening?" asked Elizabeth.

"Right, but her maid verified she was indeed at home."

"So, Sarah Catherine talked to the lawn-service people. She still could've left her house Wednesday morning and gone to the Beans and Leaves before the service arrived."

"Not according to my calculations. Even speeding, it takes at least twenty minutes to drive to the Beans and Leaves and back to her place. The lawn-service employees showed up at around five-thirty. One of them remembers waving at Mrs. Kendrick when she retrieved her newspaper at around six."

"That sounds pretty definite," Elizabeth said.

"Yeah, and no one remembers her leaving the premises until sometime around six-thirty when Floyd showed up to collect her."

"How did she react to the news of Bryant's death?" My curiosity stirred. She had been rather cool Saturday night at The Hook after the funeral. How had she handled the shock of the news?

"Floyd said she was quiet. She didn't chatter away like some people do when they're nervous or upset, but she didn't cry either. Floyd said she was pensive."

"Knowing her, she was trying to figure out what this meant to her financial situation." My words were soaked with my snarky attitude. But then I guess if I had been married to Bryant Kendrick for almost seven years, putting up with his wayward behavior, I might want to be compensated for my troubles as well.

While I was wrapped up in my thoughts, Gabe changed the subject from the bereaved wife to the fire marshal's decision on the fire.

"The report says the fire marshal determined the fire was an accident. Do you think that will help Matt in any way? It shows it wasn't insurance fraud."

"It can't hurt." Elizabeth swung her feet from off the desk back to the floor and fished under her desk for her shoes. "It'll help him work on his store without the question of the fire hanging over his head. He needs something to keep him busy while we sort all this out."

"Yeah, Matt's a good guy. I hate to see him and Lilly going through this. And I want to make sure the D.A. doesn't railroad him, since this is election year." Gabe sat in the second chair. "He was so sure this was an open-and-shut case. That's why I agreed to be so helpful." He loosened his tie and crossed his leg over his knee.

"Elizabeth, can I see the fire marshal's report? Didn't you tell me, Gabe, they thought the fire was caused by a coffeemaker?"

"Yes, that's what Floyd told me when he called this morning. The crime-scene unit had determined it was the cause of the fire."

Elizabeth handed me the report. "Okay, I remember Samantha saying something today about Bryant not liking all the fancy-flavored coffees. He preferred the regular stuff. She said he always had a pot of plain black coffee ready to drink after the tastings." I mulled this over for a minute as I looked over the report. "Gabe, where did they find the poison? What was it in?"

"It was in the coffee he was drinking. The coffeemaker and the urns were in pretty bad shape, though, after the fire, so it's going to take forensics a while to sort out which one had the poison in it. For all we know, it could have been in his cup."

The report stated the fire had been started by the coffeemaker being knocked over onto a pile of coffee-bean sacks. The cloth sacks caught fire and caused the damage.

"I hope forensics comes back soon because if the poison was in the grounds basket of the coffeemaker, it tells us Bryant was the intended victim and the killer knew he always had a pot of black coffee after the tastings. That means the killer not only knew about the early-morning meeting Wednesday, but they knew Bryant well enough to know his habits."

CHAPTER SEVENTEEN

Lilly Murphy's car was still parked on the square when I left Elizabeth and Gabe discussing the possibility of Samantha Holiday having an affair with Bryant Kendrick. Since I had hashed it over with both of them and didn't want to belabor the topic any further, my time would be better spent figuring out what was going on with Lilly and the late Mr. Kendrick.

The feeling of misgiving came over me again as I tried to think of a reason why Lilly would have called Bryant and not Matt the morning of the fire. It didn't compute with me.

I decided to approach my trip to the antique store as a shopping trip for a thank-you gift for Theresa Thornton, my new best friend. It might put Lilly at ease if she thought I was shopping instead of snooping. I don't do deception well, so I knew I would be leaving with something for Theresa, but it was a small price to pay to make the nagging feeling go away.

The bell on the door announced my arrival. Lilly was busy with a customer. It was around five, and the Junk in the Trunk closed at six. I was hoping the foot traffic on a Monday evening would be light enough for me to speak alone with Lilly without it seeming like a private conversation.

The customer said thanks to Lilly, assuring her his wife was going to love the treasure in the bag. Once Lilly discovered I was the one who had entered the store, the smile on her face faded. It was plain she was not happy to see me.

"Hi, Lilly." I tried to sound upbeat.

"Hi, what can I do for you?" A sigh hung at the end of her question.

I knew I had to make everything casual quick, or I would lose any chance of persuading her to open up. "Actually, I'm looking for a thank-you gift for Theresa Thornton." This had the desired effect. Like the flip of a switch, she became a warm, welcoming saleslady.

"Oh, okay. I was afraid you were here about the case, and to be honest, I don't think I could handle one more question." She stepped over to the trash can and stuck her hand into her pocket, pulling out several pieces of ceramic and paper. She must've broken something and put the fragments in her pocket in a hurry to clean it up.

I was going to have to tread lightly. "Really? I guess it has been hard on you and Matt, considering the two of you knew Bryant the longest of anyone here in town. Everyone must think you would be the best source for information about him."

"I don't know why. We knew him in college, but then it was years before he showed up here."

Lilly turned her back to me and rearranged the knickknacks to fill the empty spot on the shelf. "And he's caused nothing but trouble since he arrived." The figurines clanked against the glass shelf as she plunked them down.

I decided it would be wise to change the direction of the conversation. "So, Lilly, what would you suggest for a gift for Theresa?" This seemed to settle her down.

She turned and surveyed the shop. "We recently got in some lovely angel figurines that might look nice on a desk. They aren't very big and could be placed by a framed picture or even set in a planter to give it some flare."

"Ooh, perfect. Are they expensive?" My budget was tight. I didn't have any money to spare for a gift I hadn't planned on buying.

"No, actually they're quite reasonable. I believe they run around twelve dollars apiece, not bad for antiques." Lilly waved her hand in a dismissive manner as if the price was a mere inconvenience for something so special.

She led me to the display, and I started picking them up and looking them over. None of them shouted Insurance Agent to me, but the price was right, and I wasn't leaving the store without some trinket to make my trip here look genuine.

"These are lovely," I said, making small talk, hoping for an opportunity to discuss the case. "Have you had them long? I don't recall seeing them before."

"No, a gentleman who's an antique hunter brought them into the store this past Tuesday. We haven't even had them a week, and we've almost sold out. Sarah Catherine bought one as well as two ladies from the sewing circle. Even Tammy from Curls Salon stopped in to purchase one. They won't be around long."

"I can see why." I admired the little porcelain angels with their scalloped wings. Each figurine had a one-word message like *love* or *hope* imprinted on a scroll held in its hands.

Then my window of opportunity flew open. The phone rang. The conversation was a short one, but it gave me the chance to bring up the phone records without it seeming as if this had been my purpose all along. I quickly chose an angel and hurried to the counter so I could be there when the call ended.

When Lilly hung up, I stood ready with my angel and my remark. "Oh, Lilly, the phone ringing reminded me about Bryant's phone records."

Lilly picked up my angel and scanned the barcode on the bottom. "Yes, what about them?"

"They showed that you had called him before you called the fire department. I was curious. Why?"

"Isn't it obvious?" Her voice held a slight edge. She was back to being guarded.

"No, not really."

"I was trying to see if he was in the coffee shop. I wanted to warn him about the fire."

"Oh, I see." I watched her wrap the angel in tissue paper, then deposit it into a Junk in the Trunk bag.

"But if you called Bryant from the front of the building like Mrs. Culpepper says, then you didn't know for sure that the building was on fire."

"It was apparent something was wrong. Remember, I told you I smelled the burnt coffee. Besides, you can't believe everything Mrs. Culpepper says. She's excitable."

"Yes, but why did you call Bryant and not Matt?"

"Because Matt wasn't in the building," Lilly shifted from one foot to the other. I could tell she was becoming impatient with me.

"But you told me Wednesday the reason you didn't call Matt was because you knew he was in the building, and you wanted to get the fire trucks there as soon as possible." At this, Lilly put the bag on the counter and sat on the stool behind the register.

"Yes, I did say that." Her lips tightened into a straight line and a crease formed on her brow. "I called Bryant because I knew his habit was to arrive at the coffee shop early for the meetings. I figured he was already in the shop, and I wasn't sure if Matt was in there or not. To be honest, I hadn't noticed if Matt entered the shop. I was distracted by my own thoughts while I was walking and hadn't paid any attention to the things going on around me." Lilly sighed deeply. "But I knew Bryant would be in there."

"So, you called him to warn him?" I was a little confused.

"No, I called him to see if there was something wrong, and if I should call the police or not. When he didn't answer, I ran around the building and saw all the smoke, so I called 911."

"Oh." I hesitated for a moment. "I still need to know something."

"Go ahead, ask away. At this point, it seems useless to resist since this is the only topic of conversation in town. Why should it be any different with you?"

I felt bad for prying into her private life, but I had to get rid of the feeling I was missing something when it came to Lilly and Bryant. "You told me you had known Bryant in college and that he was charming. Did he ever try to work his charms on you?"

"Do you mean were we ever together?" Lilly asked and then answered her own question. "Yes, we were . . . together." Her shoulders drooped and she slowly shook her head.

I felt small for having to put her through this pain because her expression told me it was painful. "How long? If you and Matt married after graduation, you couldn't have been with Bryant long."

"Long enough." She looked at me and paused as if she were

deciding something. "I guess I need to tell someone the whole truth. It might as well be you. It'll have to come out anyway, right?"

"Probably." At this point, I was all ears.

"Bryant chased me our entire junior year. Both he and Matt tried to date me, and I kept telling them I wasn't interested. I wanted to be friends, but it wasn't true. I was madly in love with Bryant, but I knew his reputation. I knew it, and still I couldn't help myself. He was so charming and handsome and persistent." Lilly lowered her gaze to the floor as if she were reliving those days of her junior year.

"So, what happened?" I was enthralled with the tale.

"He asked me to marry him at the end of my junior year, and I did. We eloped."

"I thought there was more to the story."

"Yes, well, you know that old saying 'love is blind'? In my case, it was deaf and stupid too." Lilly scowled. "At first, he was very attentive. Every day was filled with romance and sweetness, but then things started to change. He picked up his old habits again. Bryant the Cad had returned. It was as if he couldn't help himself. I knew right away I had made a horrible mistake, and I went home to my parents."

"What did you do then? About Matt and all."

"My parents helped me to get an annulment. I was back in college that fall as if nothing happened. I kept my marriage to Bryant to myself."

"How did Matt handle it?"

"That's the thing. Matt doesn't know."

"Matt doesn't know?" I stood gawking for a few moments, letting this piece of news soak in. "Not at all?"

"No, he doesn't. Bryant went his own way our senior year. I'm sure he thought Matt knew and didn't want to hear about how wretched he was for treating me the way he did. That's why when Bryant showed up here six years ago, I knew he was here to cause trouble. At first, everything went along fine until Bryant figured out Matt didn't know anything about us. Once he set his sights on selling Java Veins to the Benson company, he used our past to force me to pressure Matt to sell, threatening to tell Matt that I had lied to him all these years."

"I'm sorry."

"It's all right. I just couldn't bear the thought of how hurt Matt would be finding out I had married Bryant. I never wanted Matt to think he was my second choice. I love him too much for that."

"I'm sure he'll understand. He has to know how much you love him."

"It is what it is." She shrugged. "I'm just glad someone knows. It was bound to come out sooner or later. It's better to tell someone who would understand about being young and foolish and in love."

I wasn't sure I understood about being in love, but I did understand about being young and sometimes foolish. "You know, I'm going to have to tell Gabe what you've told me."

"I know."

"Does anyone else know?" I asked, thinking I already knew the answer.

"Yes, Sarah Catherine knows. That's part of the reason why we spent the evening of the funeral together. We were mourning our losses."

"If she knows, I think it's time you told Matt the whole story. I wouldn't want him hearing it from someone else." My heart filled with compassion for the woman who sat before me. "It would be better if he heard it from you."

"Yes, you're right. I should've done it a long time ago. Being foolish isn't exclusive to the young. Could you hold off telling the lieutenant for a couple of days? I want to pick the right time to talk to Matt."

"I don't know. With the investigation going on and this having a direct connection with Bryant, I'm not sure I can wait to tell him."

She shrugged. "Do what you think is best." She handed me the bag with the angel in it. "I'll tell Matt tonight. No sense in putting it off, but this will break his heart."

I walked toward the door but stopped before stepping out. "The lieutenant will consider this motive. You might want to be ready for the questions that will come."

I left Lilly sitting behind the counter deep in thought.

Outside the shop, I took a moment to look at the angel

figurine I had bought for Theresa Thornton, Insurance Agent Extraordinaire. I discovered I had bought the one that said peace. How ironic.

Things were not peaceful in Pine Lake since Bryant Kendrick's murder, and I had the feeling it would be a while before it was peaceful again.

~

Home sounded so good, and as I pushed open my apartment door, delicious aromas floated out to greet me. Gizmo, my Scottish terrier, stood on his hind legs and wagged his tail, begging to be picked up.

I hung my things on the coat stand behind the door and picked up the waiting pup. He wiggled his body in excitement, licking my hand as I petted him. Julia was humming from the kitchen.

Once I released Gizmo, he took off like a bullet, running laps in a big circle around the sofa, down the hall and back. As the dog made his third lap, Julia came into the living room. "Hey, stranger."

"Hey, yourself. I smell something wonderful. I hope it's dinner because I'm starved."

"You're in luck. It is dinner. I saw this show on one of the cable stations, and the chef made this wonderful-looking stew. So, I raided the fridge and voilà, Julia's 'A Little Bit of Everything Stew' was invented."

"Oh my gosh, if we don't eat soon, I might gnaw off my arm." My stomach agreed with a low rumble of its own.

"Come on, let's feed that monster you call a stomach." Julia headed to the little dining area of our kitchen. "You set the table while I dish it up."

"Deal." I inhaled the rich aroma and thanked the Lord for giving me a roommate who was a chef.

After we said the blessing, Julia wanted to know how things were going with the insurance claim.

"Excellent, I finally got all the quotes together today and turned them in to Theresa, which means all the paperwork is done, and now I'm just waiting on the check." I savored a bite of stew. The beef melted in my mouth. "I have to say it feels good having part of it finished."

"I can only imagine." Julia blew on her stew to cool it. "Which of the repairmen are you hiring to do the work?"

"I decided on Mr. Shine. He seems easy to work with, and since we'll be sharing a space for a week or two, that was important to me. Also, he gave me the most reasonable estimate and can start tomorrow."

"Sounds like he's exactly what the insurance adjuster ordered."

"Definitely. So, have you received any new orders for Pure Sweetness? The last one I heard about was the wedding cake for this past Saturday. How did it go?"

"It went pretty well, but the wedding cake orders have slowed down. Most people go for spring and summer weddings, but I've received a few new orders from some of the local restaurants for pies and cakes for their dessert menus. So, it's not going too bad."

"Awesome." Julia was a hard worker, and I admired her for it. She had started Pure Sweetness as a side business, and I enjoyed having a comrade-in-arms traverse the road of business owners together.

"How is your new job going? Have you caught the killer yet?" She teased.

"Not yet, but I'm working on it. Gabe and I interviewed Samantha Holiday and Casey Russell today."

"Oh, you and Gabe. Wow, you sure have changed your tune. Last time I heard anything about Gabe the Babe, you had dubbed yourself the blond fainting floozy, and weren't sure you could ever look him in the eye again."

"Yes, but since then, we went on a date of sorts."

"What?" Julia exclaimed, almost spilling her spoonful of stew in her lap. She used her napkin to sop up the broth from the table.

"I told you about the two dates I planned for Saturday."

"Yes, and I was surprised I didn't receive a distress call from you or the emergency room." Julia liked to goad me about my dating track record.

"Everyone survived."

"Glad to hear it. So, how does Gabe fit in with your two dates?"

"One of my guys was a no-show, and Gabe happened to be there. So, we had dessert and coffee, and guess what? I didn't burn down the restaurant or hurt anyone including myself while in his presence."

"You're kidding. Are you sure you were you, and Gabe was Gabe? Because according to what you told me last week, you should have exploded or something."

"I know, but as you can see, I didn't." I lifted my hands in a ta-da stance. "But I made up for it today."

"I'm all ears." She leaned one elbow on the table and rested her cheek in the palm of her hand.

"Gabe had suggested we ride together to Inkster to interview Casey Russell. He has a beautiful red Corvette."

"I know. I've seen it around town. He looks really good in it too, I must say."

"Yes, he does." I wiggled my eyebrows. "Anyway, when we returned to my car after the interview, his car kept eating different pieces of my clothing."

"What do you mean it ate your clothing?"

"I mean his car wouldn't let me go. First, my purse strap got caught in his car door. Then it was my skirt. Gabe brought up Ivanhoe—"

"Ivanhoe," Julia interrupted. "Why on earth would he bring up Ivanhoe?" She looked confused.

"Because he wanted me to pay him a ransom for releasing me from the clutches of his evil car door."

"You are the funniest thing, Amy Kate. It couldn't have been that hard to get out of the car."

"You weren't there. It was a lot harder than it sounds."

"Okay, you're here now, and I don't see a car attached. I assume Gabe negotiated a ransom. What was it? Instead of his car door holding you hostage, does he get to . . . kiss you?" Julia cocked her left eyebrow.

"No," I blushed and swatted my hand in her general direction. "He wants oatmeal raisin cookies by Sunday."

"Oh, that sounds harmless, I suppose." Disappointment colored Julia's tone. I'm sure she was hoping for something a little more romantic. To be honest, I was too.

"Yeah, but the cookies led me to the favor I need to ask."

"Let me guess, you want my oatmeal raisin-cookie recipe, right?" A little half-smile played on her lips.

"He said his favorites were his mother's, but she's been so busy with her new job she hasn't had time to bake any for him. So, yes, if you don't mind too much, I would like your recipe."

"His mother, hmm?" Julia pursed her lips.

"That's what he said."

"I'll be glad to give you my recipe, but if you have any interest in Gabe whatsoever, I'd get his mother's recipe. That way you'll know you have a sure thing."

At times, Julia is a genius. "Besides, being Southern women, we should know the secret to catching a man isn't simply how you look but how you cook."

"Amen to that, sister." I held my hand up.

Julia high fived me.

Throughout dinner, we caught each other up on our lives. I told her about the interviews with the suspects and entertained her with the tale of my date with Chet Baker.

She was impressed I was keeping up my bad-first-date track record with the mud-sloshing experience. Then she told me about her sous chef, Miles, and some of the things happening at the Whispering Pines.

While I was doing the dishes, I told her how Samantha responded when I wanted to look in her boss's office, and I mentioned the indentation I saw in the carpet. Then I said, "I wonder if Samantha got rid of the missing plant? Maybe it was a foxglove, the plant used to poison Bryant. If so, what do you think she did with it?" I placed the last of the stew in the refrigerator.

"I don't know. How would you dispose of a plant you didn't want anyone to find?" Julia tilted her head as she contemplated her own question.

"Well, I might burn it." I said.

"Yes, but wouldn't the fumes be poisonous if the plant were poisonous?"

That was a good point. I knew if poison ivy was burned, it could have terrible repercussions. "I don't know. I hadn't thought of that. Okay, how would you get rid of it if you couldn't burn it?" I placed the cups in the dishwasher.

"I would bury it in a deep hole or throw it out," Julia said.

I stopped dead in my tracks. "Yes, I would throw it out, but not in my own trash can in case someone found it. I wouldn't want it to be linked back to me, so I would put it in someone else's trash can or in a dumpster, where anyone could dump their trash, and there would be no way to link it back to me." I squealed and whirled to face her. "Julia, you're a genius. Do you think you're up for some dumpster diving?"

"Some what?" Julie's face scrunched into a network of lines.

"You know, dumpster diving. Digging around in a dumpster."

"I'm getting a bad feeling about this. Are we about to get our little selves in trouble?" Julia crossed her arms and leaned her hip against the counter. "Because I have a feeling that is exactly what we're about to do."

"Not if we do it right." I grinned.

"Okay, I know I'll regret this." Julia rolled her eyes. "I'm in. So, what's the plan?"

CHAPTER EIGHTEEN

The dumpsters for Java Vein's office building were in the back of the building at the far end of the parking lot. The area was narrow. If the lot were ever full, it would be tight. It was clear the main parking was out in front of the building. I noticed two black SUVs with the Java Vein logo parked next to one another under one of the security lights about midway down.

I pulled the van over, grabbed my flashlight, and hopped out to look in the windows of the SUVs but didn't see anything of real interest. Besides, I figured the police had searched them since I told Gabe about Lilly seeing a black SUV the morning of the murder. Note to self—ask Gabe if they had found anything.

I parked in the last space closest to the dumpsters, thinking it would draw less attention. Of course, two women dressed in black and fishing around in the dumpsters at ten o'clock at night weren't going to draw any notice whatsoever, right?

"Gloves," I said.
"Gloves," my cohort responded.
"Flashlight," I said.
"Flashlight." Julia said.
"Ready?" I asked.
"Ready." she said.

There were three dumpsters, all of which had lids located on the top.

Rats. Being vertically challenged as I was, I was glad I had thought to pack the ladder.

"Ladder." I grinned at Julia.

"Let's go pull it out." She giggled. "I feel like one of those army special-agent chicks we see in the movies."

We pulled the ladder from the back of the van, dropping it to the ground only once. The clatter made us freeze and wait to see if anyone came out of the building. No one did, so we proceeded.

Julia and I threw open the lid, and I propped the ladder next to the dumpster nearest the building.

"Okay, what do we do?" Julia whispered.

"Your job is to hold the ladder secure while I climb into the big blue box, and then keep a lookout in case anyone shows up," I whispered back. The cold, the dark, and the fact we were sneaking around lent itself to whispering.

"Aye, aye, Captain." Julia saluted me.

I mounted the ladder and was surprised to find the dumpster was close to empty. "Julia."

"Yeah?"

"This one doesn't have much in it. Do you think they've already been dumped?" I made my way back down the ladder rungs.

"I don't know. I hadn't thought about it."

"Me neither." My feet hit the pavement. "Let's try the other two since we're here anyway."

"Okay, Captain," Julia said, maintaining her army special-agent chick-movie persona.

We lugged the ladder to the second dumpster, flipped the lid open, and discovered a mound of garbage waist deep.

"It looks as if I'll have to go in if I want to find anything in this one."

Julia stood up straight and saluted me again. "If you're not back in ten minutes, I'll notify your next of kin, but I'm not coming in after you."

"Chicken." I smiled at my friend.

"I'm a chef. I have health codes to think about." She grinned and flashed her light on the ladder so I could see my way up the rungs.

There was no ladylike way to lower myself in, so I hoisted myself over the side and hoped I landed on something solid. Thankful for gloves and boots, I began my swim through the trash.

After about fifteen minutes of turning over old lunches, empty boxes and discarded piles of paper, I spotted some wilted dark foliage with a limp pinkish flower attached. It was trapped under a huge old computer monitor.

I groaned as I moved the piece, trying not to damage the plant underneath it, when I heard the whoop, whoop, whoop sound of a siren. Moments later a loud voice commanded, "Hands in the air."

I stood up, hands in the air, and peeked over the side of the dumpster.

Everything was in shadows. Police lights flashed blue, and the outline of a man came near us with his gun drawn, ready for any sudden moves. I knew enough to stay still until told otherwise.

"You in the dumpster, come out slowly. Keep your hands where I can see them."

"Yes, Officer," I called loud enough for him to hear me. "I can explain, but I'm going to need some help getting out of here. I'm not strong enough or tall enough to get myself over the edge, so I may need my ladder."

"Amy Kate, is that you?" The deep, husky voice sounded familiar—the one that went with the handsome face of Lieutenant Gabe Cooper.

"Yes." Embarrassment washed over me. Caught red-handed going through other people's trash, trying to score a clue. The one person I didn't want to see while dressed à la garbage was the one who showed up.

Gabe holstered his weapon and jogged over to the dumpster.

Julia backed up, probably trying to melt into the parking lot, but Gabe gave her a blistering look of disapproval before looking at me.

"What on earth are you doing in the dumpster?" His face colored with irritation. "Are you trying to get yourself arrested? What if I hadn't been the one to answer the call and dispatch had sent someone else? What were you thinking?" He asked these questions in rapid succession, not giving me a fair chance to answer any of them. I started to sputter an answer, but he cut me off.

"You, Amy Kate, are trouble waiting to happen. It's like you can't help it. It just seeks you out wherever you go. You're a . . . a . . . a—" Gabe fumbled to find an appropriate description.

"Trouble magnet?" I suggested.

"Yes," he said. "A trouble magnet."

"That may be true." I peered over the edge of the dumpster. "But look what I found." I handed him the pot filled with the limp plant that was still identifiable even after its stint in the cold dumpster.

"Foxglove." He recognized the plant. "Let's get you out of there, then I want some answers." Gabe sounded a bit calmer. The shock of finding me in the trash was wearing off.

Gabe and Julia lifted the ladder sideways and swung it into the dumpster. I caught one end and leaned it up against the wall, planting it on top of the not-so-solid trash under my feet. From outside of the dumpster, Gabe steadied the end sticking out.

I climbed up to the edge, but then it became apparent to everyone I needed another ladder on the outside of the dumpster to climb out.

"All right, try to swing your feet over first, then jump and I'll try to catch you."

Even if I am the right height for it, I am not a gymnast. I am a bookworm. Bookworms do not swing and jump. I could feel the sweat starting to form on the palms of my hands, even in the thirty-degree weather.

Gabe let go of the ladder and hurried to the area beneath me.

I lifted one leg over, my belly teetering on the thin edge of the dumpster, trying hard not to fall in either direction. Gabe grabbed my arm and rolled me from the edge of the blue tin can into his strong arms.

I smiled up at him, grateful he had rescued me from my predicament. He held me in his arms, smiling back, shaking his head in disbelief.

Julia cleared her throat once—or maybe it was twice—and then I removed my arms from around Gabe's neck, and he slipped me to the ground.

There I stood decked out in this week's produce and day-old bread. Chanel would be so proud. I made introductions. "Gabe, this is my roommate and co-conspirator, Julia Jacobs." I glanced at my roommate, who stuck out her hand to shake his. "Julia, this is Lieutenant Gabe Cooper of the Pine Lake Police Department."

Gabe took a step forward and shook her hand.

"So, I figured from the flashing blue lights and the 'hands in the air' comment—" Julia poked a little fun, then she asked with a measure of seriousness, "—are you going to arrest us? Is dumpster diving illegal in Alabama or something?"

"No, but trespassing is, and you two are on private property. The station received a call from the night guard. He saw you scoping out the SUVs and thought you might be car thieves."

"Oh," I said.

Gabe reached over and pulled a piece of wilted lettuce from my hair. "I suggest we leave before anyone else calls this in, and I have to explain why Lucy and Ethel are digging around in the trash bin." He smiled at his *I Love Lucy* reference. "Is there somewhere we can go to talk? Because I still want those answers."

Julia piped up, "You can come back to our apartment, and we'll have some hot chocolate and warm up."

I held up my right hand to stop the conversation. "You can join us as long as you don't make any sarcastic remarks about how I smell."

"Would I do that?" Gabe asked.

"You most certainly would."

"Okay, I'll behave myself. Let me bag this plant. Then on the way, I'll radio into the station to let them know what I found when I got here."

How I wanted to be a fly on his dashboard.

He headed to his car, opened the trunk, and pulled out a plastic bag big enough to hold the plant.

~

The hot chocolate felt like warm sunshine as it slid down my throat, and the steam rising from the mug helped melt away the frosty nip from my face. We chitchatted about general topics. Gabe tried to make friends with Gizmo by tossing his favorite rope toy. I could tell he was trying hard to make polite conversation before jumping into the heart of the matter. Why was I digging around in other people's trash at this late hour? He did a good job holding off until we finished our mugs of hot chocolate.

As I swallowed the last drop, Gabe asked, "Okay, ladies, what were you two doing in the trash bin?"

"This morning when we were at Java Vein, I caught a quick glimpse of Bryant's office before Samantha had the chance to shut the door in my face. I saw an indention in the carpet from where something had been sitting near the window."

"So, you thought something had been moved?"

"Yes." Excitement ran through me. "And with the shape of the indention and how close it was to the window, I thought that 'something' might be a plant."

"And it was," Julia said, just as excited.

"Okay, you found a missing plant in the dumpster, but the foxglove was already in the coffee shop accessible to everyone. What does a missing plant prove?"

"It proves the killer didn't have to know there was foxglove in the coffee shop—someone like Samantha or Casey. What if the killer didn't go to the shop much but knew enough about gardening to know what the plant in Bryant's office could do? What if the foxglove in the coffee shop isn't the foxglove the killer used?" I gathered the empty mugs and placed them in the sink.

"If that were the case, the murder was planned, not a spur-of-the-moment decision because it was there—handy. The murderer would've had to bring the foxglove with him or her. I need to take the plant into the evidence lab, and have it tested for fingerprints to see who's been handling it," Gabe said. "But even if Samantha's prints are on it, that wouldn't be unusual. Secretaries usually water the plants in the offices, which means if she used it to kill him, it would be hard to prove."

I corrected Gabe. "You mean administrative assistant." He cut his eyes toward me and frowned, not responding to my comment.

"I wonder who gave Bryant the plant?" Julia asked.

This caught my attention.

"Yes, who would give a man like Bryant foxglove?" I asked, more to myself than to anyone else.

"Yeah, so far everything we know about this guy makes him out to be less than nurturing. He was all about making a buck—not the kind of guy you'd give a plant to."

"No, he's not." I rubbed my chin deep in thought. "I wanted to ask you about the SUVs. Did someone ever search them after I told you about Lilly seeing one of them leaving the scene of the crime?"

"Yes, we went over them, but there wasn't anything out the ordinary. All we found were a few petrified french fries under the floor mats in the back and some paperwork left by Casey with the Inkster logo on it."

"Did you ask her when she had used the SUV?"

"She said she used it Monday and Tuesday because her car was in the shop but signed it back in with Samantha late Tuesday afternoon. Floyd checked out her story with her mechanic, and it appears to be true."

"Did Samantha send you the log yet?" I wanted to get a look at it, though I didn't expect the person who drove Wednesday morning to have signed it. Knowing who had what vehicle and how many were parked outside the office building might at least eliminate one or two people from the list.

Casey, it seemed, wasn't the one driving away from the murder of Bryant Kendrick, but someone did, and it was starting to look like it might be Samantha, the administrative assistant.

"No." Gabe frowned. "I'll try getting in touch with her tomorrow." He stretched, then stood. "Lucy, Ethel, it's been delightful, but I should let you ladies get some sleep."

"I'll walk you to the door," I stood to push my chair under the table. I'd been meaning to ask Gabe about the shard of porcelain I'd found at the scene of the crime but hadn't found the right moment. Perhaps it was time.

When we reached the living room, we stopped in front of the door. "Gabe, I've been meaning to ask you. Did anyone find any pieces of broken porcelain at the crime scene?"

"No, why?"

"I figured there should've been some broken mugs or something. The way Bryant knocked everything off the counter when he fell to the floor. It just seemed likely, that's all." I wasn't going to tell him that I had a piece of porcelain I was trying to match. Nor was I telling him I had inadvertently taken it from the crime scene. No sense in stirring up any extra trouble tonight. The smell of garbage was too fresh.

"No, we didn't find any broken mugs."

"So, Bryant's mug was intact, not broken or chipped?" I asked.

"Yeah, it was intact. Now I have a question for you." He took his jacket from the coat stand from behind the front door. "Did you catch Lilly tonight at the store?"

"Yes, I meant to tell you. She knew Bryant a great deal better than we thought. She was married to him."

"Married to him? We haven't found anything in our records."

"You may need to dig a little deeper. Lilly's parents had the marriage annulled. From what Lilly said it didn't last long, maybe two or three months over the summer after her junior year. Both she and Bryant were back at college for their senior year, and no one was the wiser about their romance."

"No one, not even Matt?"

"Not even Matt. He still doesn't know."

"This will have to come out."

"I know. I told Lilly she needed to tell Matt before it's out in the open. She knew I had to tell you and Elizabeth," I said.

"Elizabeth isn't going to like this."

"What do you mean?"

"It gives Matt motive. If he found out Bryant and Lilly were married and no one bothered to tell him, Matt could feel betrayed—or even worse, he could have thought they were still involved with one another. He could've killed Bryant out of jealousy."

"I hadn't even thought of that." I sighed and slumped onto the couch.

"Yeah, Elizabeth's not going to like this. That was the one thing in Matt's favor. He didn't have a motive for killing his partner since they had signed the new contract."

With that thought hanging in the air, we said our good nights. Even Gizmo was too tired to walk Gabe to the door, so he wagged his tail a couple of times instead.

Sleep evaded me as I tossed around ideas like I'd been

tossing around bags of garbage. Gabe told us Bryant's computer hadn't given them any new leads. They'd checked his emails over the past year. It was as Samantha and Sarah Catherine had said. Ed Philips contacted Bryant several times after he lost his job and up until the month his wife had passed away. Why had Ed gone to the visitation for Bryant, the man who had cost him his living? It struck me as strange that he would have gone.

The fact we had found foxglove in the dumpster had me wondering about who had given Bryant, the guy who only cared about himself, a plant—a living thing to be loved and nurtured. From what I knew about Bryant, I wouldn't have trusted him with a pet rock much less something that required attention.

The one person who loved gardening and was mixed up in all this was Lilly. Or Samantha. She was the one who threw the plant out. Did she know anything about gardening?

And then there's Ed Philips, someone I don't know much about either. All I had on him was the stuff I had read in the police reports. As I drifted off to sleep, I decided to remedy the situation first thing tomorrow morning. I needed more information, and for Matt's sake, I was going to get it.

CHAPTER NINETEEN

First thing Tuesday morning came earlier than I wanted. My alarm buzzed with a fierceness I couldn't ignore, causing me to throw my feet over the edge of the bed and zombie-walk across the room to turn it off.

Once I had a shower and half a cup of coffee in me, my eyes began to focus. The day outside was cold but bright. I drove to the bookshop in order to meet Mr. Shine for his first day of the rebuilding effort. My heart squeezed tight in my chest with anticipation. I had high hopes for Mr. Shine.

My Twisted Plots gang was holding a staff meeting this morning to plan the upcoming book signing with Tom Perkins. After today, our doors would open again, and we'd be back on the old schedule with Flora coming in at nine o'clock and Carter joining us at one. I worked from nine until five, Monday through Friday, and then I caught the evening shift with Kirk on Saturdays.

Maybe that's why I had to turn to a dating service for help. I had no time to get out into the real world and mingle.

Not stopping at the Beans and Leaves for my second cup of liquid motivation felt strange. I'll admit it. I am spoiled for any other coffee. A fast-food foam cup filled with sludge just won't cut it now.

Matt was in his shop clearing out some of the charred remains of the bags that had held coffee and tea leaves. Since the police had released the crime scene, a.k.a. his shop, on Saturday, Matt was getting it cleaned up and ready for his own version of the repairmen's march. He had to be relieved the fire marshal's report had ruled out arson.

I waved as I passed the window. He nodded and smiled since his hands were full.

"You're late," Flora said in her no-nonsense voice when I entered the shop.

"I know. Is Mr. Shine here yet?" I glanced around for any sign of him, hoping to avoid Flora's typical lecture about being on time.

"No, he called a few minutes ago to say he was stopping at the hardware store first to pick up some of the needed materials. He also said he was bringing paint samples so you could choose the new color for the work area."

"That's awesome. We can choose something different. No more depressing gray." I clapped my hands in anticipation. "I never did like how the darker color made the room feel small and cluttered."

"I don't know about the cluttered part being the fault of the paint, but I didn't like it either. Your Aunt Maude's decorator, though, swore the color was the new neutral." Flora adopted a slight European accent imitating the flamboyant decorator. "Darling, it's the new in. It's all the rage in New York. Even Trump Towers went Gravel Gray."

I tried to smoother my giggle. Her impression was spot-on. Feeling relieved I had skirted one of Flora's speeches on responsibility and promptness, I went to the counter to deposit my belongings in one of the cubbies underneath.

The Twisted Plots employees showed up around nine thirty, and our creative juices joined us somewhere around ten.

Mr. Shine appeared with materials, tools and a helper named Ben. Ben was in his early twenties with shaggy blond hair that he kept out of his eyes with a flip of his head, which seemed to be a continual battle. His jeans were nonexistent due to all the holes they had in them. Maybe appropriate for the summer weather, but in the month of January with the temperature around thirty-five, I wondered about his sanity.

Carter, Kirk, and Flora were helpful in laying out a plan for getting the word out about the mystery writer's visit. I had two weeks to saturate the city of Pine Lakes with the news of the book signing. We agreed hosting a private event on Friday night at the Twisted Plots for our book-club members would be a great way to get the weekend started.

Carter was put in charge of posting the plans on our website. Flora, being a pen-and-paper gal, said she was itching to check out the new office-supply store. The staff there would help her make an amazing flyer to hand out to customers.

I asked Kirk if he could get us an ad in the college paper. "No prob, boss lady," was his reply.

Everyone left the meeting as Kirk would say, "stoked." The end of this smoky trial was near. Mr. Shine whistled a tune to the beat of his hammer, which to me sounded like heaven.

Once Flora was done checking the online orders and doing some research for a first edition for Mrs. Darcy, one of our best customers, I confiscated the one computer that was still plugged in and working. I wanted to check the Open Hearts site, hoping to make another date with Chet, the reporter, and see if he had any information on Samantha. I was willing to offer up a little information myself if his intel was worthwhile. He'd been angling for an interview. I'd use that as bait.

I opened the site, delighted to find I had another interested party. My ego needed the boost. After checking his information, I decided not to pursue a meeting with him. There was something fishy about his profile. Besides, he liked mountain climbing, and my vertigo prevented me from going to the top of any mountain, not even for love.

I left Chet a message on the private chat site, mentioning an interview, hoping it would be enough to entice him to contact me. I let him know I wanted to meet him for lunch today and left my cell phone number since we hadn't exchanged contact information. Our first date through the chat site had ended with a lot of cold and wetness and teeth chattering. It didn't lend itself to the customary "and here is my number. Call me sometime."

~

My stomach made a nuisance of itself again as I found a seat inside the Deli on the Square. The place buzzed with people. The aromas of soups and hot sandwiches wafted around me like carpenter bees around wood.

I grabbed a menu from the stand beside the napkin holder

and perused the choices while waiting for Chet. He had called, sounding anxious to meet.

Impatient, I decided to go ahead and order. After all, this wasn't a date. It was a business meeting, and I wanted to quiet down the gurgling of the monster from the black lagoon in my midsection before Chet arrived. I didn't want him thinking I was a starving entrepreneur, even if it was somewhat true.

Chet entered the deli as if he owned it. He spoke to several people, shaking their hands and patting them on the back. Thanks to the 'Around Town' segment in the newspaper, he was one of those people who knew everybody, and everybody knew him. He was dressed casually in a tan pea coat with dark wooden buttons. Around his neck he sported a red and brown striped scarf. His blond hair was once again flawless.

A smile came to his lips when he spotted me at the back of the deli. He finished socializing by giving his public one last wave in the direction of no one in particular and then made his way to my table. "Hi, Amy Kate, I was glad to get your message."

"Yes, I was glad you could meet on such short notice."

The waitress deposited my food in front of me.

Chet grinned. "Couldn't wait, huh?"

"No, I'm starving. Do you mind if I bless my food or would you feel uncomfortable?" Maybe I shouldn't have asked. Perhaps I should've blessed my food and went on as if it was nothing special, but I didn't want to do that to Chet. After all, he had been so sweet to me on the drive home. It was my turn to show him some courtesy.

"No, problem, my dad's a Baptist preacher. I grew up saying grace at every meal. I still bless my food unless I'm somewhere it might cause—let's say—a stir." He bowed his head and blessed my food and his forthcoming food with a humility that—shall we say—'stirred' me.

Once Chet's food arrived, we got down to business. "So, what did you want to talk about? I know it wasn't the water conditions at Pine Lake."

"Ha, ha, Mr. Funnyman. I wanted to see if you had any information on Samantha Holiday. Have you come across anything you would consider interesting?"

"I might've, but what's in it for me?"

"An even trade. I give you what I know on Samantha in exchange for what you know."

"I recall you saying something about an interview in your message?"

"Yes, I can't give you an interview now because the case is ongoing, and my sister, the lawyer, would kill me. But—" I raised my hand to stop him from backpedaling before I could finish. "I am in a position to offer you an exclusive interview with the investigator who is working for my sister on the case, once it's been resolved." I said this like he didn't know I was the one working on the case. I half expected some sarcastic jab.

"Hmm, that's not a bad offer. Who's the investigator?" Chet asked with a straight face.

Suddenly it became clear. He didn't know I was the investigator. Since he had gone to such great lengths trying to interview me Saturday, I assumed he knew, but he didn't. He must've wanted to interview me because I owned the Twisted Plots. "I am," I said.

He laughed—not a slight "oh, that's a good one" laugh. No, he let out one of those howling kinds of laughs that makes everyone turn and stare. I looked around the deli to see if anyone had noticed his outburst. Several curious faces looked back at me.

"Oh, Amy Kate, I'm so sorry, but all I could think about was you running and screaming from the big, hairy raccoon, which landed you on your backside in the lake. What would you do if you ever had to tackle something bigger and hairier and maybe even meaner?" He wiped the last few tears of laughter from the corner of his eye. "Your screaming wouldn't scare off a real threat the way it did that raccoon."

With my dignity a little bruised, I sat up straighter in my chair and retorted to Mr. Baker it was none of his concern. Tired of his tomfoolery, I asked, "Do you want the interview or not?" He may have all day to clown around, but I didn't. I had a business to run and a murder to solve.

Contrite, Chet said again he was sorry. "Yes, I want the interview."

"All right, what do you know about Samantha Holiday?"

"I've been digging around in her past and discovered she moved here about the same time as Bryant and Sarah Catherine. They arrived within months of each other."

"Why did you find that interesting?"

"Because she doesn't have any ties to this place. At least none I can find. She doesn't have any relatives who live here, and there's no record of her ever living here in the past. Most people who move to this town come because they have relatives here or for work-related purposes, but she didn't."

"Hmm, odd," I said.

"Yes, and the fact she showed up maybe three months after the they arrived seems too convenient."

"Lots of people move here throughout the year." I took a bite of my chicken salad, which was my attempt at eating healthier.

"Yes, but most of them don't get hired the first place they put in an application."

"What?" My estimation of Chet's research skills rose with this revelation.

"She moved here the week of June eighteenth, and according to the hire date on her application, started working at Java Vein a week later. Plus, and this is the good stuff, she rented a house through one of those real estate agencies who manages rental properties for the owners. I nosed around and found out the property she's renting was owned by Bryant Kendrick."

"Okay, I'm officially impressed."

Chet relaxed back into his chair throwing his right arm over the back. "You should be."

I had devoured half my salad by this time, and my stomach settled down.

"Your turn, what can you tell me about Samantha Holiday?"

"I can tell you she's acting strangely over the death of her boss. Gabe Cooper and I went to interview her yesterday, and she was nothing but business, but when I realized I had left my purse in her office, I went back to get it and discovered her sobbing at her desk. It was weird. They had worked together for six years, but she seemed almost too upset. Does that make sense?"

Chet watched me with his piercing green eyes. It was hard to concentrate.

"Yes, sometimes by sheer instinct we know when things don't add up."

"I also discovered a plant missing from Bryant's office."

"What's the significance of that?"

"Do you know how Bryant was killed?" As a precaution, I asked. There was only so much I could give in this exchange. I had to keep Matt's interests in mind.

"I know he was poisoned."

"Do you know what kind of poison was used?"

"No, do you?" Chet leaned in closer to me.

"Let's just say the missing plant caught my eye."

"Got it. So, Bryant was poisoned with some type of plant, and Samantha Holiday had access to one."

"Maybe." I didn't want to divulge too much. "But if I tell you for sure, I would have to kill you." I smirked.

The waitress overheard my remark when she dropped off our checks. She looked me over once to make sure I wasn't packin' and then moved on to the next table.

I pulled my check out from beside my empty plate, glanced at it, and threw an appropriate tip on the table with a little extra for not patting me down. I closed my wallet, then gave Chet the serious look I used to give my students when they were in trouble. "I want to remind you if any of this appears in the news before the case is solved, I will consider this our last meeting. Are we clear?"

He smiled. "Clear as the water in Pine Lake."

CHAPTER TWENTY

"**Ms. Holiday isn't** in today." The lady who sat behind Samantha's desk informed me. "She's not feeling well and took a sick day."

Disappointed, I made my way through the reception area of Java Vein and took the elevator to the lobby. On the way down, I decided to go see Samantha Holiday at her home, the one owned by Bryant Kendrick. I slid into the driver's seat of my blue minivan and dug through the pile of papers that sat in the passenger side. I knew I had her home address in the notes I'd taken at the lunch with Gabe and Elizabeth.

Sure enough, I located it right below a ketchup stain. I noted the time on the console when I cranked the van. It was going on one o'clock, so I texted Flora before leaving the parking lot. A tinge of guilt reared its ugly head for leaving her to deal with the repairman.

My Text: *How's everything going?*
Flora's Text: *All is well.*
My Text: *Should I come back or continue on the trail?*
Flora's Text: *Stay on the trail. Fill me in later.*

I stopped to gas up, then went west toward the city limits. Samantha's rental house sat out in the new annexed section of town where there was a mix of farmhouses, trailers, and subdivisions elbowing each other for the right to be there.

I turned down a dirt road, which transformed into a path, barely wide enough for my van. Before I found a spot to turn around, a house emerged from behind a row of tall oak trees.

Since there were no other houses in view, I concluded I'd reached my destination. The GPS system on my phone told me the same thing with a little black and white checkered flag.

I parked off to the side of the gravel driveway and eased from the car, not wanting to announce my presence just yet. I needed time to scope out the yard.

The small white shotgun house had a porch running across the front, and on either side of the steps sat an empty flower bed prepared for spring planting. The remnants of three hanging plants swung from S hooks along the front rail. Good, she gardens. I'd found a second gardener on our list of suspects. Now to find out if she knew a foxglove plant from a hole in the ground.

Careful to stay out of sight, I snuck around the side of the house into the backyard. In the left corner, I discovered a small metal shed, which looked big enough to hold a lawn mower and some tools. I crept to the faded tin building, the eerie snap and crackle of the dead dry leaves amplifying in my ears.

I glanced over my shoulder to make sure Samantha hadn't heard the noises. Once I reached the shed, I found to my delight it wasn't locked, so I cracked the door and peeked in.

Just as I'd thought, it contained a lawn mower, carpenter tools, gardening supplies, and some bags of topsoil. There was also a varied collection of ceramic pots as well as those plastic ones that look like orange pottery but aren't.

Great, now all I needed to find was the smoking gun or rather the smoking foxglove.

Bang.

A door slammed.

My hand flew to my heart, and I whirled to see if I'd been caught snooping. No one was at the back door, so I stepped inside the metal building and left the door cracked to listen.

Someone moved around in the front yard. The minivan.

Samantha must have spotted it and wondered who it belonged to. For a moment, I thought about hiding in the shed, but then how could I explain being in there if she found me?

Instead, I double-timed it back to the side of the front porch where I pressed myself up against the house. I peeked around the corner. Samantha stood on the porch looking at my vehicle. I hoped she might go back into the house, but she seemed rooted to the spot.

What to do?

A piece of dad's advice popped into my mind. If you can't face your opponent head-on, distract them. I decided on a bit of misdirection. Noticing a rose bush next to me, I squatted and started a conversation with myself like I was supposed to be there.

"Look at this soil." I clucked while I picked up some of the dirt. "Such a shame." I glanced up and feigned shocked expression.

Samantha Holiday peered at me from the porch, her mouth pulled into a firm line, and her eyes swollen. She wore a pink fluffy robe with a tissue hanging out of the left pocket, a far cry from how she was dressed yesterday, and if I didn't know better, I would swear her hair hadn't been brushed in days. Her hairdo, as we say in the South, looked like a rat's nest. Samantha Holiday was a wreck.

"What is?" She asked.

"This rose bush. They hate shade, and from what I can see, this is a terrible place to have planted this bush. Though they do alright in red clay, they do better in some sort of compost mixture." I threw down the dirt I had picked up.

"Aren't you the lady I met yesterday with Lieutenant Cooper? Amy Kate something?" The V that tangled her brows deepened.

"Yes, I am." I stood from my squatting position. "Amy Kate Anderson." I offered my hand. She didn't return the gesture, so I pulled my hand back to my side. "There are a few questions you might be able to help me with, and the lady at your office said you were home today. Would it be all right if I came in for a few minutes?" I started rubbing my arms as if I were cold. "We could talk, and I could warm up a bit?"

Samantha ran her gaze over me. Her thoughts played out on her face. She wasn't sure if letting me in her home was the wisest thing to do. In the end, Southern hospitality won out over better judgment, and she invited me in.

I sighed, relieved she hadn't thrown me off the property. My confidence grew. Now, if I could manage to get her to confess to murdering Bryant and show me her foxglove, I'd be rocking in my new role as Elizabeth's legs. Logic whispered it wasn't going to be that simple.

Samantha led the way into a warm, cozy house. I noticed a door off to the left-hand side of the living room, which had to be a bedroom. A bar between the living room and the kitchen was cluttered with unopened mail and plates stacked layers deep.

A tiny hallway led into the bathroom. The door was open. The mass of towels littering the floor testified to the fact that this homeowner hadn't bothered with cleaning or straightening for several days. The door off to the left of the kitchen completed the layout of the tiny cottage.

The stark contrast between Samantha's office and her home troubled me. There was no way the same woman maintained both spaces. Even to my amateur eye, everything screamed Samantha was in full mourning for Bryant Kendrick.

Samantha motioned for me to take a seat on the couch. I leaned down and moved the blanket which was covering up the portion of the couch that was not covered by magazines. She offered me something to drink. From the looks of the kitchen, I wasn't sure she would be able to find a clean glass, but I accepted her kind offer and waited in the living room while she went to the kitchen to pour us two glasses of sweet tea.

I heard the refrigerator door open and took the liberty of surveying the small living room. I caught sight of a picture frame lying face down on the shelf of one of those ladder-shelving units and couldn't resist the urge to see who was in the picture, so I hurried toward it, hoping she wouldn't see me. Through the opening above the kitchen bar, I could see Samantha with her back to me.

I picked up the framed picture of her and Bryant. Her eyes shined with warmth and love. The picture itself wasn't incriminating. The fact it was on display and she had thought to turn it over before coming to see who was here, was. I replaced the frame and hurried over to a couple of plants that sat on a modern black iron plant stand. The three healthy plants were real, but none of them were foxglove.

Samantha returned from the kitchen carrying two glasses of tea.

"I see you like plants. I couldn't help noticing you had several planters outside by the front porch steps. Do you enjoy gardening?" I took a seat on the couch.

"Yes, I find it helps me unwind. After being stuck indoors all day at the office, I enjoy some time outside. I start feeling cooped up after a while. I'll be glad when it's spring again." She placed the glasses on coasters on the coffee table and sat in the armchair that was angled to face the couch.

"I can understand the need to be outside. Sometimes if I'm indoors too long, I have to escape for a walk to get my juices flowing again. Do you have any favorite plants?" I asked this question so I could hear her talk. Yesterday, she didn't have any trace of a cold, but I wanted to make sure the red nose and swollen eyes weren't from some sickness she may have developed overnight. After all, the lady behind the desk had said Samantha was home sick.

"From the number of bushes scattered throughout the yard, you can tell that I favor roses. However, I also tend to love hydrangea bushes. The flowers remind me of colored snowballs." Her lips lifted in a slight smile.

No, no sign of a cold here. She hadn't sniffled, sneezed, coughed, or hiccupped once since I arrived, nor had I seen any evidence of medications sitting around on the counter or the end tables, not even a cough drop. She was in mourning.

"Yes, hydrangeas are beautiful indeed. I was wondering, do you ever grow foxglove?" I asked.

Samantha drummed her fingers on the arm of the chair. "I've grown several things over the years. It's hard to keep track. As you can see from the planters on the front porch, not all my plants survive from spring to spring."

"No, mine don't either." I paused to take a sip of my tea. "I happened to notice yesterday when the lieutenant and I were at Java Vein that a plant was missing from Mr. Bryant's office. Do you know what happened to it?"

"You mean when you entered his office without permission?" She lifted her chin and cocked a brow.

I started to say something, then thought better of it. "Yes, when I looked in the murder victim's office."

Samantha took her own sip of tea before answering. "Yes,

Bryant got rid of it. He wasn't the nurturing sort, and it had died."

Since the plant I'd found was healthy enough, Samantha was lying. "If he did get rid of it, what do you think he would've done with it?"

"I'm not sure." She shrugged. "One day it was in his office and the next it was gone. I didn't concern myself with its disappearance. I figured Bryant got tired of looking at it. Really, Miss Anderson, there's no mystery there."

"Umm, I guess not," I said. "Did you happen to know what type of plant it was?"

"No, I hadn't noticed."

"Even though you love to garden, you didn't notice." I hesitated, but when she didn't answer, I went on. "What other hobbies do you have, other than gardening, if you don't mind me asking?"

"I don't mind, but I don't see how it could help you with your investigation."

"Sometimes it's the small things that get one to thinking," I said as if I had worked on hundreds of cases and knew this as a matter of personal experience. I'm as much a fraud as she is.

"I do like movies. Romances are my absolute favorites."

I held up my hand for her to stop. "That's not exactly what I meant. Let me try again. What do you do in your off time?"

"Isn't that the same as asking me about my hobbies?"

She wasn't going to make my job easy. I'd have to be blunt. "Not quite. I'm wondering more who you spent your time with instead of how you spent your time." There, to the point.

Samantha leaned back in her chair, and with a slight tilt of her head, asked her own question. "So, what you're really wanting to know is if I spent time with Bryant away from the office?"

"Well yes, that's what I'm asking." I met her gaze, and for a split second, we sat there in complete silence, the question standing between us.

Samantha sprang from her seat and marched to the door. "I believe this interview is over, Miss—" She flung the front door open and pointed the way out, never looking me in the eye.

"Anderson," I filled in for her.

I walked toward the door but stopped beside the picture and set it up straight. Her loving eyes focused on Bryant while he looked at the camera.

"If you did spend time with Bryant outside of work, I will find out. I don't want to hurt anyone. Just need the truth, so I can figure out who did this and why. Matt Murphy is an innocent man, and if you have any information which might help him, I need to know."

If she were as loyal to Bryant as others said, maybe she felt some sort of loyalty to Matt too.

Her staunch silence held my answer.

I stopped in the doorway. "I hope you get to feeling better, Miss Holiday."

"I'm sure I will."

"I don't know. A guilty conscious is a hard thing to shake."

If looks could kill, I would've dropped on the spot. Thankfully, her only recourse was to slam the door as soon as I stepped across the threshold.

So much for a confession. No foxglove seemed to be floating around either. At least I now knew the indention in the carpet had been from a planter. That was something. I also knew Miss Holiday had been involved with Bryant Kendrick.

Oh, she could deny it, but between the information Chet had supplied me and the framed portrait of the two of them, I was confident they had in fact had an affair.

But believing it is one thing. Proving it is another story. Someone in our small town of Pine Lake had to know something about it. All I had to do was figure out who that was and get them talking.

Chapter Twenty-One

I pondered my interview with Samantha on the trip to the shop to pick up the delivery for the post office. It was the least I could do for Flora and Carter after they had handled everything today with Mr. Shine.

When I arrived, I mumbled something to Flora about bringing the coffee tomorrow, flashed her a thank-you smile, and ran for the door with the boxes to be mailed.

The post office was dead, so I made it in and out in record time, which suited me fine since I wanted to get to Ed Philips' place and hear what kind of alibi he had for the time in question. So far it seemed everyone had an alibi except me and Samantha Holiday. In her interview with Gabe the day of the murder, she said she was home alone.

Ed Philips lived in a trailer park called Addie's Haven, which was off the beaten path, but I wouldn't have described it as a haven. Mr. Philips' trailer was close to the end of the narrow-paved road. A swing set sat in the sliver of a side yard, which made sense because according to my notes, he had a seven-year-old daughter named Claire.

At almost three in the afternoon, no one appeared to be home at the Philips estate. After knocking with no results, I tried to peek in the window that was in the middle of the front door but being five foot two is not always conducive to spying. The little section of the living room I could see indicated the place was empty.

I jiggled the doorknob to no avail, so I decided to renew a

skill my father had taught me as a teenager—the old credit-card door pick. This would be the first time I used it on someone else's property. If I wasn't running out of time, I wouldn't resort to such tactics, I told myself as I went to the car to get my gas credit card. But Bryant had died almost a week ago, and I didn't want the trail to grow any colder. If bending the fourth amendment a little helped to clear Matt, it would be worth it.

Feeling a little nervous, I approached the door of the trailer. I looked over my shoulder to make sure no one was watching. What stared back at me was a plastic pink flamingo wearing a Santa hat. I didn't think he'd rat me out.

Even with the metal bar running along the edge of the door, there was a gap. It was large enough I could slide my card in between the door and the mortise plate. I needed to move the edge of the card between the actual lock and the notch in the door where it rested.

I shimmied the card just so and heard a snap. Pulling the card out, I examined it. Broken. I flipped the card over and used a different corner. To my great surprise, the lock pushed into the door frame allowing the door to open.

I tucked my card in my back pocket and entered, calling out hello as I went. Again, no answer.

I stood in the middle of the living room and surveyed my surroundings. The trailer was small but tidy. Everything was picked up and put away except for a few breakfast dishes left in the sink. The place was homey.

The family pictures on the bookshelf caught my eye. One was of a man and his bride on their wedding day—Ed Philips and his deceased wife, if I had to guess.

How sad to have left life so young.

Another photo was of the wife and a baby girl about two years old. The most recent photo on the shelf was of the three of them at Christmas. It must have been taken before the wife became ill.

The little girl in the picture appeared to be about four or five. She wore a frilly dress made of red velveteen, and her light brown hair was curled with great care. She sat in her mother's lap while the father stood, his protective arms around them.

This picture brought up my own longings, reminding me of

my own Christmas pictures with family—my mother, my father, my siblings, all huddled together smiling for the camera, capturing the moment. No one ever tells you that you can't capture moments. That it's an impossibility. Rather, the moments slip away, growing dimmer and fainter with time. One day I was going to find the person who took my mother from me, but that wasn't today.

"Hello," said a sweet voice from behind me.

Startled, I turned to find an older version of the girl in the picture. She had to be around six or seven. She stood inside the door with her backpack dangling on the floor.

"Hello." I replaced the picture, mortified I'd been caught.

"Who are you?" The young girl asked as she turned to shut the door to the trailer.

"I'm Amy Kate. Are you Claire?"

"Yes, is my father here with you? I didn't see his car outside." The little girl furrowed her brow, obviously trying to decide if I was a friend or foe.

"No, he's not here with me. I'm waiting to see him. I had a few questions I wanted to ask him about—" I paused, fishing around for the right words to use with a seven-year-old. I landed on "some business." That seemed to satisfy her.

"Oh, you must be one of Daddy's new employees from his company." The little girl didn't wait for an answer but went down the hallway. "I'll be right back. I'm going to put away my backpack. Daddy gets mad if I leave it out in the living room."

The girl wasn't gone but a minute. She rounded the corner of the hallway, still talking as if she hadn't left the room at all. "I saw you looking at our pictures. The Christmas one is my favorite. Mommy looked happy there. It was before she got sick."

"Yes, I've heard about your mom, and you're right. She does look happy in that picture."

"Hey, do you want a snack?" Claire offered. "I always get one first before I do my homework."

"No, I'd better not." I watched her move around in the kitchen, climbing up on the counters to reach the glasses. She seemed like an old pro at it.

As if she read my mind, Claire said, "Dad doesn't like me

climbing on the counters, but it's so much easier than pulling out the stepladder that's beside the refrigerator. Besides, it lets me practice my gymnastics."

"Oh, are you a gymnast?" I was glad to stumble on a topic other than who I was and why I was in her home.

"Not anymore. After Mom became sick and Dad lost his job, I had to give it up. I was five then, and I'm seven now. Dad says I should be able to catch up when I start back."

"Are you starting back?"

"Maybe, if Dad's new company works. What do you do at my dad's company?"

"Claire," a male voice said from the doorway. The man stopped short when he spotted me and assessed me the same way his daughter had moments earlier. "Who are you?" His voice was crisp and direct.

"I'm Amy Kate Anderson."

Mr. Philips turned to his daughter, "What have I told you about letting strangers into the house when I'm not home, Claire?"

"But Daddy, I didn't let her in. She was already in the house when I got home."

Uh oh, I steeled myself for what was about to come as Mr. Philips turned his attention from his daughter back to me.

"Okay, lady." He pulled his cell phone from his pocket.

"Amy Kate." I tried to come off as non-threatening.

"All right, Amy Kate, I don't know what you're up to or why you're here, but you have exactly thirty seconds to straighten this out, or I'm calling the police and having you arrested for breaking and entering."

I could hear Gabe now. I'd never be able to live it down, and his theory about me being a liability would be proven right.

"I'm working for Elizabeth Anderson, the lawyer. I'm trying to find out information on Bryant Kendrick that might help in solving his murder case."

"Yes, I read about that in the papers. Why'd you come here? I haven't worked with Bryant Kendrick in over a year, and trust me, we didn't keep in touch." Mr. Philips still held his phone posed to hit the call button.

"I heard you'd been pressing Mr. Kendrick to help with

your wife's medical bills. Is that true?" I wanted to say I'd heard he had been stalking Bryant, but I didn't think the implications of the word would go over too well. I tried to keep my comments professional, since I didn't relish the idea of being arrested. The blue lights last night were enough of a scare. Twice and Gabe would ban me from the case altogether.

"Claire, why don't you take your snack to your room and start on your homework, okay?" He said.

"Okay, Daddy." Her faced scrunched up, but she didn't argue.

We waited while she gathered up her snack and left for her room. She glanced back before she turned the corner. "It was nice to meet you, Amy Kate. I hope I see you again." Then she disappeared into the depths of the trailer.

"Can I sit down, Mr. Philips?" I asked.

"No," Mr. Philips said. "You may not. I didn't invite you into my home, so we'll conduct this meeting standing."

I caught myself before my backside hit the couch cushion, and thanks to some serious wall squats I'd been doing in my exercise routine, I pulled myself to a standing position. "Okay."

"Now, Miss Anderson, ask me your questions, and I'll see what I can tell you."

"Is it true you asked Bryant to help with the medical bills?"

"Yes, I did," he said.

"Why?" I asked.

"Because he had cost me my job with his complaints, and because I really wasn't thinking straight."

"You mean because of your wife's illness?"

"Not how you mean. It wasn't just because I was devastated, which I was, but when you're taking care of a sick wife and a small child, there isn't a lot of time for sleeping or eating. I was worn out. Even when I took a minute to rest, sleep rarely came, and I was grabbing stuff to eat on the go. Poor Claire was dragged from one friend's house to another while I tried to take care of her mother."

"Not the ideal situation."

"No. But once my head cleared, I knew how foolish it was for me to have asked a man like Bryant Kendrick to help with anything."

"Were you surprised to be fired?"

"You could say that. Bryant wasn't happy over the recent delays, but as difficult as he could be, I thought he'd have the decency to extend a little grace. I found out the hard way I was wrong."

"Samantha Holiday said you showed up at Java Vein corporate one evening. What was that about?"

"I was trying to convince Bryant to help me get my job back. I needed an income, with Claire to take care of and the medical bills piling up. Insurance only goes so far."

"How did that go over?"

"He was unmoved by my arguments. Said there was nothing he could do. He remarked if I valued my job so much, I should have done it better. Cold-hearted—" At this point, Mr. Philips muttered something under his breath and rubbed the back of his neck. The frustration over his last conversation with Bryant played out on his face. "Anyway, let's just say he declined to help. Does that tell you what you need to know?"

"Yes. I have one last question. Why did you go to the visitation for Bryant if you disliked him so?"

"I went for Sarah Catherine's sake. She was good to me and my wife during the last month or two of the cancer. She even apologized for Bryant's behavior and made excuses for him. I wanted to let her know it had meant something to me." He stood with his arms crossed, an unmovable mountain.

I nodded my understanding.

"Anything else?" He asked.

"Yeah, where were you at five o'clock Wednesday morning?"

"Like I told one of the cops on Thursday, I was here with Claire. She was sick with a stomach flu. She came down with it sometime after dinner Tuesday evening, and I placed a call to her pediatrician's answering service around two. I was worried about her dehydrating. The doctor returned my call right after five." Mr. Philips turned his phone off and returned it to his front pocket. "Now, if that's all you need from me, I should check on Claire and get some dinner started."

I thanked him for his time and proceeded to the front door, but before I had shut it all the way, he said, "Oh, and I know the doormat says, 'Come on in,' but next time, I'd wait until someone is actually home. It might help to keep you out of trouble."

I nodded but didn't say anything. I counted my blessings Mr. Philip was a man who understood grace. Bryant Kendrick hadn't understood that concept in life, and I feared his inability to grasp the human need for grace, compassion, and mercy was the very thing that led to his death.

It was after five, so I made a quick trip to Twisted Plots to check out the progress of the repairs and make sure everything was locked up tight. I was surprised to find the lights on and Flora and Carter still there. "Hey guys. I thought you'd be gone by now."

"Yeah, me too, but Carter and I started searching online for the rare edition that Mrs. Darcy wanted, and I lost track of time." Flora bent to retrieve her purse behind the counter.

"It's my fault," Carter said. "I got drawn into the history and the background of the author we were researching. Once we started with the actual search for the edition, it was later than we thought. Herman is going to have my head for keeping his gal out past suppertime." he chuckled.

"I'm out of here," Flora said. "See you tomorrow."

"Tomorrow, it is." Carter rounded the counter to get his coat from one of the cubbies.

I was turning off the lights when the phone by the register rang.

"Finally," Elizabeth said, sounding frantic. "I've been trying to reach you on your cell all afternoon."

"Oh, I'm sorry. I was out doing some interviews, and I turned my phone on vibrate. What's up?"

"The police arrested Matt this afternoon for Bryant's murder."

Chapter Twenty-Two

"What? Why now?" What had changed so abruptly that they had made an arrest?

"Gabe said the information you gave him about Lilly and Bryant having been married years ago was enough to warrant an arrest."

"How did that give the D.A. cause for an arrest? Oh right, I remember. Motive."

"Yes, motive had been missing in their case against Matt. They knew he hadn't wanted to sell the Beans and Leaves, but in the contract they found at the crime scene, Bryant was leaving Matt the store on the square, and Matt had already signed the contract. So, there was no apparent motive. But this thing with Lilly and Bryant gave Matt a different reason for wanting Bryant dead—jealousy."

Gabe's warning from last night played in my ear. I leaned against the counter feeling tired. "Elizabeth, Matt didn't do it."

"I know, but the D.A. believes whoever killed Bryant knew him well. It was someone close to him. They knew his schedule and his habits and had access to the shop. To the D.A., that sounds like Matt."

"Yeah, to me too."

"Right, the one thing missing was a motive. But once Lilly told you about the annulment, the D.A. had the final piece to the puzzle."

I groaned. I had given the D.A. the final piece. Now, I *had* to prove Matt was innocent. I couldn't be the one to send him to jail. "Matt didn't do it."

"I know, but we need to hand-deliver someone else to the D.A. as a suspect. At the very least, someone to muddy the water a little, making the D.A.'s case against Matt not so clear-cut. You said you were out doing interviews. Anything there?" Elizabeth asked.

"It seems Ed Philips has a rock-solid alibi. Samantha Holiday, however, is acting like she and Bryant were involved, but she's not like Casey, who was casual about her indiscretions. Samantha did have a picture of the two of them on display in her home, and she looked like she'd been crushed by a steamroller. She didn't even go into work today."

"Oh, you went to her house. I hope you didn't do anything impulsive."

"No, I was invited in after a little persuasive acting." Pleased with myself, I leaned my elbow on the counter.

"Okay, if you say so. But try to keep out of trouble. I don't need my investigator and my client both in jail. That wouldn't be good for my reputation."

"No, I guess not. Hey, let me ask you a question. If you wanted to find out about someone through the Pine Lake grapevine, who would you talk to?"

"Flora, of course. She'll either have the information or know who might."

I mentally kicked myself in the pants for being so dense. "Yes, why didn't I think of that?" Elizabeth was right. My dear Flora would know. I had better plan on picking up some cinnamon raisin bread to go along with the coffee I owed Flora. She loved cinnamon raisin bread.

"All right, Sis, I'll let you go so you can go home, but let's plan to meet at the police station tomorrow at ten. It might be beneficial if we both have a chat with Matt." Elizabeth disconnected, and the dull quiet of the evening settled in around me.

All Elizabeth wanted was to prove Matt's innocence, but I wanted to find the killer and the opportunity for that was flowing out of the window with every minute. I hated to admit the ambitious D.A. was right. The killer had to be someone close to Bryant, but which one of the women he'd hurt had the chance and the means to make him pay?

~

I arrived at work early to have everything ready for Flora's arrival. I hoped Flora wouldn't be so shocked she'd have a heart attack. My being early wouldn't go without notice or comment.

With the exception of a few pieces of equipment and a chair or two, the shop was back in order. There was still the painting to be done, but we had moved the big stuff back into the work room under a couple of tarps.

I couldn't wait to flip the "Open" sign over, the anticipation conjuring up hopes of the shop teeming with customers. Though it had only been a week, it felt like we plowed through at least a month's worth of obstacles to get to this point. I was fortunate compared to Matt and Lilly, who had weeks' worth of work ahead of them. That's if we could get Matt out of jail.

"Amy Kate, do I smell cinnamon raisin bread?" Flora asked. Even with the hint of a smoky stench still lingering, the enticing aroma of the warm bread filled the room. The cinnamon wafted into the air and drew Flora to the temptation, as I had hoped it would when she arrived promptly at eight-fifty, as she did every morning of the week.

"Yes, Flora, I promised you coffee yesterday, and I thought you might enjoy having some of your favorite comfort food to start the day off right." I could tell she wasn't buying it.

"Really, you bought my favorite bread and showed up early just because?"

"Yep, just because."

She laid her purse and coat on the counter. "Hmm. Amy Kate Anderson, God is going to strike you down one of these days for telling such bald-faced lies." She snatched up a piece of the yummy-smelling bread. "I won't hold it against you if it keeps the bread comin'. Now, what's this all about?"

"Well—" How to broach the subject? I took too long because Flora decided to put her purse and coat away behind the counter while she waited for my response.

"Spit it out, girlfriend. What do you need?"

I sidestepped all the hemming and hawing and got to the point. "Information."

"About what?"

"Not what, but who."

"Oh, I see why you were hesitant. No one wants to be thought of as a gossip." A wicked grin spread across her face. "Especially after the sermon Reverend De Luca gave last Sunday." She took a bite out of her bread, swallowed and then asked, "So, who's our topic?"

"Samantha Holiday regarding her relationship with Bryant. I have my suspicions, but I don't have any proof, not a word from the Pine Lake grapevine. Do you know anything about these two being friendly?" I raised my eyebrows.

"Friendly is a bit of an understatement, dear. After all, the girl followed him here because he promised her a job. Surely, she knew he was up to something. You don't invite someone to follow you when you move for a job. But from what I've heard, the relationship didn't start until three years after they arrived in Pine Lake."

"Oh, I understand from a reliable source the house she rents belongs to Bryant. Do you know if that's true?"

"Yes, it's true. I heard that straight from Roxie Cuevas. She's the one who sold him the house."

"Interesting."

Flora was in the zone, though, and she continued her story as if I hadn't uttered a word.

"They were something of an item for about two years. On Saturdays, Bryant would tell Sarah Catherine he was going golfing in Huntsville, but he'd sneak down to Neville's Motel out on Highway 72 to meet up with Samantha. Nora told me they often lunched at the bed and breakfast. She heard them fighting one afternoon about him leaving his wife. Samantha said she was tired of his excuses and something about any self-respecting woman would leave him high and dry." Flora glanced over at me.

"Go on," I said.

"Nora wasn't sure if Samantha meant herself or Sarah Catherine. That's the problem with eavesdropping while waiting tables—you only get bits." Flora made this last statement with a straight face. She took her gossip seriously. "Anyway, Nora said by the time they left, Bryant had placated her with his air-filled promises. When the lunches and the trips to the motel stopped, it was assumed the affair had ended."

Here she stopped to take a sip of her coffee. "When Bryant walked into the bed and breakfast a few months later with Casey Russell on his arm, you could've knocked us over with a lead pipe. After all, Bryant had chased Samantha for three years and then kept company with her for two. There must have been some deep feelings there. But there weren't. Adultery is what it's always been—bad news."

"It must've hurt Samantha when she discovered he was willing to do for Casey what he'd been unwilling to do for her," I remarked before slipping the last bite of bread into my mouth.

"You know it did. I saw her several weeks after the snake started seeing Casey, and she was low. You could tell she'd been crying. It broke my heart, but he was a user from the get-go. And there isn't anything short of a miracle that can change a character like him. It's a shame too because he could've had such a wonderful life with his wife, but he always had to have the one just beyond his reach."

"I couldn't imagine working with that creep every day, knowing how he was." I thought about the hurt Samantha must have experienced because of Bryant. Of course, many would say she brought this pain upon herself, and they might be right. But one must pity the soul carrying a broken heart.

"Now I've given you the goods. You owe me a few updates on the case," Flora said.

"Oh, shoot a monkey, what time is it?"

Flora looked at her watch. "Close to ten. Why?"

"I've got to go. I'm supposed to meet Elizabeth at the police station."

"Police station?"

"Don't tell me you don't know."

"Know what?"

"Matt's been arrested for murder," I called over my shoulder from the front door, "Flora, you're slipping. I expect my sources to be better informed than that."

She stood on tiptoes leaning over the counter, grinning. "One old gossip can only do so much."

~

The front desk of the police station bustled with activity. I signaled to the officer on duty, a fellow by the name of Pete. He waved me on through to the elevators, so I skirted around lines and groupings of people.

The elevator arrived sooner than I anticipated, and for a moment, wished it hadn't arrived at all. I dreaded seeing Matt under these circumstances and wasn't sure what to say to him once I did. I needed a few minutes to prepare, but it wasn't to be.

Elizabeth was in the interrogation room with Matt when I arrived in the squad room. They were together on the other side of the glass pane. Elizabeth looked stressed. She stood, leaning toward Matt, and her body language screamed tension. Her face was flushed and whatever Matt said, made Elizabeth drop her hands as if in resignation.

Matt, on the other hand, didn't look stressed at all. Of the two, he seemed to be the calm one, which struck me as odd. Matt sat peacefully in a chair with his hands clasped across his belly watching Elizabeth. For a guy arrested for murder, he seemed rather chill.

Once Elizabeth noticed me standing beside Gabe's desk, she made a beeline for the door. "You're here." The moment the words left her mouth, I sensed something had gone wrong.

"What has you so hot and bothered? You looked like you were going to eat poor Matt for dinner the way you were chewing him up one side."

"Where's Gabe? Have you seen him?" Elizabeth asked, her eyes darting from one corner of the room to the other. "I need to ask him something."

As if on cue, Gabe came strolling through the glass doors leading into the squad room from the hallway.

Elizabeth hurried to meet him before he had a chance to make it to his desk. She stopped him in his tracks.

"Good morning, Elizabeth. I see you've talked to Matt."

"Darn right I've talked to Matt. What are you trying to pull here? Matt says you pulled a confession from him yesterday afternoon when you brought him in. Is that true?"

"No, we didn't pull anything from him. He just started talking."

"Likely story, Gabe. I know how this works. Get them to talk before they think to lawyer up."

"It wasn't like that."

"Then, how was it?" Elizabeth huffed and crossed her arms. I hadn't seen Elizabeth this mad in a long time, but I was curious how they convinced a man I was pretty certain was innocent to confess.

"I swear, he just started talking. He kept saying he wanted us to write up his confession so he could sign it."

"Did you? Has he signed a confession?"

"No, because I don't think he's guilty."

Elizabeth drew in a breath and when she let it out, her shoulders lowered. "You don't think he's guilty."

"No. This confession is too convenient, and some of the things he's saying don't add up with the evidence from the crime scene. It's almost like he's given up."

"Then," I said, "we'd better find out what is motivating this confession and quick, or someone other than you will hear about it, and we won't be able to protect Matt."

"Did you record his confession?" Elizabeth asked.

"No, Floyd and I volunteered to pick him up, since we were working the case. I didn't want a stranger doing it. He started rambling the minute he saw us. We told him to keep quiet until he talked with you. Now, I'm glad Floyd and I were the ones to go. Anyone else would've run with that confession."

"Okay, let's try to keep this under wraps until we figure out what's going on with him. We don't need the D.A. hearing about this." Elizabeth strode toward the interview room. "I'll see if I can get him to shed any light on his sudden need to confess."

Matt's body language told me he wasn't willing to answer her questions. He kept looking away from her as if making eye contact would compel him to tell her his story.

Then it hit me. Everyone tells me their stories. It's part of the reason Elizabeth gave in and hired me, because people seem to want to tell me things even when I don't ask. I went to talk to Elizabeth about giving me a shot at Matt when the glass doors to the hallway flew open and a rattled Lilly Murphy entered the squad room.

Gabe rushed to her. He must have figured she might cause a scene, but that wasn't Lilly's style.

I changed my trajectory and headed toward Lilly, thinking I

might be able to comfort her. But once I was within earshot of the conversation, it was plain Lilly had something she wanted to say, and she wanted to say it immediately.

Gabe guided her to the second interview room where she collapsed into one of the chairs. I followed even though I wasn't invited and shut the door for privacy.

"I've been so worried. I tried to talk to him last night after they arrested him, but they wouldn't let me. Then this morning, he refused to see me." Her words dropped off, her resolve visibly melted, and the tears poured.

"Why wouldn't he see you? Do you know?" I asked, giving her an open invitation to say what she'd come to say.

"It's all my fault. I shouldn't have told him about Bryant."

"Lilly, we talked about this. I had to tell Gabe about your marriage to Bryant. You agreed it would be better for Matt to hear about it from you," She looked so pathetic I had to console her, but I wasn't sure she would welcome it.

"It wasn't the marriage part that upset him. He said he already knew about that." She sniffled.

"That must have been a bit of a relief to you," Gabe said.

"No. He'd been suspicious that Bryant and I might have rekindled our relationship. He thought it was what motivated Bryant to come to Pine Lake in the first place—Bryant had come for me. He said he was worried sick he might lose me to him."

"What did you tell him?" I asked.

"I told him there was no way in Hades I would ever be with Bryant again. Once was enough. The man was the most selfish, self-centered piece of breathing flesh ever to walk the face of the earth. I loathed the man." Lilly fidgeted in her chair. Her lips pulled tight into a straight line. "But that's not why I'm so worried," she said. "I also told him something else, something that only my parents knew and took to their graves."

Okay, I thought, this is it. This is what's lying below the surface of Lilly's heart.

"Lilly, if it can help explain why he's confessed to killing Bryant, you need to tell us," Gabe coaxed. His voice held the right mix of compassion and strength.

"He's confessed to the murder." Lilly gasped. "It wasn't him. You know that, right? It wasn't him." She choked on the sobs.

    Finally, Lilly peered at me with pleading eyes. She needed me to walk with her. To help her carry the burden this story held. From the pained distress on her face, I couldn't imagine what this woman had suffered. I reached my hand out and took hold of hers, trying to strengthen her with my touch.

    "Lilly," I said with a calm I didn't feel, "you need to tell us what's going on."

    "Matt is confessing because he believes I murdered Bryant."

    "Why would he think that?" Gabe asked.

    "Because he knows why I loathe the man and the price I paid for marrying him." She pushed away the tears that rolled down her cheeks. "I told Matt about the baby."

Chapter Twenty-Three

Lilly's shoulders sagged from the weight of her confession.

"The baby?" Gabe asked, confusion written all over his face.

I was no better. Lilly had lost me. "What baby?"

"The one I aborted because Bryant told me to."

"Oh, Lilly, there was a baby?" I asked.

"Yes, I never should've had the abortion, but he left me no choice. Bryant was furious when he found out I was pregnant. He said I spoiled everything. He accused me of wanting a baby so I wouldn't have to work, so I could just stay home and make him support me. He called me worthless and lazy. My Prince Charming had turned into the most grotesque, vile monster. He issued an ultimatum. Him or the baby."

Gabe groaned and plopped in the vacant chair across the table from us. "What a piece of work."

"I was so in love with Bryant and wanted the marriage to work, but I should've known it was doomed. No real man reacts like that. I had always wanted kids, you see, and I never dreamed Bryant didn't. So, I had the abortion. I told myself it was to save my marriage." Lilly removed her hand from mine. My strength was no longer needed. Lilly looked down and shook her head, "I didn't know it at the time, but he was already seeing someone else on the side. A child would have been too much responsibility. Wives he could get rid of, but children are yours forever."

My heart ached for this woman who gave up so much for someone who didn't deserve it.

"Why did Matt think you killed Bryant over this?" Gabe asked.

"Because Matt now knows it was Bryant who cost us our chance for a family. You see, the abortion left me sterile. I couldn't have any more." Lilly covered her eyes, and a single tear wove down her cheek, probably the only one left.

"Matt thought I'd snapped, and to tell you the truth—" She held her head up and looked Gabe straight in the eye. "I might've if it hadn't been for him. Once we were married, I got a good look at what love really was like. Matt was so patient and kind with me. There was a time when we were first married, I cried for no reason, but Matt would sit and hold me. Let me cry it all out."

"So, you didn't want revenge for what Bryant had cost you?" Gabe asked.

"No, by the time Bryant surfaced here, I had what I wanted, a man who loved and respected me. A man who thought I was enough." Lilly's gaze didn't waver. She was telling us her story. The hole Bryant had created in her heart was filled by the love Matt provided.

Matt was the one who loved her so much he was willing to confess to a murder he didn't commit in order to keep her safe.

We left Lilly sitting in the second interrogation room

"Do you think she did it?" I asked Gabe who sat across from me at his desk.

"No, Lilly was so devastated by her actions with the unborn baby she would never have been able to take another life."

"Not even if she felt her present happiness was being threatened?"

"Not even then. But I'm not sure where to go from here. We have someone confessing to a murder he didn't commit, and all the other suspects have pretty solid alibis for that morning." Gabe twirled a pen between his fingers as he sat contemplating our dilemma.

"There is one person who doesn't seem to have a rock-solid alibi, Samantha Holiday."

"You're right. Hers can't be verified. But a lot of people live alone, and at that hour, most people aren't entertaining." He paused. "Even here in Alabama, Southern hospitality only goes so far." Those beautiful dimples of his appeared. After Lilly's story, I found his light humor comforting.

"Yeah, but I have some information which might move Samantha Holiday back to the top of the suspect list."

"Go on." Gabe leaned forward and placed his elbows on the desk.

"Flora said Samantha and Bryant used to go into the Pines for lunch sometimes. Nora overheard a few of their conversations. From one of them, it sounded like Samantha was pressuring Bryant to leave his wife. Samantha was in love with Bryant and wanted him to marry her. According to what Flora told me, they were together for about two years, right before Casey Russell appeared on the scene."

"Eating lunch at the Pines doesn't prove an affair."

"No, but meeting at Neville's Motel most Saturdays does."

"All right, rookie, looks like you've opened up our next line of inquiry. If we can establish a paper trail showing when they were there and maybe how often, along with the fingerprints we found on the plant from the dumpster, we might have enough to get Matt released. While I'm working on that angle, why don't you go see what you can find out from Nora?"

"Okay. I'd like to pay another visit to Samantha as well. Maybe if I show up with more than a hunch, she'll be willing to fill in some of the blanks for me."

"Good idea. I'll get Floyd to pull Bryant's credit-card records and start fishing through them, and I'll go have a little chat with Mr. Neville."

"I'm going to go check on Lilly before I leave, and one of us needs to bring Elizabeth up to speed," I said.

"You go check on Lilly, and I'll give Elizabeth the update. Maybe if I deliver some good news, she'll forgive me for bringing in her client."

"Maybe, but I wouldn't count on it."

Lilly sipped on a cup of water one of the officers had brought to her. I watched her through the glass. She had regained her composure and seemed less frantic now that her story was out.

I poked my head into the room. "Lilly, would you mind staying for a while? Elizabeth might have some questions for you when she's done with Matt."

"No, that's fine. I already called the Junk in the Trunk to let them know I'm going to be out for a couple of days." At this thought, Lilly's bottom lip began to quiver.

"It won't be a couple of days. Elizabeth is working her magic right now to try to get him released," I said.

"I know Elizabeth is trying—" Before Lilly could finish, Elizabeth entered the room.

"Hi, Lilly, are you doing okay?"

Lilly shrugged and continued to sip on her water.

"Um, Amy Kate, can I see you outside for a moment?"

"Sure, Sis." I sensed Elizabeth wanted to wait until we were out of earshot of Lilly to have this conversation.

"Hey, Gabe told me what you found out from Flora. He also clued me in on what Lilly had to say."

"Yeah, isn't that great? It'll help prove Matt didn't have any reason to be jealous of Bryant. Lilly couldn't stand to be in the same room with the jerk. She wasn't interested in anything he had to offer."

"Don't you see, Amy Kate? This might pull the plug on the jealousy motive, but it gives the D.A. bigger and better guns. Now, he can say Matt killed Bryant out of anger over not being able to have kids. The way I understand it, Lilly clearly blames Bryant for their loss."

"Oh." I groaned, not realizing until this moment the implications of Lilly's story. "There must be something I'm missing." I chewed on my bottom lip. "There is one question I still need to ask Lilly, so I might as well ask her now."

Elizabeth followed me into the room where Lilly waited. It would be best if I brought up the plant we had found in the dumpster from a gardener's point of view. I pulled out the chair across from Lilly and took a seat. "Lilly, I know you're an avid gardener. You even have a hothouse, right?"

"Yes, I do." She stared at me with a strange expression on her face. "But I don't see what that has to do with any of this. The detectives decided anyone could've killed Bryant since the foxglove was displayed as centerpieces on the tables in the shop."

"No, my question isn't about the foxglove in the shop. I was thinking of a plant that was in Bryant's office, and for the life of me, I can't figure out who would've given a man like Bryant a plant. Everyone who knew him knew he wasn't the nurturing type."

"Oh." Lilly winced. "To be perfectly honest, I gave Bryant the plant. I saw him the day after his birthday when he came around to talk to Matt about something with the Benson deal. While he was waiting, he mentioned something about his birthday. I wish you could've seen the pathetic look on his face when I asked him how he had celebrated it. He mumbled something, and when I asked him to repeat it, he said he'd celebrated it alone. All I could do was take pity on him, so I gave him one of my plants."

"You won't believe this, Lilly, but he kept that plant in his office."

"I figured it had gone the way of the trash bin."

"That was its final resting place, but Bryant wasn't the one who put it there. Your act of kindness must have touched him. Funny, what things reach people."

Matt entered the room with Gabe never taking his eyes off Lilly. She rushed to him, diving into his open arms.

"Matt, you didn't seriously confess, did you?" Lilly asked.

"Yes, I did. I thought you might've gone and done something foolish, trying to make things right for me like you so often do."

With these words, Matt kissed her forehead as she leaned into him. "I'm so sorry. I should've known better. I haven't been thinking clearly since . . . all this. You know I'd do anything to protect you, darlin'."

"Promise me you won't say another word about being guilty. I don't need your protection. I'm a big girl. I can handle this."

While Matt talked over his case with Elizabeth and Gabe, I snuck out the door to go to Samantha's house.

~

It was nearly lunchtime when I approached Samantha's place, and the monster from the blue lagoon was gurgling in my tummy again. I know better than to ignore my hunger, but I didn't have the time or the resources to feed the monster within. I just hoped it wouldn't get too noisy while I was chatting with Samantha.

She answered the door on the second ring. Today, she was clothed in something other than a bathrobe, and the rat's nest which had passed for her hair at my last visit was tamed. "Come on in." She turned from the door, headed for the couch and plopped down.

"Hey, am I interrupting anything?" I tried to seem open and concerned, although if truth be told, I didn't care if I was interrupting anything or not. As far as I could see, she had the answers I needed.

"No, you're not. I was trying to get motivated to clean up this mess. I've kind of let things go lately." She looked around the living room.

"That's to be expected. After Bryant's death. I understand you two were very close."

"Yes, you made that clear last time you were here."

"Um, I did, didn't I?"

"Yeah, and I didn't appreciate your insinuations, so why don't you tell me why you're here this time, and we'll skip the pleasantries."

"Okay, suits me. I've heard from reliable sources you and Bryant were in fact an item for about two years."

"I see the Pine Lake grapevine has been in rare form this week." She straightened in her seat so she could look me right in the eye.

I blushed. She had guessed my reliable sources.

"Why should I tell you? How will telling you help me?" She asked.

"I don't know how it'll help you, but it might help Matt Murphy. He was arrested yesterday afternoon."

"Matt was arrested?" Her brows furrowed.

"Yeah, he was." I hoped this news would loosen her tongue.

She thought for more than a moment, making me wonder if she regretted telling me anything. "Yeah, we were an item for about two years. The rat had the nerve to promise me he was going to leave his wife. He chased me for four years and wore down my resistance. Bryant could be rather charming at times. Now I know while he was chasing me, he was seeing some other girl in the office."

"How do you know that?" I asked, rather impressed with Samantha for being quick on the uptake.

"Let's just say some of your reliable sources are also some of mine. You can't sneeze in this town without half the population saying, 'Bless you.' It's ridiculous." She rolled her eyes.

I couldn't help but chuckle. She had our small town pegged.

"The funny thing is, I still loved him." She leaned over and pulled a tissue from the box sitting on the coffee table.

I moved from the armchair to a spot on the couch next to her and found myself wrapping my right arm around her shoulders.

She laid her head on my shoulder and dabbed her eyes with the crumpled tissue. "I know I shouldn't, but I do. And I hate myself for it. I swore after the way he dropped me for Casey, I'd never give him the time of day, but I was fooling myself." She nestled her head on my shoulder and sobbed.

I let her finish her cry before I pushed on with my questions. After all, I didn't want to appear heartless. Once she calmed down, I moved back to the armchair where I could be detached and free from bias for our next topic.

"Did you drive one of the SUVs to the Beans and Leaves the morning of the murder?" I asked.

"I had to see him. I was going to give him my resignation, but I had to try and talk to him one last time. A better word for it would be plead. How pathetic is that?" The disgust in her voice tinged her words. "I wanted him to know I was willing to take him back on his terms, that I was through badgering him to marry me. If all he wanted was to be together, I was good with it."

"What was his response?"

"He said he hated to see me go. I was a good administrative assistant, but I had to do what I had to do."

"What about the pleading?"

"He stopped it before I ever started by informing me, he'd replaced me in his bed with ease. Replacing me in the office wouldn't be hard either. So, there was no pleading. In that moment, I grasped the fact it had to be over for me. I'd given him everything, so I decided to leave while I had a shred of self-respect left. If I begged him to let me stay, he would've taken advantage of my vulnerability and even that shred of dignity would have been gone." She sighed. "So, I gave him my letter of resignation, climbed into the SUV, and tore out."

"Did the car alarm on the SUV go off? Do you remember?"

"Of course, I remember. It was five o'clock in the morning, for Pete's sake. You don't forget almost waking the dead. I was so upset about what happened I pushed the wrong button while I was trying to unlock the truck. It took me forever to get the blasted thing to shut off."

"That explains the alarm Lilly heard that morning. You do understand in telling me this, you're putting yourself at the top of the suspect list."

"I don't have anything to worry about. The last time I saw him, he was alive and walking through the back door of the coffee shop."

"Maybe, but what you told me places you at the scene of the crime, and once Lieutenant Cooper finds the paper trail from where you and Bryant spent some cozy Saturday afternoons at Neville's Motel, it will be enough for the D.A. to release Matt and start looking in your direction. And since several in Pine Lake know he threw you over for Casey Russell, I'm betting the D.A. might take a hard look at the woman scorned as motive for murder. So, if I were you, I'd find a good lawyer."

I picked up my purse from beside the armchair. I didn't want to mention the fingerprints found on the plant from the dumpster. She could find out about that through the regular channels. A person can only handle so much bad news at one time.

With my purse in my lap, I glanced at Samantha. "I'm sorry to have to do this to you, but my job is to give the D.A. somebody other than Matt Murphy to look at as a suspect." I stood and walked to the door, knowing in less than an hour, Samantha Holiday's world would fall apart. I wasn't feeling particularly great about it. After all, the woman had just sobbed her heart out on my shoulder. My blouse was still damp from her tears, and here I was using her to get what I wanted, which was Matt out of jail. Boy, I felt lower than the wolf that was buried last Saturday.

With my hand on the knob of the front door, I turned. "Like you said, though, if you didn't do it, then you shouldn't have anything to worry about."

She nodded and managed a weak smile.

If I was her, I'd still call a lawyer.

On my way to the bookshop, I sent Flora a text to see if she wanted me to pick up some Chinese takeout for lunch. I could use some comfort food, and we both loved the food at Wrong's Place. It was supposed to be Wong's Place, but there had been a mix-up with the lettering on the sign for the grand opening.

Since Mr. Wong had been divorced three times to date and was working on the fourth, he doesn't mind being called Mr. Wrong. As he likes to say, marriage has proven he is not Mr. Wright.

While I waited for the food to be ready, I called Gabe and told him what I had learned from Samantha. He said with the credit card receipts, along with the information he obtained from Mr. Neville and his wife, the D.A. should be picking Samantha up for questioning by the end of the day.

"What about Matt?" I asked, the scent of beef and broccoli wafting in my direction, making my stomach growl.

"He should be released soon. I'm so glad Floyd and I were the ones to pick him up. He doesn't know how lucky he is. If anyone else had gotten hold of him while he was confessing ninety-to-nothing, it wouldn't have ended up as well for him, even with the evidence on Samantha."

"I'm sure he's learned his lesson. Lilly's tougher than he gives her credit for and can take care of herself."

"Yeah, you're right. She's got a lot of gumption. Did you ever make it to Nora's?"

"No, but I can go over there after lunch if you need me to." I handed Mr. Wong my debit card to pay for the food.

"No, I can handle it from here. You did your job and got Matt off the hook."

"So, you don't think he's still considered a suspect by the D.A.?"

"No, I wouldn't think so. The evidence against Samantha is solid. We have e a potential murder weapon with her fingerprints on it. We have the love affair gone wrong, and we have her at the scene of the crime. That's a hefty list."

"Yeah, it is when you put it all together like that. I have this feeling we're missing something though. Something obvious."

"No, if you ask me, I think we've wrapped things up pretty neatly. It's hard for you to imagine anyone being capable of murder, especially someone like Samantha. Someone whose only fault is falling in love with the wrong guy."

"You're right. So, I guess that leaves Matt in the clear, and Elizabeth will be breathing a sigh of relief." I thought about some of the glares Elizabeth shot Gabe earlier that morning and chuckled. If it was up to Elizabeth, Gabe would be walking around with a few extra holes in his body. "I'd better go. The food's ready, and Flora won't be pleased if it's cold when she gets it."

"No, she won't, and we need to keep our connection to the Pine Lake grapevine happy."

I clicked off my cell and hefted the bag of sweet-smelling Asian goodness into the car, filling it with the aroma. Today was a good day.

The food hit the spot, and the monster living inside me was once again quieted. As we were finishing up, Carter's wife, Maureen, bounded into the shop with Carter on her heels.

"Ladies, Carter has been telling me so much about you two I had to stop in and introduce myself." Maureen drawled with a South Carolina accent. Dressed in the latest fashion, she wore some rather large beads and bangles, but it seemed to complement her short, stout body and her silver hair. I knew within minutes Maureen Cooper was going to be someone I liked.

"This is Amy Kate Anderson, my boss, and this feisty young woman is Flora," Carter said.

Flora giggled.

"Don't mind him, ladies." Maureen turned to watch her husband. "He's often up to no good. I can just imagine what kind of mischief he gets into here without me keeping a watchful eye on him." She laughed.

"Oh, I can't imagine our Carter getting into any trouble," Flora said.

Maureen leaned closer to us with a conspiratorial air. "If he ever gets to be a handful, you two let me know. I have the cure for that ailment." We laughed.

"I am so glad you came by today, Mrs. Cooper," I said.

"Oh, please, it's Maureen."

"Okay, Maureen. You were on my to-do list."

"Did you hear that, Carter? I was on her to-do list. It seems I've made the list. Have you?" She poked her husband in his ribs with her elbow.

"No, I don't think I have, dear. But there's only one list I care to make and that's yours." Carter lifted his wife's hand from off the counter and kissed it.

She giggled like a teenager in love. What a wonderful pair these two made.

"How in heaven's name did I make your to-do list?"

"Your son asked me to bake him some oatmeal raisin cookies in payment for bumping into his car." I thought it better not to mention the whole scenario about his car eating my clothes.

"You bumped into Baby?" Maureen gasped, wide eyed.

"If Baby is his car, then yes." I made a mental note to rag Gabe about calling his car Baby. "I was wondering if you could give me your recipe for the cookies. Since he bragged so much about how good yours were, I thought I'd make him what he likes."

"What a splendid idea. Now, these cookies are for Gabe and not Michael, right?"

"Michael? Do you know Michael Cooper?"

"Certainly, we know Michael." She gave Carter, who was standing right next to her, a knowing look. Carter winked at her, and then she turned her attention back to me. "And from what I understand, so do you. You had a date with him this past Saturday night."

"I think you're confused. I had a date with a Michael Cooper, but he was a no-show. But I did run into Gabe, and after my date didn't appear, he joined me for coffee and dessert."

"Oh . . . I see," Maureen said as both she and Carter shook

their heads and grinned at me. "I believe my confusion is clearing."

Carter chuckled. "Yes, I'm getting a clearer picture too."

Chapter Twenty-Four

"You see dear, Michael and—" The bell on the door announcing a customer interrupted Maureen. It was Mrs. Darcy coming in to purchase the elusive first edition of *Little Women* she wanted.

Flora swept from behind the counter and went to greet Mrs. Darcy. Both Flora and Carter were so pleased to have located the first edition they beamed with pride at their accomplishment, and Mrs. Darcy could not say enough nice things about them or their research skills.

Once Mrs. Darcy had caught up on the latest town chitchat with Flora, she said her good-byes.

"Maureen, I am so sorry for the interruption." I turned my focus back to her. "I sure appreciate your willingness to share your recipe with me. Hope it's not some sort of family secret."

"Good gravy, no. I got it off a box of raisins years ago. Carter and the boys all loved it, so it became the one I made. I'll be glad to email it to you if you'll give me your address."

"Sure. Let me grab a business card, and I'll write my personal email on the back. That way you can have both."

"Fine, fine, I'll be sure to send it to you today. When do you have to deliver your payment of cookies?"

"Sunday. He was merciful to me and gave me a little time since I've been working on getting the shop up and trying to help Elizabeth with the murder investigation. I told him I was a little busy this week."

Maureen grinned at my humor.

"You know that was always one surefire way I could tell the boys apart. Gabe and Seth would eat the oatmeal raisin cookies until they were about to pop, but Michael didn't care for them as much. So, he'd stop after one or two."

"Oh, so Michael is your son too. That must be why you think I've met him, but I haven't. I only know Gabe."

"No, sweetie, you've met Michael. You just don't know it," she said with an air of mystery, glancing over her shoulder at Carter, who looked at me with a lopsided grin on his face.

"Go ahead and tell her, Maureen. She deserves to know. They've had their bit of fun with her. Now, it's time she knew."

"I'm not following."

"The man you had dessert with at Hooks Saturday night was Michael Cooper," Maureen said slowly, as if she were giving me a clue to something.

"No," I answered in the same slow manner. "it was Gabe."

Maureen shook her head. "You're not getting it, dear. The man Saturday night was Michael. I know because he told me what a wonderful time he had with you, and how much you two seemed to have in common."

"No, the man I had dessert with—" The pieces of the puzzle started to fall into place. "Oh, I see. The picture *is* getting clearer." I was a little miffed at being taken.

"Yes, sweetie. Michael and Gabe are twins. We named them after the archangels in the Bible, Michael and Gabriel. They were such strong names."

A picture of Uncle Bob's extra, extra hot sauce popped into my brain. It was going to be a prominent ingredient in Maureen's famous oatmeal raisin cookies—at least the batch I was going to whip up for the Cooper men. What's the saying, "Liar, liar, pants on fire"? Well, come Sunday afternoon a lot more was going to be on fire than some stinking pair of pants. I was going to make sure these two culprits got what was coming to them, and I was not above spicing things up. Literally.

~

Elizabeth called later in the afternoon to say Matt had been released. I heard the relief in her voice. "Amy Kate, you did a great job for me on this case. I wouldn't have been half as far along in the investigation had I tried to do it myself. You have a knack for this. I'm glad you talked me into hiring you."

"I appreciate the compliment, Sis."

"What would you say about teaming up with me on a permanent part-time basis?"

"I'd say you've lost your mind. I've had my fill of interviews and clues."

"That's what I thought you'd say." She sounded amused. "But I want you to consider it. I've been using those guys from out of town too long. I need someone local, and it won't be the creeper."

"Now, you know the creeper is a town icon like Uncle Cyrus. You can't go around decimating his character like that. You could be sued for libel." I enjoyed prodding her a little.

"So, let him sue me. But unless doomsday hits, I am *not* working with that guy."

"Got it."

"So, what about my offer? Will you at least think about it?"

"Elizabeth, I appreciate the fact you took a chance on me for this case, and I really needed the money. But I already have a job. I love my bookshop."

"Come on, it could be fun." She lowered her voice. "And think of all the time you could spend with Gabe the Babe." Elizabeth sure knew how to play dirty.

"No, I'm good. If Gabe wants to see me, he can ask me out on a date."

"All right, I understand. I also wanted to let you know I have your check."

"Hallelujah." I'd be able to make payroll. Now if the book signing with Tom Perkins could make up the difference, Twisted Plots might be back in the black.

~

Julia was pumped when I told her about the evidence Gabe and I had found, connecting Samantha to the crime. As we discussed the day's events over dinner, I confided in Julia that I felt as if I were missing something about the case, but for the life of me, I couldn't put my finger on it.

She assured me I had done my best, and with Matt off the D.A.'s radar, there was nothing more to worry about. She was right.

Once we finished dinner, I went to my room and pulled out the porcelain angel I had bought for Theresa. I wanted to get it ready to drop off on my way into work the next day. I placed it in the center of the tissue paper and contemplated the best way to wrap it. Since I hadn't remembered to bring a box, I opted to use a pretty pink bag instead.

I gazed down at the delicate piece, and the beauty of the angel struck me. The scalloped wings gave it a uniqueness all its own. The wings. Something about the angel figurine felt so familiar.

Where had I seen this before?

The feeling I was overlooking something washed over me again, but it waned when I concentrated on what to write on the card.

After I wrapped the gift, I went to the kitchen to load the dishwasher. I asked Julia, who had gone to the living room, if she would be interested in a cup of coffee to top off the wonderful meal, she had made for us.

I loved it when the wedding season was over because it meant Julia was home most evenings to cook, but it also meant I would have to diet before swimsuit season. Oh, the seasons of life. How they rule my world.

I pulled the coffeemaker out from under the counter and rinsed out the residue from yesterday's pot, then dug around for the coffee and filters in the pantry. Julia likes to keep them together. It makes sense to her, and since she's the kitchen diva, I do things her way to keep her happy. I decided to use the decaf coffee since I wanted to sleep tonight. Regular coffee in the morning is great. Regular coffee at night, not so much.

"Julia, are you going to want one cup or two?" I called into the living room from the kitchen.

"Are you making decaf or regular?"

"Decaf."

"Make enough for two then, please."

I fumbled with the measuring cup, counting by twos to

myself. Placing the pot into the machine, I pushed the "on" button, thinking I should redo this process before bedtime, so we could have our coffee ready in the morning. Nothing compares to waking to the smell of fresh coffee. How I love that delay button.

"The delay button."

"Stupid, stupid, stupid," I cried. "Of course."

"What is it?" Julia's feet padded across the carpet toward the kitchen.

"The delay button. That's what I was missing."

"Do you mean in the case?"

"Yes, I know why Samantha didn't seem worried. It's because she had no reason to be. She's innocent."

"Okay, but what does the delay button on the coffeemaker have to do with Samantha's innocence?"

"Everything. We've been looking at everyone's alibis for the morning of the murder, but they're useless. The killer didn't have to be at the coffee shop in order to commit the murder. He or she could have waited until the evening shift left and then prepared the coffee pot the night before, the way we do with our delay button. The poison must have been in the coffee when Bryant went to drink his first cup of the day."

"Talk about packin' a punch. That's a cup I'd rather miss."

"Yeah, I'm sure Bryant would agree with you."

"Okay, that makes sense. Both the urns and the regular pot you said Bryant liked to drink would have been set up the night before."

"Not necessarily. I think Matt did the urns for the taste tests himself. So, they might not have been set up ahead of time."

I started pacing back and forth across the kitchen floor. "That means the poison was in the coffeemaker. Gabe's probably not received the report back from the lab. Everything was so damaged in the fire, including the half-melted coffeemaker. It's taking a while."

Julia leaned against the door jamb, immersed in our conversation. "But if it were set up the night before, then that means the killer would have needed a key to the store."

"You're right, it does, my clever friend, and Samantha, Casey, and Ed didn't have keys to the Beans and Leaves, nor would they have had easy access to them."

"What about Matt and Lilly? I hate to say it, but they're the two who have the easiest access to the shop, and no one would think anything odd about seeing them going in and out of the place after hours. No one would even notice."

"True, but there is one other person who would've had easy access to the keys, and who made darn sure to have a tidy alibi for the time of the murder, and she fits our woman-scorned theory." I whisked by Julia and proceeded to the coat rack to grab my things.

"Where are you going?" Julia asked.

"Lawn service in January, my eye," I muttered. "Call Gabe. I'm headed to Sarah Catherine's. Tell him to meet me there."

~

I rang the bell three times at Sarah Catherine's door. The porch light popped on. I squinted against the brilliant light until my eyes adjusted. The curtain in the small window beside the door moved. Her face appeared in the pane seconds before the door opened.

"Oh, Amy Kate, what are you doing here at this hour? I hope everything's all right." She sounded concerned.

"Yes, everything's fine. Do you mind if I come in? You and I need to have a little chat about the Beans and Leaves."

"About the Beans and Leaves? You do know Matt is now the sole owner of the Beans and Leaves shop. I don't have any interest in it any longer since Bryant and Matt signed the contract before Bryant's death."

"Yes, I'm aware of that, but you'll want to hear what I have to say, since it concerns what happened there on Wednesday."

Her face turned pale under the glare of the porch light. "You mean the day of the murder?"

"Yes, it's about that day." I was determined to have this conversation with Sarah Catherine whether she wanted to hear or not. She looked as if she was going to tell me to come back at another time, and I was ready to stick my foot in the doorway, but she invited me in.

Once the front door closed, Sarah Catherine led the way down a hall past a flight of stairs to her study. She stopped outside the door. "I was about to have some tea. It's one of the specialties from the shop. Can I interest you in a cup?"

Realizing that I had forgotten all about my coffee, I accepted Sarah Catherine's offer. "The tea sounds great. It'll warm me up."

"The study is in here." She pointed to her right. "I'll go get the tea." She continued down the hall disappearing through a doorway.

I turned and entered a room filled with books and maps and two leather chairs that were angled toward a fireplace. The room looked to be straight out of a Victorian novel.

She returned a few minutes later and placed the tea tray on the oval table between the two chairs. It held two small teapots and two cups along with a sugar bowl and creamer.

"Sugar?" Sarah Catherine smiled as she stood to serve.

"Do you have any honey?" I asked.

"No, I'm sorry."

"Okay, sugar will be fine. Thank you." I tried to be as pleasant as she had been. "I'm sorry for showing up like this, but I thought we should have a talk about the night of the murder. I might have found some new information."

"You mean the morning of the murder, don't you?" she corrected.

"No, I mean the night before the murder, or I guess the night the murder was prepared."

Sarah Catherine moved to the second leather chair and took a seat. "What do you mean the night the murder was prepared?" Her brows furrowed.

"Is it all right with you if I'm frank?" I asked.

"Certainly." Sarah Catherine added a spoonful of sugar to her own cup and stirred.

"You see, I believe whoever killed Bryant put the poison in the coffeemaker the night before, so there was no need to be present that morning. Bryant either drank the poisoned coffee that had been brewed by the use of the delay button, or—and this is kind of sad—he pushed the button to start the brew dripping himself. Either way, the murderer could have prepared the coffeemaker any time between closing Tuesday night and Bryant's arrival Wednesday morning." I took a sip of my tea to buy some time, wanting to see how Sarah Catherine reacted to this news.

She pursed her lips, and I could tell she was thinking over what I said.

"Oh, I suppose that means it had to be someone with access to the store. To get in after hours and all. Have the police started questioning the employees who had keys?"

Was it me, or was she fishing for information?

"No, not yet," I said. "I just grasped all this myself. I haven't had time to talk it over with the lieutenant, but once he knows, they will." I nodded, taking a sip of tea.

Sarah Catherine put down her own cup and leaned back in her chair. She had finished her tea and watched me as I finished mine. "So, you haven't discussed this with the police?"

"No, but I was wondering. Do you have a key to the coffee shop?"

"I'm sure I have one around here somewhere, but I have no idea where. Bryant did keep a spare at one time."

A feeling of relaxation passed over me. "Of course, that makes sense." I found myself fighting the overwhelming desire to curl up in the chair and sleep as the warmth of the fire surrounded me.

"I see you've finished your tea, Amy Kate, and I don't suspect you'll need any more." Sarah Catherine stood and removed a pair of gloves from her front pants pocket and without rushing, poked each finger into its assigned hole. She then moved toward me.

Slumped in the chair, I tried to get up, but my arms and legs wouldn't cooperate. I was glued to my spot, helpless. *Oh Julia,* I thought as I fought the need to sleep, *please make that call.*

My eyes drooped although I fought to hold them open. Whatever was in the tea was winning.

Sarah Catherine took a piece of paper out of the drawer in the oval table. She then took my limp hand and laid it on the paper, pressing my prints all over it. Once done, she leaned over me and poked it into the pocket of my coat.

"You see, I couldn't let Bryant take anything else from me. I couldn't. He'd already taken so much. My hopes for children, my dreams of love. He'd run through my fortune, spending it on other women. I couldn't let him cheat me out of my share of the millions from the sale of Java Vein. That's why he'd pushed Matt so hard to sign the contract. He needed the money." She sighed. "If he'd simply been able to love only me. But—" She stood straight. "—we know he couldn't. It wasn't in his DNA.

She moved to the front of the fireplace and stopped. "When the divorce papers came, I made a decision. He wasn't getting anything else from me. I'd given him the best part of my life, and in return, he gave me nothing." Her eyes roamed over the room.

She was making sure there was nothing to place me here. *No, she's going to move me.*

She retrieved my teacup from my limp hand and set it on the table.

I willed myself to say something, anything, to stop her. "Contract," I forced the word from my lips. I wasn't sure she heard me.

"I'd seen the article about the sale of the company, and I knew he had no intention of giving me my share. Even though it was my money we invested. So, you see there was no way around it. For me to get what I deserved, he had to go."

She squatted down so she was eye level with me. "And unfortunately, I don't see any way around this either. I regret having to do this, but I can't go to prison. This is the only way. They will find you in your car with Samantha's resignation letter in your coat pocket. Samantha's perfect. She had access to the foxglove and the key. Someone else has to be the killer, and as you proved by showing up tonight, I need to give them a better suspect than me." She stood.

My eyes grew heavy. I could no longer keep them open. *I must sleep.* Darkness flooded in. Quiet surrounded me. The need to drift on this wave of darkness engulfed me. I gave in to it and drifted down past the black, following the little porcelain angel of peace into the stillness.

Somewhere from far away, noises and voices sounded and then a crash and the sound of thumping. I couldn't decide if it was the sound of footsteps or my heartbeat. Someone said, "Hold on, Amy Kate, the ambulance is coming."

A rush of cold air pushed into my lungs and someone yelled, "Out of the way."

~

When I awoke in a hospital bed in one of the emergency room cubicles, half the town of Pine Lake was in there with me. Gabe stood next to my bed.

My head hurt, my stomach hurt, and breathing wasn't much fun either.

"What happened?" Pain ran through my throat. Words irritated my vocal cords. I clutched my throat with my hand.

"You, my dear friend, had your stomach pumped." Julia sat beside me on the bed.

"I feel like I got run over by a semi, twice." My words came out sounding like a teenage choir boy going through puberty.

"No, the culprit was Sarah Catherine's specialty tea laced with foxglove," Gabe explained. "Don't you know not to eat or drink anything when you're investigating a case where poison is involved?" he asked.

"Do now," I said, humbled by his reproof.

"You had me worried there. I hate to think what would've happened to you if Julia hadn't called me when she did."

"Thank you, Julia." I squeezed my friend's hand.

"My pleasure." She leaned over and hugged me tight. "I'm going to go home and let you have a minute with your family. Gabe said he'd give you a lift to the apartment, and we'll go get your car from Sarah Catherine's tomorrow."

"Sarah Catherine." I pushed up on my elbow. "Did you get her?"

"Yes," Dad said, "but if Gabe had been any later, I'm afraid you wouldn't have survived."

I turned to Gabe and winked. "My hero." I figured it was a gesture he could appreciate.

~

Gabe was kind enough to drive me home from the hospital. As I unlocked my apartment door, I made my confession. "I have something I need to give to you."

"Is it something I want?"

"Maybe," I answered with downcast eyes. "But you probably wanted it before now."

The stairwell light threw shadows on Gabe's frowning face. "What are you talking about?"

"Wait here." I entered the apartment. It didn't take me long to dig the shard of porcelain out of my jewelry box where I had placed it almost a week ago. I found Gabe leaning against the door jamb. "Here." I handed it to him.

"What is it?" Gabe held the piece up toward the light.

"It's a piece of porcelain I found at the Beans and Leaves the day of the murder."

"What?" He stood up straight.

"I took it...from the crime scene."

"You what?" Gabe's lips pulled tight and the nerve by his jaw throbbed. "You do know I could haul you in for obstruction? Not to mention tampering with evidence." Gabe threw up his hands in disbelief and turned his back to me.

I reached out and caught his arm, moving to stand in front of him. "Gabe, you've got to believe I didn't know it was important. I knelt to clean up the stuff that had been knocked over and saw it under the counter. Since I didn't find anything else broken, I was going to throw it away. Then Mr. 'you can't be in here' came along and tossed me out. At that point, I stuck it in my pocket and forgot about it." I shrugged.

"What do you mean you didn't know it was important?" Gabe had caught that.

"Tonight, I was wrapping a gift for Theresa Thornton. It was a porcelain angel with scalloped wings. The wings looked just like the shard."

"So, how is that significant?"

"Because as I was drifting into la la land tonight, I remembered Lilly telling me the angels had come into the store on Tuesday and Sarah Catherine had purchased one. So, the only way this piece of the angel's wing could have been in the coffee shop Wednesday morning is if Sarah Catherine was in the coffee shop sometime after the antique dealer made his delivery. So, this puts Sarah Catherine at the scene of the crime."

After a few moments of silence, Gabe handed me back the shard. "You know, you are one lucky lady."

"What do you mean?" I asked, confused.

"It's a good thing Sarah Catherine tried to kill you because now we don't need that shard for our case. Otherwise, you would be up to your neck in an obstruction charge."

"I never thought I'd consider almost being killed lucky, but if it keeps me out of jail, I'll count it as a blessing."

Gabe sighed and stared at me. He took my hands in his, leaned slightly forward, and invaded my personal space. "You're done digging around at crime scenes. I can't always be there to protect you."

"Protecting me isn't your job."

"Yes, it is. As an officer of the law, it is my job. So, please don't make it any harder for me. Stay away from trouble." Then, Lieutenant Gabe Cooper ever so gently kissed me on my cheek and left.

I stood a moment not sure what had happened. It was like one of those scenes from a superhero movie where the hero saves the girl, steals a kiss, and then flies off into the night sky. Except my hero asked me, the trouble magnet, to stay out of trouble. He might as well have asked me not to breathe.

Chapter Twenty-Five

"Amen," Joe Anderson said.

"Amen," echoed the crowd gathered around his table. I sat in my usual place next to Elizabeth. Dad had invited the whole crew from the hospital cubicle to Sunday lunch. Everyone was there, my sisters and their families. Julia, the Coopers, and both Michael and Gabe had accepted the invitation as well as Chet Baker.

Chet just wanted to make sure I remembered our deal about his exclusive for the *Pine Lake Daily News*. He made a beeline to the hospital when he'd heard over his police scanner what had happened to me. I'm not sure if he came to check on me or the story. After all, it is a little hard to get an interview from a dead person.

That's why we're celebrating today. I'm not dead. Still slightly sore, a little humiliated, wary of tea, but definitely not dead.

As the bowls and platters were passed around, Dad told Gabe, "I'm so glad you acted as quickly as you did when Julia called. I'd hate to think what today would have held for us if you hadn't."

"Yeah, Gabe, I'm so glad you answered my call," Julia echoed.

"As weird as this may sound, I had my phone in my hand when it rang. I had taken it out in order to call Amy Kate."

"What were you calling her for?" Alexia asked.

"Floyd and I received the forensic report on the

coffeemaker Tuesday, but I didn't tell Amy Kate or Elizabeth about it because I asked the lab to do one more test on it. We had a hunch there might be a fingerprint on the tab of the basket that held the grounds. It was mangled, but we thought it was worth a shot."

"Was there?" I asked.

"Yes, Sarah Catherine's." Gabe said.

"Oh," Elizabeth said, "so you were going to call Amy Kate to warn her Sarah Catherine had become a prime suspect."

"Right. Then I got Julia's call telling me Amy Kate was headed to Sarah Catherine's and was convinced she was our killer. I headed over there to stop her."

"At first, I thought it was Samantha Holiday. Then it became clear to me it was Sarah Catherine. If this had been a murder mystery book, it would have been Samantha Holiday. A crime of passion."

Gabe grinned at me. "If only life were like books. Think of all the twisted plots there'd be for us to unravel."

"True, true." Chet balanced a huge helping of mashed potatoes on his fork. "But life is so full of such unexpected and twisted outcomes, who needs fiction? That's why I report on real life. Look at how reality TV has taken off."

"I hate reality TV." Elizabeth shot him a look.

Changing the subject, Carter asked, "What happened when you arrived at Sarah Catherine's?"

"Once I saw Amy Kate's car in the driveway, I panicked and called for backup. When I banged on the door and no one came, I rushed in and found her slumped back in her chair. It was then I saw Amy Kate's fists roll up, and she began to convulse. I called for an ambulance. Luckily, a squad car was on patrol in the neighborhood and heard my call. They caught Sarah Catherine as she came around the back of the house."

"Wow." Carter nodded his approval. Grant even added his sentiments by banging his spoon on the table.

"So, that makes you a real-life hero, Gabe," Dad said, "and I owe you my thanks."

Gabe's gaze met mine. "No, you don't, Mr. Anderson. I'm just glad our girl is safe."

Warm admiration flooded into his eyes, and a tingle ran

through me. *Our girl?* I liked the sound of that.

Carter cleared his throat. Lost in thought for a moment, time stood still for me in the eyes of Gabe Cooper. I blushed.

"Amy Kate, sweetie, didn't you promise someone some oatmeal raisin cookies?" Maureen asked.

I admit having a slight twinge of guilt over what I was about to do since Gabe had saved my life, but then I remembered all the chances these two Cooper men had been given to fess up about tricking me. They hadn't taken any of them. Nope, Gabe Cooper's eyes were about to be warm, but it wasn't going to be because of admiration. "Why yes, Maureen, I do have those cookies as promised."

I rose from the table and went to the kitchen to fetch the two platters of cookies. One tray, of course, was for Michael and Gabe, and the other one was for everyone else.

"Here you go." I handed off the regular cookies to my dad to pass around. I then held out the platter to Michael and Gabe. "And these are for you two. I made these special just like your mom makes them. Ivanhoe, I hope you enjoy them."

Michael stopped before he took a bite. "You know, Gabe, we do owe Amy Kate an apology for stringing her along."

"*We* owe her an apology?" Gabe asked. "I don't recall being the one who told her I was you. I believe *you* owe her an apology,"

"Now, guys, if you think about it, you both owe her an apology," Maureen said in true motherly fashion. "After all, either one of you could have cleared it up for her, but neither one of you did."

"She's right. I'm sorry for not telling you who I was the other night at Hooks. It seemed easier to let you think I was Gabe. It sort of took care of all that first-date nervousness since you thought you already knew me."

"Yeah, I should have straightened it out when you told me about our coffee and dessert. Sorry," Gabe said.

As these words left their mouths and the cookies entered, I leapt across the table to snatch the cookies from their lips.

I was too late. The shocked looks on their faces made me feel awful. They shot up from their seats, spitting and sputtering. Cookies flew everywhere.

Gabe grabbed Alexia's water glass and downed it. Looking at me, he bellowed, "You little—" He couldn't get any more words out before he broke into a coughing fit.

I decided it might be time for me to go home. On my way through the kitchen, I found Michael, with his tongue under the spigot, the water on high. His shirt was drenched, but he didn't seem to care.

As I passed by, he glanced up at me and grinned. "Now we're even," then dove back under the spigot, lapping at the water like a dog.

Note to self, half a cup of Uncle Bob's extra hot, hot sauce is just about the right amount to leave a man speechless.

As I closed the back door, I heard Maureen laughing as she announced to her two grown sons, "That girl's trouble with a capital T. I *like* her."

EPILOGUE

The book signing with Tom Perkins had turned into a major town event. Family, friends, acquaintances, book lovers, those who were out to be seen, and lookie-loos came to the Twisted Plots to meet the famous author.

My team of worker bees had spread the word so well there were times I was afraid we were breaking the fire code for the number of occupants the building could hold.

The book signing held earlier in the day turned into a storytelling fest with Mr. Perkins captivating his audience with tales from his former profession as a police hostage negotiator. To say the crowd listened intently was an understatement. They were mesmerized by the thrilling tales of murders and serial killers.

Julia catered the evening's meet-and-greet for me and outdid herself. The sweet-and-sour meatballs were a huge success along with everything else.

My workroom had been turned into a miniature kitchen with crockpots and toaster ovens plugged in everywhere, keeping food warm. For the cold food, Julia had brought in several professional-grade coolers and a small dorm refrigerator by the back wall. The entire weekend exceeded my expectations.

Everyone disbanded somewhere around nine-thirty, and we sent Tom Perkins off with a check and a hearty thank you.

I sat in one of the club chairs by the window, rubbing my aching toes, which felt so good after being on them all day.

Julia was in the back cleaning up the last of the platters and bowls. A swish of cold air came in the shop when the door opened. I glanced up to find Matt Murphy standing inside the doorway.

"Matt." I jumped up to greet him. We hadn't talked much since the arrest. "Come in. Sit with me."

"No, I can't stay long. I wanted to see how the book signing went. It looked like the whole town was here."

"I know. We planned for maybe a hundred, but I think we had closer to two. I don't know how Julia pulled it off. She had to send Kirk out for a few items and wound up doing some improvising."

"She's good at that." Matt smiled.

"Yes." I gestured toward the chairs. "Are you sure you don't want to sit down?"

"Gotta go. I was in the middle of prepping the store for its opening on Monday and I need to finish. I just wanted to thank you again for all that you and Elizabeth did for us. I haven't seen my Lilly so happy in years."

"Secrets do have a way of weighing us down."

"Yes, they do. But Lilly and I agreed no more secrets between us." He chuckled and turned toward the door. "We've learned our lesson. I guess I'd better get back. She'll be looking for me."

I stopped him before he could push the door open. "Are you still going through with the deal with Benson Corporation to sell the other stores?"

"Yes, it's a good deal, and we'll need the money so Lilly and I can fix up the old place and plan our retirement. She wants to enlarge her greenhouse." He shrugged. "We have always dreamed of growing old together in this little town. It seems—thanks to you—we'll be able to do just that. Me with my piece of heaven and she with hers." He opened the door, then stopped. "The simple things, Amy Kate. That's what makes life worthwhile."

I contemplated those words as I walked to the door to lock it. He was right. It was the simple things in life that added to its richness: family, friends, people you love and those who love you. Matt was on to something.

I was settling into my chair when a rap on the glass door

broke my train of thought. I slipped my shoes back on before going to see who it was.

The sight warmed my heart. Standing on the other side of the glass was Gabe Cooper, holding up a bag from Mr. Wrong's Place.

He yelled through the glass, "Can I come in?" Then he flashed a boyish grin and pointed to the bag.

There was no way I was going to tell him how stuffed I was from all the food Julia had supplied for the event. I couldn't refuse his offer of good company and great food, especially after the Uncle Bob's hot-sauce incident.

I pushed the door open, and he hurried through to keep the cold air out.

I wasn't sure what to say to him, having not seen either Gabe or Michael since the cookie delivery. As I relocked the door, I tried to think of a way to apologize.

But I shouldn't have worried. Gabe had thought of everything, including how to get the conversation rolling. "So, I thought it was time I made good on that invitation for you to join me for Chinese." He unloaded the bag of goodies onto the square coffee table sitting in the center of the four club chairs.

"Oh, you did, did you?" I noticed Gabe was very much at ease. He made himself at home in the chair closest to the wall. Any awkwardness of the situation was lost on him.

"Yep," he leaned forward, pointing to the containers. "Here we have sweet-and sour-pork. In this little container, we have Chicken Lo Mein—"

"Yum, one of my favorites." I couldn't hide my pleasure at his thoughtfulness.

"And over here, all wrapped up to keep them warm, are the egg rolls."

"Awesome. What would Chinese be without the egg rolls?" I took the seat across from him.

"Most certainly," he said with a serious expression that transformed into a playful smile. "You can't enjoy Chinese without the egg rolls stuffed with all those unidentifiable ingredients."

"You know, I have always wondered what those little red flecks are. But at the same time, I'm not sure I want to know." I reached for the chopsticks buried at the bottom of the bag.

Gabe looked down at the table. "I didn't think to bring any plates, but if you're not opposed to sharing, we can eat out of the same containers. Of course, we'll have to sit a little closer to share."

Now, a parade of thoughts marched through my mind. For one, I knew for a fact we had paper plates in the back. A quick and easy solution. But I also knew I didn't mind the prospect of sitting close to Gabe and sharing our little dinner.

Then there was the fact that not only were the paper plates hanging around in the back workroom, but so was my friend, Julia. What would she think if she found me all cozied up with Gabe the Babe sharing a tasty treat from Mr. Wrong's Place? Who was I kidding? She'd be thrilled.

About then, Julia stepped from around a bookcase. "Hi, Gabe, I didn't know anyone was here."

I hadn't heard her come in from the workroom. "Yeah, he dropped by with some Chinese food. Wasn't that sweet?" I tried to get Julia to catch on about the food.

"Wow, I don't know how you can be eating, Amy Kate. I'm about to explode." She placed her hand on her tummy. "I know I've grown a pant size tonight."

Gabe's smile faded, and I gave Julia the *don't you get it* stare. She got it but too late.

"I'm sorry. What a dunce I am," she said. "Ignore me. Amy Kate can eat Chinese whenever. It doesn't matter. Besides, it's her comfort food, and after a day like she had today, she could use a good dose of chow mein." Julia paused, glanced at Gabe, then at me, and said in a matter-of-fact tone, "I think I'll see myself out the back door. Will you be alright here alone?"

Gabe cleared his throat, and when Julia realized what she had said, she turned two distinct shades of red. "I wasn't implying she wouldn't be safe here with you."

"It's okay, Julia," Gabe said. "As long as you don't offer us any paper plates, I'm good."

"Paper plates?" Julia asked, not understanding the comment. "Do you need paper plates? Because if you do, I—"

"No," we interrupted in unison.

"Okay, no paper plates for you guys." She shook her head.

"I don't get it, but that's okay. I'll be leaving now." Julia disappeared back into the work room.

Gabe stood and moved his club chair next to mine. Then he slipped his feet out of his shoes and propped them up on the square coffee table, leaning back while eating a big glob of sweet-and-sour pork. He looked so comfortable.

I followed suit, taking off my shoes and pulling my feet up under me in the chair. A little sigh of contentment escaped.

"You know," I said in a conspiratorial tone, "This might not be safe, us eating together. We don't exactly have the best track record for safe encounters. The only one that went well was the one I had with your brother. So, it doesn't count since it wasn't really you."

"You might have something there. So, you're saying if I might want to ask you out, I'd need to increase my life insurance." A roguish grin enveloped his face, causing his brown eyes to twinkle.

"Yes, that is exactly what I am saying." The funny thing was, it was probably true.

"How about this? How about we eat our Chinese takeout and then I'll walk you to your car, and if the sky doesn't fall in on us or we don't burn the place down—"

"Bite your tongue," I said, not willing to tempt fate or God even a little bit.

"Sorry," he said, then continued, "We'll take it from there. See how it goes."

"Okay . . . but I would look into more insurance—life, car, and otherwise—seriously since I think your mom may be right. I do seem to attract trouble—even more when I'm around you."

"Then I will, because I'm not planning on going anywhere anytime soon."

From the way he planted himself in the club chair, chowing down on lo mein with his stockinged feet propped on the coffee table, I was inclined to believe him.

"So, you're not worried about this wildly uncanny force I have that attracts trouble?"

"Trust me, Amy Kate," his deep voice taking on a husky timber, "that's not the force that I'm worried about." And then the self-assured lieutenant winked at me before downing another glob of Chinese food.

Bonita Y. McCoy hails from the Great State of Alabama where she lives on a five-acre farm with two cows, two dogs, two cats, and one husband who she's had for over thirty years. She is a mother to three grown sons and two beautiful daughters-in-law, one who joined the family from Japan. She loves God, and she loves to write. Her blog, articles, and novels are an expression of both these passions.

Drop by and visit her Facebook Author's Page or Instagram page or visit her website bonitaymccoy.com where you can find her books, blog, and all the other things she might be doing.

Sign up for her newsletter and stay in touch.

Books by Bonita Y. McCoy

Sawyer Sweet Romances
Truth Be Told
No Room in His Heart
Seeds of Love coming soon

An Amy Kate Mystery
Twisted Plots

Contributed to:
Chicken Soup for the Soul Thanks Dad

Dear Friends,

Thank you for delving into the life and crime solving hi-jinx of Amy Kate Anderson. I hope you enjoyed the journey and felt very much at home in Pine Lake, Alabama with Flora and Carter and the whole gang.

As I wrote this story, there were times that Amy Kate reminded me of myself, making her lists and trying to solve all her problems herself. Don't we often do that. We try to face our unexpected struggles ourselves without turning to God in our moment of need. I know I do.

There were times I wanted to tell Amy Kate to stop and pray, but she is young and on a mission.

However, we, dear friends, as Christ followers, can stop and pray when life seems difficult and especially prickly. This is a lesson I must learn over and over and over, again to lean my full weight on Jesus.

Maybe one day, Amy Kate will learn this lesson. Maybe one day, I will too.

Thank you again for joining me on this amazing adventure of writing and loving God.

God's Best,
Bonita Y. McCoy

Made in the USA
Las Vegas, NV
31 May 2024